THE PIRATE'S INDECENT PROPOSAL

HIGHLAND SCANDAL: BOOK ONE

JAYNE CASTEL

All characters and situations in this publication are fictitious, and any resemblance to living persons is purely coincidental.

The Pirate's Indecent Proposal, by Jayne Castel

Published by Winter Mist Press

ISBN: 978-1-991280-23-7 (paperback)

Edited by Tim Burton
Cover design by Winter Mist Press
Cover images courtesy of Deposit Photos and generated by Midjourney
Chapter header images generated by Midjourney.

Visit Jayne's website: www.jaynecastel.com

A pirate's promise is a perilous thing. When a lady strikes a scandalous bargain with a plunderer of the seas, neither of them suspects where it will lead. Revenge and high stakes on Medieval Isle of Mull.

After Liza Maclean's cruel husband decides to do away with her, she finds herself tied up and left to die on a rock in the middle of the sea. All hope seems lost until she is unexpectedly saved … by pirates.

Alec Rankin's name is legend among the Western Isles. He and his crew have carved a reputation as bloodthirsty and ruthless. But when he rescues the distraught lady from certain death, Alec's life takes an unexpected turn.

Desperate to get revenge on her husband and be reunited with her son, Liza tries to strike a bargain with Alec to gain his help. However, when he responds with an indecent proposal, she is torn between outrage and despair.

He'll help her, for a sizeable amount of coin … and one night together.

It's her choice—but how far will Liza go to take back what her husband has stolen from her?

Full of impossible choices, forbidden love, and steam, Jayne Castel's new series, HIGHLAND SCANDAL, is set on Medieval Isle of Mull and follows three unconventional sisters, and the men who put everything on the line for them.

CONTENT WARNINGS

THE PIRATE'S INDECENT PROPOSAL is a steamy Historical Romance intended for mature (18+) readers. Here is a list of content that some readers may find triggering:

Sexual coercion (threatened)
Marital and child abuse
Graphic sex
Violence and murder

*To all my readers who have been hanging out for me to write a pirate hero
… your patience has been rewarded!*

"What does not kill me,
makes me stronger."
— **Friedrich Nietzsche**

1: NOTHING BUT A THORN

Loch Buie
Off the southern coast of the Isle of Mull
Scotland

Early March, 1318

"I WAS NEVER enough, was I?" Liza rasped, her throat tight. "I was never *her*?"

A muscle in her husband's jaw flexed.

She was brave to bring up his first wife, Greta. In all their marriage, she'd avoided doing so, for Leod's temper could be terrifying. But she had nothing to lose now.

"No," he replied, his gaze glinting. "She was a rose, but ye have been nothing but a thorn."

His voice was harsh, his words designed to wound.

Even after years of weathering his scorn, Liza flinched. Her sister Kylie had warned her not to marry this man. "I know his sort," she'd said one evening, as they sat by the hearth in their father's hall, Highland collies curled at their feet. "And if ye agree to wed him, ye shall end up unhappy."

There had been a knowing edge to her sister's voice, but Liza had dismissed her words at the time. Kylie's loveless and childless marriage had embittered her. Leod was a taciturn sort, yet he'd grieved his first wife deeply, which meant he was capable of love. Liza had been certain that she'd crack the ice around his heart.

How wrong she'd been.

And now, her husband was going to kill her.

She'd known it from the moment he trussed her up like a goose and threw her into the boat. He'd then rowed her out into the loch—and with each long draw of the oars now, fear cramped Liza's bowels.

She couldn't believe no one had tried to stop him. Leod's men knew what he was about to do—she'd seen it in their eyes—but not one of them had prevented the laird. Base cowards, all.

Liza's eyes grew hot and prickly. Her jaw throbbed from where he'd struck her when they'd argued in the solar, yet it was difficult to focus on anything but the twisting dread in her belly and the ache in her chest.

I'll never see Craeg again. Lord have mercy, her son had no idea where she was, and soon, he'd be left alone with his violent, cruel father. She'd no longer be his shield.

The rhythmic splash of the oars, the cry of gulls, and the whistle of the wind—much colder now that they weren't on land—became her world. Loch Buie was a salt-water loch, and eventually opened out into the sea, where a wide channel, between Mull and the mainland, stretched.

Despite the biting wind, sweat trickled down her back, between her shoulder blades. The end was surely close. How far would Leod take her before he dumped her into the deep?

They were distant from Moy Castle. Its grey-stone tower was little more than a smudge against the rugged outline of Ben Buie to the north. However, her husband didn't stop rowing, and as they drew farther out into the loch, Liza's gaze settled upon his pitiless face.

"Ye'd rob our son of his mother?" Her voice faltered then, her vision misting.

Leod's face darkened. "Aye … he's better off without ye."

"No, he's not!" Fury ignited in her gut, smothering her fear. She lunged forward in the rowboat, causing it to rock precariously. "Ye have no right to say such vile things!"

Her husband stopped rowing. An instant later, he lashed out, his palm catching her across the cheek. The force of the blow sent her sprawling, and the back of her head smacked against hard wood. With her wrists bound before her, she was unable to catch herself.

Biting down a cry of pain, she rolled onto her side. Hot tears now slid down her cheeks.

"I'll say what I like, woman," he muttered picking up the oars and resuming his task. "And after today, I'll never have to hear yer nagging voice again."

Panic slammed into her breastbone. "I tried to love ye," she choked out. "But ye have made it impossible."

Something rippled across Leod's face then, his dark eyes shadowing with what might have been guilt. "I should never have tried to replace Greta." He cut his gaze away. Sweat gleamed upon his brow as he increased the tempo of his rowing, the oars foaming through the glistening water now. "And ye were my punishment."

Grief strangled Liza then, tears blinding her. Frantically, she blinked them away. She couldn't lose control. There had to be a way out of this. She had to master her fear of this man. She had to plead with him.

"Please, Leod," she said huskily. "Don't kill me."

Her husband didn't reply.

"Ye aren't a murderer," she plowed on, even as sickly fear churned in her belly. "Not in yer heart … and if—"

"Silence!" he barked, cutting her off. "Or yer end will be all the nastier."

Dizziness swept over her at this threat, and she bit down on her tongue to stop more desperate words from spewing forth.

Meanwhile, he'd rowed her out far, beyond the headland and out into the sea itself. Smooth swells lifted the rowboat like a child's toy. They were crossing the channel now, where birlinns and cogs traveled between Oban and the southern coastline of the Isle of Mull.

Her pulse started to thump in her ears.

Where's he taking me?

Leod angled the boat west then. Twisting, Liza's gaze alighted upon a grey rock that thrust out of the sea. Little grew upon it, save clumps of yellowed grass, although gannets and shags had made this lonely spot their home too. They flapped their wings, screeching in warning as the boat inched closer.

Heart pounding, Liza turned back to face her husband. His eyes glittered now, a look of grim satisfaction upon his features. So, this was his plan—not to dump her into the icy water, but to leave her here to die alone.

"No," she whispered. "Ye can't."

"I can," he replied, his lips curving into a cruel smile. "And I will."

2: PLUNDERER OF THE SEAS

Oban
Scotland

Two days later ...

"YE ARE SITTING at our table, Rankin."

The gruff voice caused Alec to lower the tankard of ale he'd been about to drink from. He then flashed the broad-shouldered man striding toward him a dismissive glance. "Oh, aye?"

MacDonald's green eyes narrowed as he drew to a halt. "Aye ... and ye know it too."

Alec cocked an eyebrow. "I don't see yer name carved here, Camron." He gestured then, at the numerous unoccupied tables. "Sit somewhere else this eve."

The mercenary's frown deepened. "Move yer arses, or we'll do it for ye." He looked around at the crowd of rough men behind him. "Won't we, lads?"

"Aye," one of them growled. "Nobody takes our seats at *The Baited Creel.*"

Alec shrugged and glanced at his crew. A dozen of them sat with him around the long oaken table in the corner of the dingy, smoke-filled common room. Tucked into a wynd behind the docks, and frequented only by mercenaries and pirates, *The Baited Creel* was a rough establishment. But the ale was good, as were their mutton pies.

And it was the best place to go looking for a fight.

Indeed, Alec had chosen this tavern especially, for he knew that Camron MacDonald, a blade-for-hire with a mean streak, was a mouthy sort and liked a scrap. He was also more territorial than a boar.

"What do ye think?" Alec drawled, favoring his crew with a goading smile. "Should we give up our table to these dung eaters?"

"I don't think so." His second mate, Gunn, put down his half-finished pie and started to crack his knuckles. The pirate had huge scarred hands and a battered face to match. Gunn's nose had been broken so many times that it was now lumpy and shapeless. "I'm comfortable here."

"Aye." His first mate, Cory—a whip-thin pirate with close-cropped black hair and a wispy beard—agreed coolly. "We *all* are."

"I don't care if ye're as happy as pigs in shit," Camron replied, flexing his large hands at his sides. "This table is ours."

"We aren't moving," Alec said, taking a gulp from his cup of ale. "So, what are ye going to do about it?"

Camron's lip curled. He then pushed his long dark hair back from his face and stepped forward, his eyes glinting. "Ye strut about like a stag, Rankin ... the legendary 'spùinneadair-mara', whose very name strikes fear into the hearts of sailors." He paused then, sneering. "But these days, I hear rumors that ye are little more than Loch Maclean's dog."

This comment brought murmured curses and scowls from those seated at the table, although Alec merely inclined his head. "Was that supposed to insult me?"

Camron spat on the dirty reed-strewn floor between them. "Aye."

Limping out of The Baited Creel a short while later, Alec spat a gob of blood onto the ground. He then cast a glance over his shoulder at where Cory emerged from the tavern behind him. His first mate had taken a heavy punch to the eye. It had already swollen closed.

With his good eye, Cory regarded his captain. "Ye made a mess of MacDonald," he wheezed, still breathless from the brawl. "His face wasn't pretty before … but now bairns will run screaming at the sight of him."

Wiping blood from his lips with the back of his hand, Alec flashed him a violent smile. Camron had played straight into his hands. "Good. Serves the shitweasel right for trying to break my leg."

The rest of his crew had already left the tavern. They now waited in the narrow wynd beyond, grins on their battered faces. It had been a bruising fight, but they'd bested Camron and his friends in the end, leaving them bleeding, and groaning curses through swollen lips as Alec flicked the proprietor an extra coin for his trouble.

Camron was vicious and fought dirty, but Alec did too. Even so, the mercenary had loosened one of his teeth and his left knee now throbbed in time with his heartbeat.

A crisp, salty wind sprang up as the crew of The Blood Reiver made their way out of the wynd, ducking under washing lines and emerging on the quay beyond.

"Do ye think that worked then?" Cory murmured, falling back to walk alongside his captain.

Alec shot him a side-long glance. "It's a start."

"I suppose the lads look happier now," his first mate admitted.

"They'd better be." Alec wiped once more at the blood that still trickled down his chin. Indeed, they were laughing and ribbing each other in the aftermath of the fight, in contrast to the surly faces and glowers he'd witnessed of late. "There's nothing like a good brawl to improve yer mood."

Cory snorted at that but didn't contradict him.

If he were honest, Alec didn't share his crew's high spirits in the aftermath of the fight. Camron MacDonald's insult earlier had hit closer to the mark than he'd ever admit. The fact was that most of his crew weren't happy about the 'agreement' he had with the Macleans of Duart these days, whereby they left their ships and ports be. Three years earlier, they'd come to the clan's aid during a battle against the Mackinnons of Dùn Ara—and ever since, The Blood Reiver had raided elsewhere.

Silence settled between the captain and his first mate. Eventually, Alec glanced at Cory again, noting he was stroking his wispy beard, something he always did when deep in thought. Alec frowned. "What is it?"

"Time was, just the mention of Alec Rankin and The Blood Reiver's crew would have men pissing their braies," Cory replied warily. "But people don't fear us like they once did."

Alec stiffened, scowling. He didn't like to admit it, but these days he was flirting with mutiny. Cory was still unfailingly loyal—the only one among them whom he could trust not to sink a dirk into his back—but he'd heard the whispered insults of late.

Rankin's losing his edge.

Ever since he fought alongside the Macleans, he minds them too much.

When was the last time The Blood Reiver lived up to her name?

Our captain's balls have shriveled.

Aye, Alec needed to do more than drag his men into a brawl. He needed to give them the adventure they craved. The truth was they hadn't reived as much of late. The Blood Reiver spent more time at port than she did at sea. And Alec had no excuse for it—except that this life was starting to exhaust him.

There had been a time when he'd thought he'd never tire of sailing the high seas—of boarding a merchant cog and terrorizing its crew before taking his plunder—but, these days, it was difficult to dredge up his old enthusiasm.

Meanwhile, his crew walked on, their boots thumping upon the wooden quay, their rough laughter echoing off the water. It grew late, and a waxing gibbous moon was playing hide-and-seek with scudding clouds. Cogs and birlinns nudged against the docks, while laughter and raucous, drunken singing drifted out from the town.

Alec flexed his hands, his knuckles still throbbing from the fight, at his sides.

He never liked to linger long in Oban, for it brought back memories, most of them unpleasant. He'd grown up here, a port urchin, scavenging and living rough. They'd been hard years.

Up ahead, he spied the mast of his cog, The Blood Reiver, piercing the night sky like a schiltron pike. Her single large emerald woolen sail was furled, the ship's high clinker-built sides frosted by moonlight.

His chest tightened then as pride swelled. At first glance, she appeared a merchant's cog. But The Reiver was fast and could outpace even the swiftest birlinns when the wind was right. And her crew were all seasoned sailors and warriors who lived to pillage the seas.

Curse him, his crew was right about him. He'd lost his focus and gotten soft, and when a pirate lost his edge, he was as good as dead. If he wanted to remain at the helm of The Blood Reiver, he needed to take steps to claw back his reputation. He needed to ignite a fire in his belly once more.

Wincing as pain lanced through his injured knee, he quickened his pace to close the gap between him and the waiting cog before clearing his throat. "Ready to go plundering, lads?" His voice carried along the quay, causing his men to halt and swivel around to face him. An instant later, grins split their faces.

"Aye, Captain!" Gunn shouted back.

Alec's gaze swept over them. "Loch Maclean warned me off stirring up the Mackinnons of Dùn Ara after the Battle of Dounarwyse" —it was true, the clan-chief wanted a long-lasting peace to settle upon the isle— "but it's now time we looked after our own interests." He marked the hungry glint in their eyes as he continued, "We shall take The Reiver around the southern tip of Mull and head up the western coast into Mackinnon territory … what say ye all?"

Nods and approving murmurs followed before Cory spoke up. "A good choice, Captain. Let's make their young clan-chief gnash his teeth."

Alec grinned, violence kindling in his veins. That was more like it. Maybe he was in the mood for some reiving, after all. Bran Mackinnon would be entertaining to rile. The hot-tempered lad had stepped into his father's role three years earlier, after a humiliating defeat at the hands of the Macleans and their allies. Ever since, he'd struggled to earn his people's respect. The Mackinnons of Mull were vulnerable at present. "Plenty of cogs leave Dùn Ara, bound for The Small Isles and Skye," he added. "We shall prey upon them."

"Aye!" one of the older pirates called out. "We shall turn the sea red with Mackinnon blood … like we did at Dounarwyse!"

"They'll be crying for their mothers," a younger pirate, Athol, added with a savage grin. "Soon, they'll fear us as they do the Ghost Raiders."

Athol's comment made a few smiles around him slip. Gunn even crossed himself and then cuffed the younger man around the ear. "Clod-head, they aren't men … but demons."

"Lucifer's host," someone else muttered. "It's ill-luck to mention them."

"Enough," Alec cut in, eager to turn the conversation away from the 'specters' that had been terrorizing The Western Isles of late. They sailed into shore on misty nights upon a phantom ship and left devastation in their wake—talk of them made people, even hardened pirates, uneasy. "The Ghost Raiders are nothing more than superstition and exaggeration," he said, a harsh edge creeping into his voice. "But we are real … as are our blades. Let's bloody them!"

The shouts of his crew were resounding. "Aye!"

3: WE MEAN YE NO HARM

SHE WAS GOING to die upon this rock, with only seabirds for company. There was no doubt about it.

Liza's throat was so dry, she could hardly swallow.

It hadn't rained since her arrival here. Two long days had passed, and it was the morning of the third.

She couldn't go on much longer without water. Lying upon her side, she listened now to the cry of gannets and wondered how long it would take for them to feast upon her corpse after thirst eventually took her.

Her wrists were still bound tightly before her, for Leod knew his wife was able to swim. The distance between this lonely rock and Mull's southern coast was considerable, yet her husband was wise enough not to underestimate a mother's desperation to be reunited with her child.

Liza stared north at where the wide mouth to Loch Buie beckoned. Heat ignited in her empty belly then, throbbing.

How was Craeg faring without her? Right now, he'd be finishing his morning porridge in his bedchamber. Alone. He'd be wondering where she was, and likely fretting over it. A shudder passed through her then as she imagined his father's callous response.

The ache in her gut deepened.

Leod thought he'd get away with this, but he wouldn't. Word would reach her father of her death, and surely, someone would tell him what his son-by-marriage had done. And then Bruce MacGregor would rally his warriors and descend upon Moy Castle.

Regret twisted under her ribs. How she wished she'd managed to get away, as she'd planned. The past autumn, she'd organized a trip to Perthshire, to her family at Meggernie Castle. She'd promised her parents she'd bring Craeg, for neither of them had seen their grandson as yet. But, a day before her departure, Leod had announced that she couldn't go. Perhaps he'd sensed his wife might never return to him if she visited her kin. But—whatever the reason—he was intractable. Tearfully, she'd written to Makenna, telling her that Craeg was suffering from a grave fever, and she wouldn't be visiting.

I should have taken Craeg and run. My family would have sheltered me.

They would have, although it was likely she wouldn't have gotten farther than Craignure before her husband caught up with her.

Tears stung her burning eyes.

When she died, she'd come back as a vengeful ghost. She'd haunt that whoreson until the end of his days.

Pushing herself up onto her backside, Liza pulled her knees toward her chest, tucking them under her chin. She started to shiver then. The wind had a bite to it, for it was only early spring.

She wanted to retreat from it, but there was no shelter upon this barren rock.

Teeth chattering, Liza shifted her attention from Mull and let her gaze sweep over the open stretch of water around her. She couldn't see the mainland at this distance, but she knew it was there, just over the eastern horizon.

Boats often traveled this coastline, and she'd hoped to spy one.

However, ever since Leod had dumped her here, the sea had remained empty.

Liza's already hurting throat started to ache piteously. The Lord have mercy on her, she was doomed.

A wave of regret washed over her then. About agreeing to become Leod's wife. About not listening to her wise elder sister. About not keeping in touch with her sisters, Kylie and Makenna. She'd been too unhappy and hadn't wanted her family to know, but she was sorry about that now.

But one thing she didn't regret was Craeg.

He was her one light in the darkness. Her son.

Tears trickled down her wind-chapped cheeks then, grief clutching at her chest. *I never said goodbye.* He'd grow up without her. She'd never see him grow his first whiskers on his chin or hear his voice deepen. She'd never get to throw rose petals at his wedding, when he eventually took a wife, or kiss her grand-bairn.

Leod had stolen it all from her.

Scrunching her eyes shut, she bowed her head, resting her forehead on her knees, and let sorrow take her. There were no more tears now, for her body was too parched to release them, yet the sobs that tore through her made every part of her ache.

Eventually, the storm passed though, and she raised her head, staring out to sea.

This was it. All she could do was wait for the end to come.

And it was then that she glimpsed something.

It was distant, no more than a speck upon the horizon, but her gaze fixed on it. And as one shuddering breath followed the next, she made out a billowing green sail.

Her pulse leaped into a gallop.

She could hardly believe it. Struggling to her feet, she gingerly climbed up to the highest point of the rock, causing the gannets perched on it to take wing, screeching in indignation.

Liza clenched her jaw. Good. The birds would draw the eye to the rock, and to where she stood.

And all the while, the ship drew closer.

It was a cog, its well-maintained clinker-built sides gleaming in the bright morning sun.

"I'm here!" Liza shouted, cursing as the wind ripped her voice away. She started hopping up and down then, wishing her hands were free so she could frantically wave her arms. "Help me!"

Standing upon the castle of *The Blood Reiver*, hands clasping the great wooden wheel that steered the vessel, Alec's gaze narrowed. "What's that up ahead ... starboard?"

"A great rock, Captain," Rabbie, a gangly lad of around eighteen winters, who'd recently joined the crew, called back from where he was coiling rope below the raised platform.

"I can see that," Alec growled. "Take the plank out of yer eye and tell me what's *on* the rock."

"Birds?" Gunn quipped, unhelpfully, from where he stood next to Rabbie. This comment drew sniggers from other crew members.

Alec cut Gunn a hard look. He'd thought the tavern brawl, followed by his announcement of the night before, would have been enough to improve his crew's attitude. But it was only the morning of their first day at sea, and already morale was failing. He didn't like some of the looks his men shared when they thought he wasn't looking, or the sluggish way a few of them followed orders. Alec wasn't a fool; he sniffed the stench of a brewing mutiny rising.

It looked as if he was going to have to make an example of someone before long.

However, Gunn didn't even meet his eye. Instead, he was sharing a loaded look with Egan—a thickset pirate with a bald head that gleamed in the watery spring sunlight.

Alec scowled. Those two were trouble.

Meanwhile, Rabbie put down the rope, neared the railing, and peered out at the rock. "Satan's turds … there's someone marooned there."

Indeed, as *The Blood Reiver* sailed closer, Alec made out the figure standing atop the rock's highest point.

His frown deepened. "It's a woman."

The wine-red gown she wore flapped in the wind like a sail. She was moving around, jumping up and down, although strangely, she wasn't waving her hands.

Muttering an oath, Alec spun the wheel. Moments later, the cog lurched right, cutting through the swells toward the lonely rock. "Ready the rowboat," he shouted.

Thank the merciful saints, the cog was turning, angling toward her.

Relief bloomed hot and bright in Liza's chest. "Aye!" she shouted. "This way!"

However, as the ship drew closer, she marked something she'd missed earlier. In her desperation to gain the crew's attention—for she saw them now, watching her from the railings—she hadn't noticed the flag the cog was flying.

Red.

Blood red.

Liza stopped hopping, cold washing through her veins and dousing the heady relief. And then, she swore—a low, vicious oath that would have made her mother clutch at her crucifix.

She was a clan-chief's daughter and had grown up sheltered from the harshest aspects of life, but she'd heard of the bloody flag.

Curse her, she'd attracted the attention of pirates.

They'd just dropped anchor too and were now lowering a boat into the water.

Liza's already shaky legs turned to porridge at the sight. Sinking down onto the rock, she whispered a prayer.

The woman sat atop the rock watching them approach.

Perched at the bow of the rowboat, while his crew rowed in long strokes toward their destination, Alec observed her with interest.

The woman's dark hair was wrapped in a braid around the crown of her head, although strands had come free and whipped across the sun-kissed skin of her face. She was lovely. Her body was strong and shapely, the dark-red surcote clinging to her curves, and emphasizing the lush swell of her hips and breasts. The fine cloth she wore indicated that she was high-born.

A merchant had once told Alec that he'd met an Arab princess on one of his trips, far to the south. He'd described her exotic beauty, limpid, dark eyes, and the golden cast of her skin. The woman kneeling upon the rock was how Alec had imagined her.

"What do we have here, lads?" he murmured. "A lady in need of rescuing?"

"Now that's something we don't get enough of," Cory called back, causing the other men rowing to laugh.

However, when the boat nudged against the rock, and Alec leaped nimbly off, he marked the fear on the woman's face: her features were rigid, her eyes wild. She hadn't moved from atop the rock either, and it was then that Alec realized the woman's wrists were bound before her.

He frowned. Had someone left her here? Straightening up, he raised his hands. He then moved forward, his gaze fusing with hers. "Fear not … we mean ye no harm."

Her throat bobbed. "Ye are pirates," she called down to him. Her voice was hoarse, unsteady.

"Aye, lass."

"Then how can I take ye at yer word?"

He flashed her a grin, enjoying her defiance. The lady trembled now, yet her voice was steady, and the glint in her eye spoke of strength, not terror. "I swear to ye, *my lady*" —he couldn't help mock her a little— "that no harm shall come to ye aboard *The Blood Reiver*."

She swayed then, sinking onto her haunches, the color draining from her face.

He cocked an eyebrow. It was heartening to see that the name still struck fear into some people's hearts.

Alec climbed the slippery rock to reach her. "So, ye have heard of us then?" he asked, pulling a knife from his belt.

The woman raised her chin, her dark eyes wide. They were as beautiful as the rest of her, fringed by long black lashes. "Everyone's heard of *The Blood Reiver*," she said huskily. Her jaw firmed then. "Ye must be Captain Rankin."

He flashed her a grin. "Aye."

Moments passed, and then a groove appeared between delicately arched dark eyebrows. "Ye are friends of the Macleans, are ye not?"

He inclined his head. "Some of them."

She cleared her throat. "I'm Elizabetta Maclean, wife of the chieftain of Moy Castle … and I request safe passage back to the isle."

Alec's grin slipped. "Ye are Leod Maclean's wife?"

A nerve flickered under one eye, and then she nodded.

"And why are ye out here, alone on this rock … trussed up like a fowl at market?"

She stared back at him, those lovely dark eyes guttering. "My husband put me here."

Alec stilled.

He didn't know what to say to that. No flippant reply came to him.

He was a pirate and had seen much in his time that was unsavory—but what kind of man dumped his wife on a rock and left her to die?

After a moment, he moved forward. He then stretched out a hand toward her.

Lady Maclean flinched, and he halted. Leod Maclean's wife was used to rough handling, it seemed. "I'm just freeing yer wrists," he murmured.

She stared back at him for a heartbeat. Then, jaw setting once more as she mastered herself, she held out her wrists so he could cut her bindings.

4: INTO THE FIRE

HEART POUNDING, LIZA followed the pirate captain down to where the boat waited.

Captain Alec Rankin.

She'd heard many tales about this man, most of them terrifying. Nonetheless, in amongst them was the story of how he'd saved the Maclean clan-chief's sister, after she'd been shipwrecked, before coming to the Macleans' aid in their hour of need against the Mackinnons.

That meant this man, despite his formidable reputation, wasn't rotten to the core. Hopefully, he'd help her. Heat flared in the pit of her stomach then. Leod had to pay for what he'd done. She had to get Craeg safely away from him.

Even so, her mouth and throat were parched, and she was shivering with cold after her ordeal. Her priority was to get out of this wind and slake her thirst before she could turn her thoughts to revenge and being reunited with her son.

Sliding down the slippery rock, Rankin stopped at the bottom, near where the water lapped, and held out a hand once more. This time, it wasn't to cut away the rope around her wrist, but to help her onto the boat.

His gaze met hers, the challenge in his eyes—sea-green, the color of the water surrounding them—unmistakable.

Liza's lips thinned.

The pirate was all arrogant swagger, someone used to having no master, to others obeying him. And she'd have had to be blind not to note that the rogue was unfairly handsome. Tall and muscular, with high cheekbones, his unbound fair hair tangling in the wind, he wore a loose lèine tucked into braies and high boots, with a dirk belt across his hips.

There was no mistaking the male appreciation in his gaze either as he stared back at her. Steeling herself, she took hold of his hand, trying to ignore its heat and strength, as he helped her into the boat.

Meanwhile, the hungry gazes of the four pirates who'd rowed him out to the rock raked over her.

"Who's this then, Captain?" A huge pirate with a mashed nose asked.

"Lady Elizabetta Maclean," Rankin answered, letting go of Liza's hand as she settled down at the bow of the boat. "Her husband left her on this rock to die."

All four men stilled at this, their gazes sharp with curiosity now.

"Come on." Rankin's tone turned brusque as he lowered himself down next to Liza. "Let's get her back to The Reiver."

With grunts of acknowledgment, even as some of the men exchanged veiled glances, the pirates obeyed. They turned the boat around and hauled back on the oars, propelling the small craft back to the waiting cog. Liza raised her face, her gaze alighting once more on the bloody flag that snapped and billowed in the wind.

Her gut tightened then, dread clutching at her. *Mother Mary, preserve me.*

Why did she suddenly feel as if she were going from the frying pan into the fire?

Rankin handed Liza a large earthen cup. She took it eagerly and raised it to her lips, gulping down the cool ale. It was the best thing she'd ever tasted.

"Easy, lass, or ye shall make yerself ill."

Liza ignored him, draining the cup, and then handing it back to him. Refilling it from the jug he held, the pirate captain passed it to her once more. "Slow down."

She heeded him this time, sipping at the brew, and enjoying the way it soothed her parched throat. It was nectar.

They stood in Rankin's private quarters, a wood-paneled cabin underneath the castle—a raised platform at the stern of the cog. Glancing around her, she noted that it was simply furnished and dominated by a scrubbed oaken table and chairs. A heavy curtain hid the back of the space, no doubt where the captain slept.

Liza's pulse quickened once more. She was inside a pirate's lair, and as such felt vulnerable. As soon as she'd climbed out of the boat onto the deck of The Blood Reiver, assaulted by more predatory male gazes, Rankin had taken her directly to his cabin.

They hadn't even raised anchor. It was clear he wished to speak to her first.

Pouring himself some ale, Rankin nodded to the table. "Take a seat."

Belly fluttering, Liza obeyed. She slid onto the long bench seat. The captain sat down opposite her and placed the jug between them.

She noted that his fingers, which wrapped around his cup, were long and surprisingly refined for someone who made his living plundering and slitting the throats of those unwilling to part with their cargo.

"Elizabetta." Her name rolled smoothly off his tongue. "That's a bonnie name … if unusual. Why not Elizabeth?"

His question took her aback. Taking another sip of ale, she viewed him over the rim of her cup. "My mother chose it … she's from Iberia, the daughter of a spice merchant." She halted then before admitting. "No one calls me by my full name though … it's just Liza."

His mouth quirked. "Liza … I like that too."

She tensed, fighting the urge to squirm under his assessing gaze. She didn't care if he liked her name or not. Nonetheless, this man had rescued her, and she was grateful.

"Tell me then," Rankin went on, his gaze never leaving her face. "Why did yer husband leave ye to die on that rock?"

Liza's throat grew tight. "He hates me," she replied, wishing her voice didn't sound so raw.

"A man can hate his wife," the captain said, swirling his ale in his cup as he continued to study her. "But killing her is something else entirely."

Liza swallowed with difficulty. "We had an argument," she admitted after a lengthy pause.

"What about?"

"Our son … Craeg."

Rankin didn't answer, waiting for her to recount what had happened, but Liza hesitated. She didn't want to relive the ugliness that had preceded Leod dragging her out of the castle and down to the shore.

However, it appeared that the pirate captain wanted an explanation.

"He married me for a son … but once he got one, he treated him cruelly," she admitted finally. "Craeg is only in his fifth spring, yet Leod expects him to behave like a man." She paused, swallowing once more. "He drowned his puppy … and then when the lad wept over it, he knocked him across the room." Nausea washed over her as she recalled the scene. "I stepped between them … and Leod didn't like it."

Rankin stared back at her. His handsome face gave little away. Only the slight hardening of his gaze hinted that her tale had affected him at all. "I met yer husband at Dounarwyse … and remember him as an ill-tempered bastard," he said then, his voice as difficult to read as his expression. "But this tale surprises me."

Liza's mouth pursed. Whether or not her story surprised him mattered not. What she needed from this man wasn't his understanding, but his help.

Her mind scrabbled then as she planned her next steps. Her first thought was to ask him to take her to Duart Castle, so she could throw herself at the mercy of Loch Maclean. But she checked herself. She'd only ever met the Maclean clan-chief once, a striking man with a mane of dark hair and an arrogance that rivaled Rankin's. It was said that his wife, the lovely Mairi, had tamed him, but Liza wasn't convinced.

What if Loch didn't listen to her pleas? What if he merely sent her right back to her husband?

Her bowels cramped at the thought. Leod wouldn't bother taking her out to sea and dumping her on a rock again. He'd just kill her with his bare hands. And maybe he'd do it in front of Craeg. It would be unhinged and cruel, but she wouldn't put anything past her husband.

No, it was too risky to put her fate in the hands of Loch Maclean. Instead, she needed to grab Fortuna by the throat. She wanted her son back, and she craved vengeance.

But she couldn't do it alone.

"Do ye like coin, Rankin?" she asked eventually.

He smirked. "Of course, I'm a spùinneadair-mara."

"Well, my husband has a strongroom full of it."

His head inclined. "Does he?"

"Aye … he's a wealthy man … and I will give ye half of everything he has."

His sea-green eyes narrowed. "That's generous of ye, Liza."

She stiffened. The pirate was far too familiar. He should be addressing her according to her rank, yet the only time he'd done so was to mock her. "It is," she replied coolly, staring back at him. "But such generosity comes at a price."

Her heart started to pound then. She couldn't believe she was being this bold—that she was attempting to broker a bargain with a pirate. Had she lost her wits?

Aye, she was desperate. The thought of never seeing Craeg again made her belly cramp. This man had a decent-sized crew—and most of them appeared hardened warriors who'd seen battle. She needed them.

Rankin set his cup down on the table and folded his arms. The movement pulled the lèine he wore against the hard muscles of his chest and shoulders, and she blinked.

Lord help her, she shouldn't be marking such things.

"I'm all ears," he murmured, greed glinting in his eyes.

Liza swallowed. Suddenly, her throat was parched again. Raising her cup to her lips, she took a large fortifying gulp. Then, drawing in a deep breath, she answered, "To get these riches, ye must first kill my husband."

5: HELL HATH NO FURY

ALEC REGARDED THE woman he'd just rescued with incredulity. Of all the things he thought she might propose, this possibility hadn't occurred to him.

Surely, she wasn't in earnest?

But as the moments slid by, and the hard glint in her night-brown eyes didn't soften, he realized she was.

"Christ's blood," he murmured finally. "Hell hath no fury, indeed."

A muscle flexed in her smooth jaw, and she leaned forward. "My husband didn't *scorn* me, Rankin … he tried to murder me. And now Craeg is alone with him."

Alec stared back at her, noting the flush that stained her cheekbones.

Liza Maclean was even lovelier when she was incensed. He liked a woman with spirit. He'd been taken by Loch Maclean's fierce sister, Astrid, a few years earlier—but the lass hadn't been interested in him. She'd already fallen for the man charged with protecting her.

Alec eyed her. "Ye have balls, Liza … I'll give ye that … but more courage than sense." She flinched under his crude, harsh words, yet he continued. "A wiser woman would ask me to take her to Duart Castle instead. The Maclean will surely help ye."

She shook her head vehemently. "No. I can't risk him denying me."

"Ye underestimate Loch, he's—"

"A man."

Alec snorted. "So am I, and yet ye are asking me for help?"

Anger burned in her dark eyes. "No, ye are a *pirate*. Ye love plunder more than anything else in this world, and I can give it to ye."

He snorted. "Well then, I hope yer husband's coffers are deep."

"Aye … he's a miser. His strongroom is *rammed* full of coin."

Alec picked up his cup and took a deep draft. "Is that so?"

Liza nodded. "And half of it's yers. It's the best offer ye've ever had, Rankin." She drew herself up, her dark brows knitting together. "Will ye accept it?"

"Maybe," he drawled.

A muscle in her smooth jaw flexed. "Excuse me?"

"Such a decision can't be rushed," he said, enjoying the way her eyes glinted in anger. "I have an agreement with Loch Maclean … and killing one of his chieftains will break it." Aye, that was the truth. Loch might overlook him reiving the Mackinnons, but killing the laird of Moy was sure to raise the clan-chief's ire. All the same, Liza's husband was a vile, murderous turd who deserved to die—and the coin *was* tempting. His pulse quickened then. He'd just had an idea. Perhaps he'd found a way to restore his crew's respect and quell their malcontent for good. A moment later, he pushed himself up from the table. "Now, if ye will excuse me, I must discuss yer proposal with my crew."

The woman's mouth pursed at this, yet she held her tongue. Flashing her a careless smile, Alec turned and headed toward the door. Liza's gaze tracked him.

However, upon ducking out of the cabin under the castle, he didn't gather his crew to him. Instead, he went looking for Cory.

His first mate was overseeing the swabbies who were mopping the deck. He glanced up at Alec's approach, nodding when his captain jerked his chin toward the forecastle. Without a word, Alec climbed up to the raised platform at the bow of the cog and waited for Cory to join him. They would be alone here, and thanks to the screeching of gulls overhead, wouldn't be easily overheard.

"Change of plan, Cory," he murmured. "The Mackinnons of Dùn Ara will have to wait."

His first mate inclined his head. "Aye?"

Alec nodded. "Lady Maclean has offered us a job." Quickly, he filled him in on Liza's proposal. His first mate's dark eyes glinted when he told him that payment would be half of the contents of Moy Castle's strongroom. "It's not enough though," Alec concluded.

Cory stiffened. "It's not?"

"No … not when my crewmates are sharpening their dirks behind my back."

Cory's lean features tensed. He'd marked the look Gunn and Egan had given each other earlier too—he knew what was brewing.

Alec stepped in closer to him. "It's time to give the lads a shock," he murmured. "To make them wonder what I'm capable of."

Cory inclined his head, his gaze narrowing. "What do ye have in mind?"

"Spend tonight in my bed … and tomorrow we will take Moy Castle for ye and kill its laird … for all that coin ye promised, of course."

Liza stared at Captain Rankin, disbelieving, for a few moments. The Saints help her, this knave couldn't be serious.

She searched his face, looking for a teasing glint in his eyes or a rueful curve of his mouth. Both were absent. Cold washed over her. A moment later, her heart started to kick against her ribs.

She swallowed hard then. "Ye intend to *rape* me?"

Rankin, who'd just returned to his cabin after talking to his crew, stood in the open doorway. He'd folded his arms across his chest and leaned indolently against the door frame.

"I wouldn't call it such, lass." His sea-blue eyes taunted her. "It's more of an 'arrangement'."

She stifled a gasp. The galling arrogance of him. "Vile dog," she rasped. "I have no wish to lie with ye."

His lips lifted at the corners. "Rest assured, I will ensure the experience is a pleasant one."

Fury surged up, battering at her chest, and she made a choking sound. *Liar.* There was nothing 'pleasant' about being swived, especially against one's will. Every occasion with Leod had been an ordeal she'd gritted her teeth to get through. Fortunately, her husband hadn't visited her bed in a long while. Once Craeg was born and she'd secured her husband an heir,

Leod had left her alone. But now this odious pirate wanted her to spread her legs for him—as *payment.*

"I'm not yer whore," she ground out, flinching at her own vulgarity. "Find yerself one at yer next port."

The rumble of male laughter reached her then, and shame flushed over her in a hot tide. The other pirates were listening in. Her pulse sprang into a wild gallop. Curse them all. Did they find her humiliation amusing?

Rankin smiled then, although the curve of his lips didn't match the hardness in his gaze. He stalked around the edge of the table and stopped before Liza, looming over her.

Lifting her chin to hold his eye, she tried to ignore the hammering of her heart. It was beating so fast, she was starting to feel lightheaded. Nevertheless, she held her ground.

"That's my response to yer offer, *wench,*" he said, staring down at her. "Take it or leave it."

More guffaws followed from outside, but they both ignored the crew's mirth.

Liza's breathing grew shallow. Up close, the pirate smelled of leather, salt, and a hint of something fresh and spicy, like mint. But his scent only distracted her for a moment.

This man, her savior just a short while earlier, was Lucifer.

Swaying slightly, she lifted her hand, reaching for the small iron crucifix she wore around her neck—a gift from her pious mother. The Lord forgive her, she almost wished she were back on that rock.

"And if I decline?" she asked, her voice quivering with disgust.

He shrugged. "Then, we drop ye off on the southern edge of Loch Buie later this afternoon … and ye can walk back to Moy Castle and deal with yer husband on yer own."

"Ye could take me to Oban," she countered, even as her pulse pounded in her ears. "If *ye* won't help me, I'll find mercenaries there who will."

He shook his head.

She started to tremble as both despair and anger took hold of her. "Why not?"

"I don't have to give ye a reason," he drawled.

Liza glared at him, her fingers curling into fists at her sides. Christ's blood, she wanted to tell Rankin he could burn in the fiery pits of Hades. It was on the tip of her tongue, yet she checked herself.

Calm yerself, Liza. Turning into a spitting hellcat won't get Craeg back.

Reminding herself of what was at stake made her draw in a deep, steadying breath. She had to view the situation from a distance. Letting this filthy pirate rut her would be debasing at best, an ordeal at worst. However, by dawn, it would be over. Then, he'd help her.

If she let this pirate have her for one night, they could act. Tomorrow.

The hunger for reckoning against her husband burned like a lump of coal in her belly.

She was desperate—and it made her reckless.

Heart pounding, she gave a slight, barely perceptible nod. "Very well, Rankin," she replied, her voice hoarse. Lord, she couldn't believe the knave was manipulating her, or that she was giving in to him. Nausea now churned in her belly. "I accept yer *indecent* proposal."

The moment the words were out of her mouth, she wished she could haul them back. However, instead, she flattened her lips into a tight line. Her fingers were clenched so tightly that her nails dug into her palms.

The slight upturn of his lips now made her ache to lash out. But doing so wouldn't get her what she wanted.

One night with a lecherous pirate. It was only her body. She could shut off her mind, as she had with Leod. How would it be any different?

Rankin stepped back from her, nodding. "Good." He then turned his head to the left. "Hear that, lads? Soon, *The Reiver's* hold will be heavy with coin!"

A roar of approval followed, and Liza swallowed down bile.

He moved toward the door, although he halted just before reaching it. Casting a glance over his shoulder, he flashed her an assessing look. "Help yerself to some wine. We shall discuss details of tomorrow's attack with my crew shortly."

Liza didn't reply. She couldn't. Her tongue had frozen in her mouth. Instead, she watched Rankin leave his quarters and cringed as she listened to his men congratulate him.

"I thought we didn't ravish lasses, Captain?" one of the younger lads asked, and Liza stilled, her breath catching.

"Aye, well, a man can change his mind," Rankin drawled back. "Ye've seen the woman, Rabbie … who wouldn't want to tumble her?"

Another explosion of coarse laughter followed these words. All defiance drained out of Liza then, and her legs started to wobble under her.

Breathing a curse, she lowered herself onto the bench seat. She raised a hand to her face, her heart thudding when she realized it was shaking. "Daft lass," she whispered. "What have ye done?"

6: BURY YER SOFT HEART

"I SHALL GO in first."

Rankin's announcement made Liza glance up from where she'd finished drawing upon the tabletop with a stick of charcoal. A rough plan of Moy Castle lay before them, showing the defensive wall, the gate leading into the barmkin, and the position of Lochbuie village to the west of the tower house.

"Alone?" Despite that her mouth felt sour and her hands were shaky this afternoon, she had to concentrate. She had to keep her fear and disgust leashed.

The pirate captain nodded before sharing looks with the four men who'd joined them: the first and second mates he'd introduced as Cory and Gunn, and two more pirates, Egan and Athol, who stood just inside the doorway. The latter—a lanky young pirate—kept favoring her with hungry looks.

Liza's gut clenched.

God's troth, what if Rankin decided to share her with his crew after he plowed her? She hadn't considered that when she'd agreed to his terms, yet now, ice slithered through her veins at the thought. In bargaining with the pirate, she'd made a deal with the devil.

"Yer husband knows the clan-chief treats with me," Rankin replied, glancing her way once more. "So, I might as well use that relationship to my advantage … before I make an enemy out of Loch." He leaned forward then and tapped his finger upon the line she'd drawn to show the outline of the shore. "Five of my crew will be waiting for me here." His finger slid east. "They will be joined by another five we'll drop off farther up the loch shore. They will make their way on foot and ensure they aren't seen. I don't want our numbers to make the Watch at Moy suspicious." He paused then, "And after I've killed the laird, they'll all enter the castle and deal with the Guard."

Liza swallowed, still struggling to focus—especially when her pulse thumped in her ears and dizziness assailed her. "The Moy Guard outnumber ye, three to one … will ten be enough?"

"Eleven," he corrected her. "Including me."

"This isn't a battle, but an ambush," Cory—the wiry pirate with a sparse pointy beard upon a sharp chin, and ferrety eyes—pointed out. "What matters isn't how many men ye have … but how fast ye move and how violently ye strike."

"Aye, we don't intend to kill the entire Moy Guard," Rankin added. "Ye'll need warriors to serve ye after yer husband's dead, after all."

Liza's queasiness intensified. This discussion was making the situation all too real. Indeed, she was hiring these pirates to kill her husband and take Moy Castle.

I'll be laird.

She thought then of the fortress that had been her home over the last six years—of its neglected walls and refuse-strewn barmkin. The first thing she'd do would be to clean up the mess and hire stonemasons to repair the walls. When she'd once suggested Leod take more pride in his castle, he'd snarled at her. But when Moy was hers, she could make all the changes she wanted.

Don't get ahead of yerself. Her breathing quickened, anxiety blooming again. Would those of the Guard who survived the attack follow her?

One thing at a time, Liza. Just get through today first. She started to sweat then. Good Lord, what a tangle she'd woven. How would she weather the night ahead?

"I shall need ye to remain at Moy a day or two afterward," she said, meeting Rankin's eye. If she was going to let herself be mauled by the pirate captain tonight, she would make use of him and his crew after the attack. "Just to ensure I have the loyalty of those ye leave alive."

He favored her with a thin smile. "Very well … we wouldn't want to throw ye to the wolves."

She cut her gaze from his then, pulse hammering now, and stared down at the tabletop. *Too late.*

"What time of day is best?"

She looked up to find the huge pirate with a bald head and muscles that gleamed in the light of the lantern burning on the table watching her. Gunn's deep-set eyes were unnervingly sharp and calculating.

"The morning," she replied without hesitation. "After the noon meal, Leod often takes his dogs out for a hunt. If ye want to ensure he's at home when ye come, late morn is when ye should strike."

"So be it," Rankin said.

Liza's gaze settled upon him once more, noting the shrewd look upon his handsome face. He wasn't looking at her, but studying the map she'd drawn, clearly deep in thought.

"My husband is a warrior of renown," she said after a pause. "Can ye bring him down on yer own?"

"As Cory said … this won't be a fair fight," he replied, glancing up. "We aren't going to be facing off with dirks on the field. When the time comes, Leod Maclean won't have a chance to draw his blade."

A shiver skated down Liza's spine.

Her discomfort must have shown because Rankin inclined his head. "Ye hired me to *kill* him … have ye lost the stomach for it?"

Her fingers tightened around the nub of charcoal she still gripped. "No," she whispered.

Rankin placed the flat of his hands on the table and leaned in, his gaze capturing hers. "So, ye still hunger for revenge?"

"Aye."

His sensual mouth tugged into a rueful smile. "Well, this is the reality of it. Yer husband left ye trussed up on a rock out at sea to die. He showed ye no mercy. If ye want to ensure yer son is safe, and to take Moy Castle as yer own, ye must bury yer soft heart."

Liza scowled, even as her pulse fluttered. "What makes ye think I have one?"

He huffed a laugh, while the other pirates smirked. "Of course, ye do … ye're a woman," Rankin replied with a mocking shake of his head. "And unsuited to tasks such as these."

"Aye," Gunn replied gruffly. "Why do ye think men rule? Women lack the stomach for brutality … and to lead requires it."

Heat rose like a swift tide then, washing over Liza. Her grip on the charcoal tightened, crushing it to dust against her palm.

She wished her younger sister, Makenna, were here right now, with a fighting knife in each hand. She'd show these pirates that only a fool dismissed women as lightly as they did.

Gunn was right about one thing though, it was a man's world, and if she wanted to win, she needed to play their game.

Swallowing her simmering rage, she stood up, brushing the charcoal dust off her hands. "Just do the job I hired ye for," she replied coldly, "And let me worry about my conscience."

Liza chewed a mouthful of dried plum and cheese and forced herself to swallow.

She, Rankin, and his first and second mates were all having supper together. A spread of bread, cheese, dried fruit, and salted pork lay before them, which they washed down with fruity red wine.

She had little stomach for the meal, although she drank more heavily than she usually did. She needed something to blunt her nerves and lessen the dread that gnawed like a rat at her innards.

And she couldn't stop thinking about Craeg either. He'd have finished his supper by this hour, and—in his mother's absence—Liza's handmaid, Nettie, would be playing with him before bed.

God's bones, she longed to know how he was faring.

Ye will see him again soon, she reminded herself.

Indeed, the rest of the day had passed swiftly. Too swiftly. For although Liza was impatient to return to Moy—to be able to sweep Craeg up into her arms once more—the coming of dusk heralded the first payment she'd have to make Alec Rankin.

Aye, she'd struck a bargain with this wretch, yet she wasn't sure she could go through with it.

Lifting the cup to her lips, she took another large gulp of wine. *Ye must.*

"The wine is to yer liking?"

Rankin reclined at the end of the table, watching her under hooded lids as he skewered a piece of cheese on his eating knife.

"Aye," she replied coldly.

"It was one I was saving for a special occasion."

Cory smirked at this, while Gunn huffed a laugh.

Liza's stomach lurched, and suddenly, the wine tasted like vinegar. "No doubt the fruit of one of yer plunders," she said, wishing she didn't sound as if she were being strangled.

"It was … a cog transporting wine and spice … around five years ago now. Me and the lads drank well for a while … this is the last cask."

"A pity." Cory held his cup aloft. "Looks like we'll have to find ourselves another Castilian merchant to plunder."

Liza glanced down at the wine. "Castile," she murmured. "That's where my grandfather was from." Her chest tightened as she recalled his rare visits to Scotland, quite a journey from the Iberian Peninsula. "He used to bring us wine that tasted like this."

"That's quite a match … an Iberian merchant's daughter and a Scottish clan-chief," Rankin replied, and Liza's chin jerked up. Curse it, she hadn't even realized she'd voiced her thoughts aloud.

"Aye," she said, pushing her trencher of food away. "It caused quite a scandal at the time."

She was aware of all three men watching her intently. Cory's knowing smile was starting to vex her, while Gunn's penetrating stare made her skin prickle in warning. And then there was Rankin. His lips were curved slightly as if he was enjoying a jest at her expense.

"Don't ye all get tired of this life?" she asked after a lengthy pause.

Gunn snorted. "Never."

"No one is freer than a pirate," Cory added. "We have no master but the sea."

Rankin added nothing to these replies, merely watching Liza over the rim of his cup.

"Maybe … but ye will leave no legacy behind ye." She took a deep draft of wine. "Nothing permanent to be remembered by."

This comment wiped the smirk off Cory's face and made Gunn frown, while Rankin's eyes narrowed just a little. "Nothing lasts, Lady Maclean," he eventually drawled. "And when ye die, the world moves on … whether ye were a king or a pauper."

Their gazes fused and held for a long moment before Liza heaved a deep breath and set her cup of wine down. She'd drunk enough. Any more and her head would start to spin. Although she wanted to calm her pitching belly, she didn't want to dull her wits. Not around these men.

"Thank ye for supper, Rankin," she said stiffly. "But I'm tired … and wish to retire."

Cory snorted at this, while Gunn gave a grating laugh, one that vibrated against the wood paneling surrounding them.

Meanwhile, a lazy smile tugged at Rankin's mouth. "Keen for a tumble, are ye?"

Her heart started to pound. "No." The word came out in a panicked wheeze.

Rankin set his own cup down, his gaze capturing hers once more. "Oh, but *I* am."

"Our captain enjoys the lasses," Cory quipped with a grin. "I doubt ye'll get much rest tonight."

"Aye, ye'll be walking bow-legged by morning," Gunn added with a leer.

Liza made a strangled noise, her fingers grabbing the edge of the table. "Ye are all pigs," she gasped, the blood thundering in her ears.

7: RANKIN'S RUSE

ALONE IN THE sleeping area of Rankin's quarters, Liza eyed the bowl of cold water and cake of coarse lye soap the youngest of the pirates, a lad named Rabbie, had just brought in. A linen drying sheet lay next to the bowl on the table in the corner of the cramped space.

She was loath to touch any of it.

Instead, she flexed her hands at her sides and swiveled, her gaze taking in the large straw-stuffed mattress upon a wooden pallet behind her. Covered with woolen blankets and sheepskins, it might have been a welcoming bed—in other circumstances.

However, in this one, the sight of Captain Rankin's bed made her stomach roll over.

The Lord have mercy, she wasn't sure she could go through with this. The moment he touched her, she'd turn into a clawing, spitting cat.

Squeezing her eyes closed, she counted slowly to ten, and as she did so, her rising panic settled, just a little. Her throat constricted, and the urge to weep was so strong that her eyelids started to sting.

"Courage, Liza," she whispered shakily, opening her eyes once more. "This time tomorrow, ye shall be sitting in the laird's seat in Moy Castle, Craeg on yer knee. Leod will be dead."

That last sentence made heat flare under her ribs. She'd never thought of herself as vengeful, but that was before her husband tried to kill her. Leod's callous words returned to her then. The bastard had said their son would be better off without her.

Soon, he'd eat his words.

Her gaze settled once more on the washbowl, and, dragging in a deep breath, she stepped toward it.

She started to unlace the front of her surcote, jaw clenching as her hands trembled and her fingers fumbled.

"Rankin's a base knave," she muttered, shrugging off the surcote before unlacing the kirtle beneath. "But he's my weapon to wield."

The fire burning in her chest started to pulse, even as her throat grew unbearably tight.

It was a dangerous bargain she'd struck, yet the pirate had backed her into a corner. She needed his help, and he'd exploited her desperation. Lord, how she hated him for it. But she had to remind herself that he was the only person who could get her son back.

She needed to hold that in her mind while he rutted her.

Sweating, as she imagined the pirate's hands on her, Liza stripped down to the filmy lèine she wore under her kirtle and surcote. She'd keep this on.

The water was freezing, and the soap was gritty and abrasive, better suited to washing laundry than skin. Liza went through her ablutions swiftly, washing under her arms and breasts, and between her legs. She then uncoiled the messy braid from around the crown of her head.

Her hair was sticky from three days out in the salty wind. Lathering up her heavy tresses, she carefully rinsed her hair before wrapping it up in a drying sheet.

She moved away from the table in the corner then and perched upon the end of the bed, tucking her legs up under her. She didn't have a comb, so she removed the drying sheet and teased out the knots in her hair with her fingers.

She'd almost finished her task when the creak of the door opening beyond the hanging made her freeze. A few moments later, the curtain drew back, and Captain Rankin slipped into the sleeping area.

Heart pounding, she stared up at him, taking in the way his damp hair hung over his broad shoulders. He too had bathed.

His gaze swept over her, and she held her breath, waiting for him to make an odious, lecherous comment. She'd inherited her mother's lush curves and knew that the thin material of the lèine that covered them wouldn't hide much of her modesty. Moments passed though, and he remained silent.

A sob rose up then, clawing at her throat, but she swallowed it down. Even so, her vision blurred. Mother Mary, how would she get through this?

Alec viewed the woman seated, legs folded under her, upon the edge of his bed.

Christ's bones, he'd never seen anything lovelier than Liza Maclean clad in nothing but a translucent tunic, combing out her wet hair over one shoulder.

He took in every detail, storing it away.

He liked the way the thin linen strained against her heavy breasts, revealing the shadow of her dark, peaked nipples. The light from the single lantern hanging from the roof gleamed on her tawny skin and turned her dark eyes into limpid pools. It also highlighted her proud bone structure and strong features. And that hair. Earlier, it had been coiled in a tight braid, yet freed, it was a dark-brown mane with hints of red in its depths.

Aye, she was a siren all right. A woman torn from his dreams.

And she was waiting for him. His, for one night. All he had to do was rip the lèine off that sinful body and help himself.

But he didn't.

Instead, he noted the tension in her face, the way her eyes gleamed with unshed tears, and the slight tremor that rippled through her.

"Ye have made yerself comfortable, I see," he murmured.

She stared back at him, her smooth throat working as she swallowed.

He could smell her fear, and he marked the sharp rise and fall of those magnificent breasts.

It was time to put the poor woman out of her misery.

Crossing to the bed, and marking the way she flinched at his approach, he retrieved a woolen blanket and passed it to her. "Here … wrap this around yerself."

Her dark eyes were wide and glassy, yet she obeyed, slinging the blanket around her shoulders and drawing it about her body.

Alec then pulled up a stool and lowered himself onto it. "Ye need not worry," he said, meeting her gaze once more. "I shall not touch ye."

Liza stared back at him, confusion clouding her eyes. However, the tension that shivered off her didn't abate. She didn't believe him.

"Apologies for putting ye through all that lecherous talk today," he continued, "but … I had to make this look convincing."

She still didn't reply. Instead, the woman watched him as if he'd sprouted devil horns and a forked tail.

Alec sighed. He didn't like seeing her so cowed. "It was all a ruse, Liza."

She blinked before giving a gasp that sounded like a swallowed sob. "A ruse?"

"Aye." He flashed her a half-smile. "Things aren't always as they appear."

"I don't understand," she said huskily, her gaze still shining with tears.

Alec grimaced before raking a hand through his damp hair. He'd bathed briefly on deck, suffering a ribbing from his crew as he'd done so. It was all part of the deception he'd woven, and so he'd gone along with it. All the same, he wasn't a ravisher and didn't enjoy pretending to be one.

It had been necessary though.

"I did it to fool my crew … I wanted them to think I'd take advantage of a desperate woman for my own ends."

A groove etched between her eyebrows, confusion shadowing her eyes. Her throat worked then as she struggled to master herself. "Why?"

"Reputation is a fragile thing," he replied with a shrug. "Hard to build and easy to lose."

She frowned, and Alec's gut tightened. He could see he wasn't going to get away with a vague explanation.

"Aye, I've plundered and murdered … but I've always drawn the line at rape." His mouth twisted. "A while back, one of my crew ravished a woman on a merchant cog and I killed him for it." Her eyes widened at this admission, but he pushed on. "However, of late, the lads have started to doubt me. It's not just because we leave the Macleans of Mull alone either … I'm simply not as bloodthirsty as I once was. We haven't reived as much over the past year, and the men grow restless. They sniff weakness out like hounds. I had to do something to win them over."

Alec broke off then, embarrassed at being so frank with her.

Liza drew herself up, even as her fingers clasping the blanket tightened. "And has yer ruse worked?" Anger crept into her voice now, her spine straightening. Alec sensed her rising outrage, although he couldn't blame her for it. He'd manipulated the woman, after all.

"Time will tell," he replied. "I've done my best to get them back on side of late … but they were still on the cusp of turning mutinous." He paused, shaking his head. "And so, when ye asked me to help, I decided to twist this situation to my advantage."

A muscle flexed in her jaw. A shiver rippled through her then. "So, ye have tricked them all?"

"Aye, except Cory. My first mate is the only one among them I trust."

"I imagined pirate crews were bonded," she said roughly, her mouth pursing with distaste, "like families."

He snorted. "Ye grow close with time, aye … but I'd be a fool to think my crewmates look on me as their brother. Always watch yer back when dealing with cut-throats."

He rose to his feet then, suddenly on edge. He wasn't used to speaking so frankly, to exposing himself like this. "I could do with a cup of wine. Do ye want one?" Not waiting for her answer, he pushed aside the curtain, went to the sideboard, and helped himself to a clay bottle and two wooden cups. Beyond, he could hear drunken, slightly off-key singing. The lads were already into the ale.

They were all in high spirits this eve, looking forward to spilling some blood the following day and getting their hands on the loot. Earlier, they'd slapped him on the back and grinned as he'd made his way toward his cabin.

"Make her squeal, Captain!" Athol had called out.

"Aye, give her one for me!" Bryce had added with a leer.

Alec had kept his smile fixed in place, even if he'd itched to draw his dirk and go for the bastards. Their eagerness made anger clench in his gut. All the same, he was aware he'd set a precedent now. If he punished any of them for harassing or ravishing women in the future, he'd look like a hypocrite.

8: A TWISTED GAME

LIZA WATCHED RANKIN reappear, two cups and a clay bottle in hand. Setting them down on the low table next to the bed, he wordlessly poured the wine before passing her a cup.

Liza took it.

Frankly, after his revelation, she needed something to settle her stomach. Right now, she was confused. She still wasn't sure whether to weep with relief or throw the wine in the pirate's face.

After all, he'd let her believe he was going to plow her—and his crew were no doubt all gathered outside with their ears to the door.

Her skin prickled in humiliation.

And yet, Rankin had just admitted he wasn't the brute she took him for. He wasn't a ravisher, after all. She wasn't sure whether to believe him. It occurred to her then that the pirate could be toying with her. This could all be part of a twisted game.

Her fingers tightened around her cup at the thought, her pulse quickening.

Suddenly, the night ahead seemed interminable.

She watched warily as he heeled off his boots and climbed onto the bed. The straw mattress dipped under his weight, although he moved away from her and sat with his back against the wooden paneling lining the cabin. Still perched on the edge, Liza shifted slightly so that she could keep her eye on him. Any sudden moves and she'd vault from the bed. She didn't know what she'd do after that though—she was trapped on this cog and surrounded by water.

"All is well, Liza," he said, his lips lifting at the corners. "I'm just settling in for the evening."

Still watching him warily, she took a sip of wine. It was the same rich red he'd served her earlier. She couldn't help but savor it. "Such fine wine is wasted on pirates," she murmured under her breath.

"Ye think we can't appreciate the finer things, lass?" he asked, raising a tawny brow.

She gave an indelicate snort in response. Then swirling the wine in her cup, she gave it a sniff. "Plum and cherry … with a hint of pepper," she said, wistfulness rising in her breast. "It reminds me of my family home. My parents always had Iberian wine on the table at mealtimes."

"Ye miss yer kin, don't ye?"

She managed a small smile. "Aye." An odd melancholy stole over her then, as longing tugged at her. How she wished her father were here. Bruce MacGregor would have extricated her from this mess and dealt with both this pirate and her husband.

"Are they both still alive?"

"Aye, and after over thirty-five years together … and five daughters … they are still a formidable match." Liza took another sip of wine, welcoming its warmth in her belly. She glanced away then, the years rolling back as she recalled how her parents had always looked at each other. "As a bairn, I remember feeling jealous at times … for no one, not me nor any of my sisters, could pierce the cocoon they wrapped themselves in. Their love was everything, like the roots of a mighty oak … deep enough to withstand the years."

The pirate made an incredulous noise in the back of his throat.

Liza cut him a scowl. She couldn't believe she'd told this rogue about her family. The wine had loosened her tongue, and it emboldened her now. "And what of *yer* parents, Rankin?"

He pulled a face. "My mother was a serving lass at an alehouse on the docks in Oban, and my father a sailor. He gave up the seafaring life to be with her, although he wasn't much of a husband or a father. He was fonder of ale and brawling than of his family. My mother died when I was around five … and my father drank himself to death three summers later."

Liza observed him, looking for a flicker of emotion on his handsome face—she found none. "What became of ye after that?"

He took a gulp of wine before answering, "There was just me and my elder sister … and she did her best to look out for me."

Liza stilled. "Where did ye live?"

"On the streets. We survived by begging, scavenging, and stealing."

Liza fought a grimace. Well, that explained a lot. Nonetheless, a hard childhood didn't excuse this man's choices.

He could have taken a different path at any point. "And yer sister?"

"Dead."

She caught a flicker of something then, a shadow in his eyes. It was fleeting, but she saw it all the same.

"So, ye are alone in the world, Alec Rankin?" she said, intrigued despite herself.

He flashed her a careless smile. "Aye, except for my mutinous crew."

Liza pulled a face, letting him know what she thought of the men that sailed *The Blood Reiver*. Their lewd looks made her skin crawl, and it was a relief to be shut away from them for the night.

"I find it surprising," she said after a pause, "that ye are averse to rape. How is it that a pirate captain has lines he won't cross?"

Rankin's features tightened, and Liza's heart jolted. She'd pushed him too far. Holding her tongue now, she waited for his eyes to darken with anger, as Leod's did when her tongue got her into trouble.

But they didn't.

Instead, his gaze developed an unfocused look, as if he was suddenly lost in the past. "Years ago, when my sister and I were living rough in Oban, a sailor raped her … hurt her … badly. I was only young, yet I found the man, drunk and boasting about what he'd done … and I killed him with a boning knife."

Liza stilled at this admission. She wasn't sure how to respond.

"Fi was never the same afterward," he went on, his expression shuttering. "She became weak and listless, hardly bothering to eat or drink. I became *her* caretaker, but it wasn't enough … and when she took ill with a fever a few months later, it bested her."

A strained silence followed, and Liza considered his words. It was a plausible explanation, she supposed; his tone had seemed sincere enough. All the same, his openness disarmed her, and she wasn't sure how to respond. "I'm sorry about what happened to her," she said awkwardly.

Rankin glanced her way before lifting his cup and taking another gulp. "So am I."

Another pause followed, one that put Liza increasingly on edge. Without meaning to, she drained her wine.

"Would ye like some more?" Rankin asked.

Liza nodded, holding the cup out to him. He topped up both their drinks before resuming his place on the opposite side of the bed. He crossed his long legs at the ankle, leaning his head back against the paneling. His eyes closed then, his expression impossible to fathom.

Did he regret being so candid with her?

"Thank ye for agreeing to help me," she said eventually.

Rankin's eyes flickered open, his sea-blue gaze settling upon her. "The only thanks I need is a handsome payment after we take Moy Castle for ye."

"And ye shall get it," she assured him. "I'm a woman of my word."

Her belly twisted then—a reminder that she'd never actually seen inside Leod's strongroom. All the same, he'd surely have enough coin to pay the pirates.

His mouth quirked as their gazes held. "I can tell ye are … and strong too. Ye have put up with much of late, haven't ye?"

"Aye," she murmured, breaking their stare. "The past years haven't been easy."

"Ye don't think much of men."

Her chin kicked up, and she frowned. "Is it so evident?"

"If ye are paying attention, aye."

Her pulse quickened. She didn't like the turn this conversation had taken, and yet she couldn't help but respond, "And what else have ye observed, Rankin?"

His gaze roamed her face. "I'd say Leod Maclean was rough with ye."

She snorted. "That's easy enough to guess … the bastard tried to kill me."

"I'd also wager that he's never made any attempt to *know* ye over the years," Rankin continued, undaunted by her response.

Liza's chest constricted. "No," she whispered. Indeed, she'd cried herself to sleep in the early days of their marriage after returning to Moy Castle, when it became clear that Leod was set upon ignoring her. "He was married before me, ye know?"

He nodded. "I'd heard."

"Aye, well … he adored his first wife, but she died giving birth. He lost the bairn too … a son."

Rankin observed her over the rim of his cup. "It turned him bitter?"

She nodded.

"And yet he chose ye."

"He did … reluctantly." Liza took a deep draft of wine before continuing. She wasn't sure why she was being so open, only that speaking of these things was oddly liberating. She had no real confidant, or friend, at Moy, and life had gotten lonely. She'd held so much pain and frustration inside for so long. "My father is a man who likes to collect debts from others … and Leod had one to pay." She sighed then, rubbing a hand over her face. "On the day we met, I could tell he was a man who liked his women meek, yet I wanted to please Da, and so I agreed to the match."

"And lived to regret it."

"We both did." A lump rose in Liza's throat. "But he gave me my son," she whispered, looking away. "I don't regret *everything*."

"I think ye will make a good laird," Rankin said after a weighty pause.

She couldn't help but let her lip curl at this. "Earlier, ye and yer crewmates said the opposite. Women don't have the stomach to rule, remember?"

He shrugged. "Most don't … but then, ye're uncommon." He leaned forward, his fingers wrapping around the cup he still held. "Leod Maclean made a grave mistake the day he decided to kill his wife."

Heat prickled her skin. His words flustered her, and she wished he wouldn't speak so boldly. All the same, she couldn't help but respond to the challenge in his voice. "He did," she answered firmly.

9: IF ONLY FOR ONE NIGHT

THE BLUSH THAT now stained Liza's cheekbones warned Alec that he'd almost overstepped.

He wasn't sure how they'd ended up having this conversation—but one question had slid into another, and his interest had been sparked.

There was no doubt about it, this woman intrigued him.

When he'd found her, she'd looked like a siren upon that rock, gilded by the morning sun, with the body and face to lure men to their deaths. And after this exchange, he realized that she was just as dangerous. But Liza Maclean appeared utterly unaware of how alluring she was.

All the same, he was relieved that fear and disgust no longer shadowed her eyes.

His gut tightened then. Aye, his ruse had been successful, but it had left a sour taste in his mouth—it was a reminder that much of his reputation was based on boasts, rumors, and outright lies. One day, the deception he'd woven would be ripped away, and he needed to prepare himself for it.

Would walking away be so bad?

The whispered question took him aback. He'd never considered leaving *The Blood Reiver* before, despite that he didn't enjoy this life as much as he once had.

To his surprise, Liza moved then, seating herself at the head of the bed, like him, and making a nest for herself with pillows. The bed was large, and at least three feet lay between them. Even so, her act made it clear she was lowering her guard around him. She kept the blanket tightly wrapped about her.

Alec tried not to think about the delicious body that was hidden under it.

Her bare feet peeked out beneath the blanket, and he found himself admiring the elegant curve of her arches and her pale-gold skin.

"Are we expected to make some noise?" she asked finally, cradling the cup of wine before her.

Alec raised an eyebrow. "Noise?"

"Aye." Another charming blush stained her cheeks. "Won't yer crew be listening for ... *grunts?*"

Alec stared back at her a moment before laughter dragged its way up from his belly and rolled up through his chest and throat, filling the cabin.

"Christ's blood," he said, still grinning at the affronted look she was now giving him. "Ye make us sound like rooting pigs." Her lips thinned at this comment, yet he couldn't help but tease her. "Is that the noise Leod made when he took ye?"

Tension rippled off her now, her knuckles, where she still gripped her cup of wine, turning white. "Once again, ye mock me, pirate."

"No." Alec sobered then, realizing he'd gone too far. "Not ye, lass ... but yer husband." He shook his head ruefully before taking a sip of wine. "It's clear he doesn't know how to bed a woman."

Liza drew herself up, an eyebrow arching. "And ye do?"

Alec shrugged. "Of course."

"Conceited cockerel."

Her insult washed over him, for he marked the glint of interest in her eyes. She was trying her best to conceal it, but he intrigued her.

Silence fell between them then, and Alec allowed it to draw out. It was best not to speak of coupling, since it was too easy to flirt with this woman. He didn't want to frighten her again.

"Leod hasn't touched me in a while … which is a relief because he's rough," she said finally. Alec glanced her way to see that she was deliberately avoiding his eye now. He remained silent, watching her take what looked like a fortifying gulp of wine before continuing. "I've heard some people find pleasure in coupling … but I'm not one of them."

"That's probably his fault, not yers," Alec replied.

She huffed a humorless laugh. "Maybe … although once he's dead, I'll never have to suffer another man's touch again."

Alec frowned at the resignation, the bitterness, in her voice. "Ye're still young enough to wed again, Liza," he murmured. "Just choose more carefully next time. Find someone who will take his time to woo ye … who will look after yer pleasure before his own. Someone who will teach ye what yer body is capable of."

Her night-brown eyes grew wide at his response, her lips parting slightly.

He marked the shallowness of her breathing, the way she held the cup in a death-grip once more. However, it wasn't anger he saw in her eyes now, but an awakening of sorts.

Leave this be, the voice of reason checked him then, and he heeded it.

He'd said far too much. It was time to leash his tongue.

Liza's pulse pounded in her ears.

She wasn't sure how they'd gotten onto the subject of coupling. Nonetheless, it was *she* who wouldn't let the matter go.

Rankin's arrogance was both infuriating and intriguing. And, curse him, his words had piqued her interest.

Did not all men grunt like a humping dog as they plowed their wives? Were there really some who were tender and sensual, who focused on their woman's pleasure? Of course, she should know it was the case, for she'd always suspected her parents were happy in that area. Over the years, she'd seen their lingering glances and touches, the way her father put his arm around her mother's waist or gave her backside a cheeky squeeze when he thought no one was looking.

Rankin would be a good lover.

An odd sensation clutched at her lower belly at this realization before she gave herself a swift mental slap.

Goose! What are ye thinking? The man is a knave!

Aye, he was, and he'd let her think he was going to force himself upon her. But he hadn't. Liza's instincts told her that if she fell asleep on this bed, he wouldn't molest her.

Alec Rankin did his best to hide it, but there was a strong vein of decency in him. And after hearing about his upbringing and what had happened to his sister, she'd take him at his word.

At the same time, their conversation had unsettled her.

A strange restlessness filtered over Liza. And then, after a while, a hollow sensation settled into the pit of her stomach. She'd spoken true earlier. Once Leod was dead, she wouldn't be taking another husband. If she was to rule Moy as laird, she would need to be wary of men.

A woman in power couldn't allow herself any vulnerabilities, or her position would be stripped from her. And that meant she'd never share her bed with anyone again.

Liza's reaction to this realization was mixed, complicated. She was relieved, for coupling had only ever brought her pain and humiliation. But there was a tiny part of her that longed to learn the pleasure that Rankin had spoken of—if only for one night.

Quashing the thought, which was unsettling indeed, she raised her cup to her lips and took another sip.

The hush between them lengthened, while the faint sounds of drunken laughter filtered through the walls into the cabin. It didn't sound as if the crew were focused on them, after all.

After a while, Liza cast Rankin a sidelong look. He'd set his cup of wine aside now and had slid down so that he stretched out on the bed. His eyes were closed, his chest rising and falling slowly.

She wasn't sure whether he was asleep or not, although the fact his eyes were shut allowed her to observe him.

And, she found herself drinking him in.

Mother Mary forgive her, he was attractive. Tall and muscular, yet with long limbs that gave him litheness and grace. His fair hair fanned across the pillow, and she took in his sculpted features. No man had the right to be that beautiful.

His lèine was open at the throat, and she found her gaze drawn to the smooth vee of skin it revealed. Her pulse fluttered then, and she looked away.

What was she doing, ogling a pirate? She wondered then if the upheaval of the past days had scattered her wits.

She certainly felt … different … tonight.

Bold. Angry. Reckless.

Time slid by, and she too put aside her wine and stretched out onto her back, staring up at the low ceiling. After everything she'd been through, she should have been exhausted, and yet she was wide awake.

She'd never been so alert.

Something had shifted in her this evening, but she couldn't discern what it was.

Meanwhile, it was clear Rankin was done speaking to her. Indeed, the pirate did appear to have fallen asleep.

Glancing his way once more, she studied him in the flickering light of the lantern that hung overhead. She hated to admit it, but he fascinated her. She'd never met anyone so contradictory. She wasn't sure what to make sure of him at all.

But one thing she was certain of was that she was attracted to him.

After their revealing conversation, she was no longer afraid of the pirate captain. And as such, her awareness of him resurfaced.

Eventually, the tension building within her became impossible to ignore. Heaving in a deep breath, she rolled onto her side, facing him. Then, she cleared her throat loudly.

He twitched, shifting position, but didn't wake up.

"Rankin."

The pirate stirred, one eye cracking open. "Aye," he murmured.

"So, ye're saying that coupling doesn't have to hurt?"

His other eye opened, his gaze settling upon her as his drowsiness cleared. "It *shouldn't* hurt," he replied. "Not if it's done right."

Heat flushed through her at his response. The Lord forgive her, this man's voice made her pulse leap like a prancing pony.

She stared back at him, her stomach clenching. "I will never wed again," she said firmly. "Of that I am certain … but just once, I'd like to know what it's like" —she broke off then, her courage faltering— "to be bedded well."

That got Rankin's attention.

His eyes snapped wide, and he shifted onto his side, propping himself up onto an elbow. "What are ye saying?"

She sucked in a deep breath before releasing it slowly, to try and quiet her racing heart. "I want ye to bed me, Rankin."

10: BOLD WORDS

ALEC'S LIPS PARTED, heat igniting in his gut at her bold words. When he finally spoke, his voice was rough. "Careful, Liza … ye shouldn't play such games."

She shook her head. "This is no game," she replied, pushing herself up into a sitting position. "I've thought it through."

He frowned, even as his pulse quickened. Christ's blood, what was the woman doing? He'd fallen asleep thinking she too was resting. But instead, she'd been plotting.

"Ye don't want this," he said firmly, rolling off the bed and rising to his feet. She'd ripped him from a pleasant slumber. How the devil would he be able to sleep easily now? "After everything ye have suffered of late, ye have—"

"I know my own mind." Liza climbed off the bed and skirted it, making her way toward him. She stopped when they stood just a couple of feet apart. "And I know what I want." She paused then, her dark eyes glinting. "Tomorrow, my life will change forever. If I wish to be a strong laird and a good mother,

I will have to push my desires aside … but for one night, I want to be selfish. To do something just for me."

"But I thought ye didn't want me to touch ye?" Curse it, he was weakening. He shouldn't even be entertaining the idea of bedding her. But he was. He fought his desire for her though, for only a base knave would take advantage of a woman like this, when she was at her most vulnerable.

"That was before … when I thought ye were manipulating me." Her expression was fierce, and it made her even lovelier to look upon. "But this is different. Now, I choose to give ye my body of my own free will."

They stared at each other, tension shivering between them, before Alec breathed a curse. Raking a hand through his hair, he eyed her. "What if ye regret this in the morning?"

"I won't," she said firmly, lifting her chin in that gesture of defiance he'd already noted several times during the past day. She'd been nervous when she'd first proposed this idea, but as they'd spoken, her confidence had grown. She'd dug her heels in now.

Even so, her throat convulsed as she took another step closer. "Do ye not *want* me?"

His heart kicked against his ribs. "Of course, I do," he murmured. "It's not that."

"Then I'm yers tonight." A challenge crept into her voice as she added. "Show me how a *real* man treats a woman."

Satan's cods, she was goading him now—and he enjoyed it. He liked it far too much.

And, curse it, he wasn't made out of stone.

Moving closer still, he looked down at her. "We'll take this slowly," he said after a pause.

Her eyes darkened. "Does that mean ye agree?"

He nodded. "I swear to ye, there will be no pain," he assured her. "I will be gentle."

"Thank ye," she whispered.

Liza shrugged off the blanket, letting it fall to the ground. She then reached out and tugged at the hem of his lèine. "Will ye take this off?"

Her boldness made the heat in his belly smolder, and his mouth quirked. "Aye, if ye wish."

"I do."

He reached down and untucked his lèine, pulling it over his head in one deft movement.

Tossing it aside, he noted the way she observed him, her full lips parted as her breasts rose and fell rapidly now.

Alec reached out a hand. She took it, her palm damp, a tremor in her fingers.

Her reaction gave him pause. The lady wasn't as brave as she appeared.

Lifting his other hand, he brushed the heavy waves of hair back from her face and skimmed the smooth, warm skin of her neck and shoulder with his fingertips. "Ye are lovely, lass," he murmured as his finger traced her collarbone.

"Thank ye," she whispered.

Lowering his head, he kissed her then, his lips moving across hers languidly, until she opened for him. A groan rumbled in his throat as he tasted the sweetness of her mouth, and when her tongue timidly stroked his, lust flared hot in his belly.

This woman had no idea what a temptress she was.

He kissed her long and slow, until she melted against him— until she started to make hungry noises in the back of her throat.

Breaking off the embrace, he slid his fingers over the satiny skin of her shoulders, pushing aside the straps of the lèine and sliding the tunic down to reveal the tops of her breasts.

Liza's eyes fluttered shut, a sigh escaping her.

His mouth curved. Good, she was relaxing into this. He'd show her that a pirate knew how to treat a woman in bed, better than her laird husband.

He drew down the lèine, rolling it over the swell of her bust and then letting it flutter to the floor, around her ankles.

Liza was naked now, and what a glorious sight she was. All womanly curves and sun-kissed skin. She had broad hips and strong thighs, and his gut clenched when he thought about what lay between her shapely legs.

He slid his hands under her breasts then, feeling their weight, before lifting them, his thumbs grazing over their tips.

Her eyes snapped open, a gasp escaping.

Stroking her once more, Alec smiled. Her nipples were large, like two strawberries. And he wagered they were just as sweet. Bowing his head, he tasted her.

Liza swallowed another gasp as pleasure arrowed through her left breast, straight down through her navel to her lower belly.

She watched Rankin sink to his knees before her. He then began sucking her nipple with slow, languorous determination. His eyes were closed, his long brown eyelashes fluttering against his cheeks.

Pleasure spiked through her belly once more, stronger now, and she let out the moan that had been building in her chest. A melting sensation then quickened in the cradle of her hips.

The Virgin forgive her, she was enjoying this.

Releasing her swollen nipple with a wet sound that made her knees tremble, Rankin moved to her other breast. His eyes opened then, and he glanced up, meeting her gaze. "Ye have delicious tits, Liza." And with that, he drew her right nipple into his mouth and began to suck with the same lazy sensuality as before.

Heat flared between her thighs then, and she started to tremble.

He took his time over her breasts, sucking them both until her nipples ached, until sweat beaded upon her skin and hunger gnawed at her belly.

Finally, he ceased his delicious torture and rose to his feet.

Liza couldn't help it; she dragged her gaze down over his strong, hard-muscled torso, to where his braies sat low on his hips.

She'd have to be blind not to notice the huge erection tenting the thick material.

Her heart started to pound, even as desire clutched at her once more.

"Lie back on the bed," he murmured, unlacing his braies now.

Swallowing, even as she yanked her gaze up to meet his, she caught the glint in his eye. Rankin had seen her looking at his groin and marked the way her breathing quickened.

The desire between them smoldered, and Liza shivered from the need that now pulsed low in her belly.

Obeying him, she shifted back and stretched out upon the soft sheepskins, aware of his hot gaze raking down her body, charting every inch of her like a sailor scrutinizing the night sky.

"I swear ye are the bonniest woman I have ever seen," he breathed, his expression altering then. Indeed, he looked … awed. "Lovely enough to start a war over, like Helen of Troy."

Heat flushed over Liza at these words, a blush rising across her chest and spreading up her neck. She shouldn't like hearing him say such things, but she did. Leod hadn't ever made her feel desired, not even in the beginning.

Her gaze dropped to where he was now sliding down his braies. She lost her train of thought then, at the sight of his rod, proud and strong, straining against his flat belly.

He was even beautiful down there.

Climbing onto the mattress, he gently spread her legs. But instead of pushing into her with his shaft as she expected, he lowered his head and shoulders between her thighs. Realizing what he was about to do, Liza gave a shocked gasp and reached down to push him away. However, he caught her hand in his, entwining their fingers. "Don't worry, lass," he said, his voice thick with lust. "Ye shall enjoy this … I promise."

She stilled. His voice soothed her, made her trust him.

Keeping his left hand entwined with her right, Rankin spread her wider still with his free hand, gazing upon her most intimate place.

She watched his pupils dilate, and his lips part, before he whispered. "Exquisite."

Another shiver went through Liza, her breathing shallow now.

A moment later, he dipped his head to her sex, his tongue lathing and flicking. And all the while, his hand held hers, anchoring her to him.

Warmth gathered in her stomach, pleasure coiling there like a spring. And she gave a long guttural groan.

She'd never had a man's mouth on her before—for her encounters with Leod had consisted of her on her hands and knees with him rutting her, painfully, from behind.

This new experience was wicked, yet wonderful. She melted under the play of his lips, his tongue. He explored, savored, devoured—and when he slid a long finger deep inside her, Liza shuddered, choking off a cry.

"That's right, lass," Rankin murmured, his breath feathering across her most intimate place. "Let me hear ye."

His mouth resumed its delicious torture once more, while his finger slid in and out of her. A short while later, a second one joined it. And then when he curled them up slightly, his tongue flicking the pearl of flesh he'd found, Liza went wild.

She bucked against him, her cry filling the room, pleasure rippling and throbbing through her loins.

Falling back on the bed, panting, she whispered an oath. "Lord have mercy," she gasped. "What was that?"

Rankin rose up from between her trembling thighs and sat back on his heels, his lips curving. His rod thrust up between them, its crown glistening now, although he ignored it. Instead, his gaze met hers. "Ye have never reached yer peak before then?"

She shook her head. "My peak?"

"Aye … it's when yer carnal pleasure reaches its height, and the walls of yer quim spasm." He slid a lazy finger down her slick sex then, making her whimper.

"I thought only men reached such a frenzy of sorts," she replied huskily. "When ye spill yer seed?"

"No," he said, his smile widening. "Women do too … let me show ye again."

She gasped, her eyes flying wide. "Again?"

"Aye." His eyes glinted. "The night is still young … and we have only just begun."

11: LUSTY AND RECKLESS

LIZA STARTED TO tremble then, anticipation thrilling through her veins. This pirate had just opened a new world to her.

Rankin slid his hands under her knees, pushing them up, and folding her double so that she was fully exposed to him.

For a moment, he didn't do anything. He just gazed down at her. His breathing quickened now, and his shaft jerked, impatient.

Heat flushed over Liza, pleasure coiling once more in her loins. The man's look called to something within her she hadn't known existed before tonight—something lusty and reckless.

Rankin took hold of his rod then and positioned it against her, but instead of penetrating, he rubbed himself over her slickness, teasing them both.

Her stomach fluttered, and she bit down on her bottom lip. Reaching her peak had left her sensitive. His touch had awakened a hunger within her that wasn't easily satiated.

"So wet," Rankin said then, his voice nearly a moan. A moment later, he sank into her, inch by inch. She stretched around his girth, her breath gusting out of her as he buried himself to the hilt. A nerve fluttered in the pirate's cheek as he stared down at where their bodies joined. "And so hot."

Liza whimpered. Her mind was muddled now, any thoughts eclipsed by this growing hunger. She couldn't believe how good he felt inside her. And indeed, she was wet, so aroused now that any lingering embarrassment had fled.

He pulled back slowly then, withdrawing almost to the tip. And all the while, she watched his face, fascinated by the delight that rippled over it.

But when he sank back down, rolling his hips as he went, pleasure spasmed deep in her womb, and she cried out. This position brought him deep and rubbed him up against something—a place that, when he continued to take her in slow, sensual strokes, turned her loins molten.

And she found the way he continued to watch their bodies join—the gasps that escaped him as he plowed her—exciting beyond measure. Her own pleasure grew as she observed his. Sweat gleamed off his naked body, the muscles in his arms flexing as he braced himself against her spread knees, opening her up further still.

Ecstasy twisted then, fluttering and pulsing, and she felt wetness and heat gush from inside her. "Oh, aye!" she gasped, arching against him. "There … aye!"

And he answered Liza's pleas, driving into her at just the right angle and depth to completely unravel her.

She threw her head back, a long cry tearing from her throat. Lord, she could feel it right down to her toes. Why had no one ever told her about this? How had she lived twenty-seven winters without ever learning that her body could feel so much?

Gasping, she shifted her gaze to Rankin once more. He thrust deep again, and she was sure he'd spill inside her.

But instead, jaw clenched, he withdrew sharply.

An instant later, he turned, allowing his milky seed to jet over the blanket next to him. He crouched there, one hand still braced upon her knee, his sweat-slicked chest rising and falling as sharply as her own. Head bowed, he looked as if he was struggling to master himself.

Liza watched him, fascinated. She hadn't expected him to withdraw before his own frenzy. She'd thought he'd spill inside her, damn the consequences.

Aye, this man was one contradiction after another.

Rankin moved then, climbing off the mattress and fetching a cloth from beside the washbowl a few feet away. He then wiped up the mess he made before flashing her a rueful smile. "Ye didn't think I'd be so reckless, did ye?"

Liza swallowed. It was best she didn't answer that.

He climbed back onto the bed then and stretched out next to her, his glorious body gleaming in the lantern's glow. She dragged her gaze from him and stared up at the iron lantern with a cresset of burning oil inside gently swinging above them.

"I'd forgotten we were at sea," she murmured, aware then of the cog's gentle roll.

"Aye, although if the wind gets up any more … ye won't forget it," he replied.

"Have ye ever feared for yer life … in high seas?" she asked then. It was a relief to talk about something besides what they'd just done. She didn't feel like herself and needed to regain her equilibrium. Aye, this had been her idea—but she hadn't expected coupling to feel so good. Rankin's touch had set her on fire.

"Aye … many a time."

"But *The Blood Reiver* weathered each storm?"

"She did … she's a plucky lass."

Liza gave a soft snort. "I've never understood why men talk about their ships as if they were women."

Silence followed as he considered her question. "I've sometimes wondered that. I suppose it's because sailors' lives are bound to their cogs … and we depend on them to keep us safe." He paused then, his tone teasing as he continued, "And we all know, if ye treat a woman well, she's less likely to drive a dirk into yer back."

Liza made another rude sound. "If ye are such an expert in women, Rankin, why are ye unwed?"

He cocked a tawny eyebrow. "A pirate captain can't take a wife." He gestured to the cabin walls surrounding them. "This is no life for a woman."

She propped herself up onto an elbow then, regarding him. "So, ye choose *The Blood Reiver* over a wife and family?"

"Aye … the sea is my mistress, the crew my kin."

She frowned at his flippant reply. "A dangerous family, by all accounts."

He shrugged. "I can handle them." His gaze roamed over her face then. "So, Lady Maclean … was that tumble to yer liking?" His lips quirked then. "Was there enough *grunting* for ye?"

Heat rose to Liza's cheeks. "Knave," she murmured. "Are ye trying to shame me?"

"No." His expression sobered. "I'm just making sure I satisfied ye."

Her face started to glow like a candle. "Ye know ye did."

A smile—irritatingly smug—curved his lips at this admission. "Good … well, let me have a breather, and we can go again."

Standing on the deck of *The Blood Reiver*, Liza watched as Rankin readied his crew to go ashore. They gathered around him—a motley group of scarred men of various ages—their brows furrowed.

The captain split them up into those who'd travel with him to Moy Castle, and those they'd drop off to join them later.

Eventually, he shifted his attention to the two pirates still awaiting their instructions. "Egan and Rabbie … I'm leaving ye both here to watch over Lady Maclean," he said, fixing them with a steely look. "But if either of ye touch her, I'll have yer balls."

Both men nodded. However, Egan wore a disgruntled expression, clearly vexed he hadn't been chosen to join the raiding party. "All right, captain," he muttered. "No need to start lifting yer leg and pissing to mark yer territory."

Laughter followed these words, and Liza's skin prickled, her embarrassment intensifying when she caught the looks some of the pirates exchanged and their grinning faces. She knew Rankin had to keep up his ruse and was merely continuing the mummery he'd begun the day before. All the same, she looked forward to getting off this cog and away from these men.

Flashing Egan a lazy smile, Rankin glanced her way then, for the first time since he'd begun speaking to his men, and their gazes locked.

Heat swept over Liza.

Despite that it was a still morning, her belly started to pitch. And then, the tender flesh between her thighs began to ache.

Curse him, was one look all it took for her to melt?

Rankin hadn't been full of empty boasts. He was quite a lover. He'd taught her what her body was capable of; he'd roused pleasure that she'd gladly drowned in. And he'd set something within her free. As promised, after a short rest, he'd taken her twice more, and the last time, as he plowed her from behind while his fingers played her like a lyre, she'd sobbed her pleasure into the sheepskins.

She'd collapsed onto the bed afterward, limp and panting, and he'd lain behind her, pulling her against him. Exhausted, Liza had let sleep claim her then, but when she'd awoken at dawn, the bed was empty.

Of course, when she'd emerged from the cabin, sniggers and stares greeted her.

She and Rankin hadn't been quiet—and their coupling had gone on for a while.

Liza had faced the crew down though. Lifting her chin, she'd walked across the deck to the railing. And as she stood there, watching the sun rise into the eastern sky, turning the glistening sea into a ruddy gold, she braced herself for remorse. For shame.

But there was none.

She felt alive this morning, each sense sharp. Rankin had handed Liza a piece of her that had always been missing, and in the aftermath of their torrid coupling, she felt as if she could take on the world.

"Anything I should know about yer husband?" Rankin asked then, his lips lifting at the corners.

Liza raised her chin. "Other than he's an ill-tempered brute?"

"Does he favor his left or right hand?"

"His right," she replied without hesitation.

"How fast is he?"

"Very … don't underestimate Leod." She took a step toward him then, her gaze never wavering. "And when ye kill him, tell the bastard that *I* sent ye."

Rankin's gaze widened, as if her bloodthirstiness this morning surprised him, before he nodded. He then unbuckled the sword belt he wore around his hips and handed it to one of his crewmates. He also gave the man his dirk.

Liza eyed him incredulously. "Are ye meeting him unarmed?"

"I won't be welcomed into the tower house bearing weapons." Rankin unstrapped a thin-bladed knife from his thigh and slid it into the back of his right boot. "But fear not … I'll be ready for him."

12: DISTRACTIONS

ALEC WELCOMED THE rhythmic splash of the oars churning through the water. Seated at the bow of the rowboat, looking forward at where Moy's tower house jutted against a blue sky, he tried not to think about the situation he'd willingly tangled himself up in—or the woman who'd hired him to kill her husband.

The siren who'd asked him to bed her the night before.

Careful, lad, he warned himself. *Don't let her distract ye.*

He'd never tumbled a woman like Liza before—a clanchief's daughter ... a laird's wife. It wasn't just their difference in rank that made their coupling so explosive though, but her response to him. He'd been intent on giving her a night to remember. However, in the end, it was *he* who'd never forget it.

Irritation spiked through his chest then, and he shoved Liza from his thoughts. *Enough of this nonsense.* Aye, thinking about the woman who'd hired him, allowing memories of the night before to muddle his mind, was a recipe for disaster.

It was a sure way to get himself killed.

Leod Maclean was a hardened warrior and not a man to be taken down easily. Alec would have to strike fast. He'd need to remember why he was doing this.

For bag loads of coin from the chieftain's strongroom.

The boat reached the shallows then, and Alec's men leaped down and towed the craft to shore. Stepping onto the strand, pebbles crunching underfoot, Alec looked up at the high walls of Moy Castle towering above him.

The fortress cast a long shadow.

His gaze narrowed then. He'd never been this close to the castle before and hadn't realized it was in such a poor state of repair. The walls were crumbling in places, and tufts of grass were growing in between the stones. Moy had an unloved look.

Maybe Maclean's strongroom isn't crammed with coin, after all.

The worry wreathed up, but he dismissed it. Liza wouldn't have lied to him.

She might have. Ye don't know the woman at all.

Clenching his jaw, Alec dismissed the nagging voice in his head once more and focused on the castle before him.

It was nearing noon. He'd taken Liza's advice and arrived while the laird was likely to be at home. Smoke from the cookfires rose lazily into the sky, and the aroma of roasting mutton drifted out from the keep.

"Smells like we're just in time for the noon meal," Gunn quipped from behind him.

Alec harrumphed. "Always thinking of yer belly."

"Ye'll be able to fill it after we take the castle," Cory reminded the second mate.

"Aye … we all shall," Alec murmured. His gaze had shifted now, traveling left to the thatched and sod roofs of Lochbuie village. The shrill voice of a woman, likely telling off her bairns, reached them then, and the clang of iron told him a smith was hard at work.

"A bit shabby, isn't it?" One of the men grumbled.

"Aye," Alec replied, deliberately not looking his way. "Maclean is a miser, by all accounts."

"Better for us then," Cory replied.

Alec certainly hoped so. He glanced over his shoulder, surveying the five pirates he'd brought with him. "See that top window?" He paused, waiting for 'ayes' to follow. "That's the laird's solar. When Maclean's dead, I'll wave this" —he patted the sash of red cloth he'd tied around his waist— "to let ye know it's time." He glanced right then at the oakwood that hugged the water's edge. "The others will be here shortly."

"We'll *all* be waiting, Captain," Cory assured him, his keen gaze glinting.

Alec nodded. "Good … strike fast. Don't give them time to close the gates."

He knew he could count on his first mate. He wasn't so sure about the other four though, or the five men who were currently making their way, in stealth, toward them along the eastern shore of the loch. Aye, they were impressed by his ruthlessness the night before—and had welcomed his change of plans—but how long would that last? At least the promise of considerable loot would keep them loyal, for the time being.

Turning, Alec picked his way across the swathe of stones to the path leading up to the gates, where warriors, their chainmail vests glinting in the sun, watched him. Aye, their arrival had been noted.

"What brings ye to Moy, Rankin?"

Standing in the castle's barmkin, Alec's gaze rested upon the big man who stood before him on the steps leading into the tower house. Leod Maclean's stone-hewn face was even harder than he remembered it, and his dark gaze wasn't friendly.

"I have news for ye, Maclean," Alec replied, flashing the laird an easy grin.

All the while, he was aware of stares boring into him from all directions. Nonetheless, they could see he'd left his men behind on the shore and was unarmed.

Four guards at the open gates. Ten on the walls. And another three standing nearby in the barmkin. Aye, he'd counted them all.

There'd be others too, of course, but he and his crew would deal with them. Those who didn't kneel before the new laird of Moy Castle and swear fealty to her would die.

Don't be hasty, Alec cautioned himself then. *First, ye must cut off the head of the snake.*

His words hadn't softened Maclean's grim face. Instead, he folded muscular arms across his broad chest, his mouth puckering as if he'd just tasted vinegar. "Let's hear it then."

"It's about the MacDonalds of Sleat," Alec replied smoothly. He then cast a glance around him, a smile still lingering on his lips. "However, the information I bring is … sensitive. Best we speak of it in private."

Leod Maclean's black brows crashed together, a heavy silence dropping in the barmkin.

Meanwhile, a fowl pecked at the dirt nearby, helping itself to the last of the barley a lass had been scattering when Alec entered. Moy Castle wasn't in a good state inside the walls either.

Food scraps and animal dung littered the barmkin, and the air reeked of horse piss.

Watching the chieftain's face, Alec hoped the information Liza had given him, on the recent skirmish between the MacDonalds of Sleat and the Macleans of Moy, would be enough to sway him. It was the best excuse they'd been able to come up with.

"Has Aonghas MacDonald been stirring up trouble again?" Maclean finally growled.

"Not the clan-chief but his son, Callum. He and I shared an ale or two in Oban yesterday," Alec replied. "He said a few things ye might be interested in."

Maclean's eyes gleamed at that, and Alec knew he had him. "Oh, aye?"

Alec nodded yet said nothing else. The laird would have to invite him upstairs, to his solar, to hear the rest.

Moments passed, and then Maclean huffed an irritated sigh. Stepping back, he jerked his chin toward the door behind him. "Come on then, Rankin. Ye'd better not be about to waste my time."

Swallowing a smile, Alec followed him.

They entered the tower house, stepping into a square smoky hall. To the right-hand side, stone steps led upstairs.

Servants bustled about, placing trenchers on long trestle tables, and readying the hall for the noon meal. A huge hearth burned at the far end, and before it, playing with what looked like a wooden horse, was a lad of around five winters.

One look at him, and Alec knew this was Craeg, Liza's son.

He didn't favor his father at all. Instead, he had his mother's dark hair with its red highlights, and her sun-kissed skin and large night-brown eyes. Glancing up as the laird and his guest entered, the lad's fingers clutched nervously around his toy, as if expecting a reprimand. He wasn't disappointed.

"What are ye doing down here?" Maclean snarled, not breaking his stride. "Rolling on the floor like one of the dogs." The lad blanched, his throat convulsing as the laird continued, "Get upstairs before I put my boot up yer arse!"

Maclean took the steps two at a time, impatience bristling off him.

Alec easily kept pace with him, following him to the third floor.

As Liza had told him, the laird's solar faced south. Alec stepped into a comfortable space, where deerskins covered scrubbed wooden floorboards and a magnificent stag's head hung over the hearth. Axes and shields decorated the stone walls, and two highbacked wooden chairs flanked the fireplace, where a lump of peat gently glowed. It was the only part of the castle he'd seen so far that didn't look neglected.

Maclean didn't take a seat, and he didn't suggest his guest took one either. Nor did he offer him a cup of wine as Alec had hoped.

Inhospitable turd. It was customary to always offer one's guest a drink, and Alec had been planning to strike the moment the laird's back was turned.

Now, he'd have to come up with another distraction.

The laird was making him earn his coin.

"Talk," Maclean demanded, folding his arms over his chest once more.

Alec mirrored his stance. "What did ye do to vex Aonghus MacDonald so?"

The laird's lip curled. "His men deliberately provoked mine at a gathering last year." His gaze narrowed then. "Didn't his son tell ye that?"

"He did," Alec replied. "But I thought there might be more to his story … considering what Callum is planning."

"And what's that?"

"I'd better start at the beginning, Maclean … Callum picked up yer wife from a rock at sea on his way to Oban, around two days ago."

Leod Maclean's eyes snapped wide, his big frame going rigid. A heavy silence followed before he asked, "Dead?"

Alec gave a low laugh. "No, very much alive … and saying that her husband abandoned her there."

A nerve ticked in Maclean's cheek, yet he didn't reply.

"It seems Callum MacDonald is the gallant sort. Yer wife has convinced him that ye are a fiend … and he's on his way to cut yer throat to avenge her."

Another silence followed, and Maclean's arms dropped to his sides, his meaty hands clenching into fists. "Meddling whoreson," he ground out. "How dare he?"

"MacDonald feels he has righteousness on his side … that and he's besotted. Word is that yer wife seduced him."

Maclean snorted at this, his face screwing up. "That useless bitch couldn't seduce a wet-behind-the-ears lad desperate to hump his first woman."

Heat flared in Alec's gut. *Ye shall regret speaking of her like that.* This was personal now. He was going to enjoy spilling Maclean's blood. Masking his reaction, he gave an indolent shrug. "Be that as it may, he's coming for ye … a birlinn, sixty warriors strong, would have left Oban shortly after we did this morning." Alec flashed him a hard smile then. "Fear not though … if ye are willing to part with some coin, me and my crew will join yer men and defend this castle."

13: YE NEVER DESERVED HER

LEOD MACLEAN'S CURSE was explosive.

Turning on his heel, he crossed to the window, grabbing the ledge as he glared out at the glittering waters of Loch Buie. "Attack me at yer peril, *whelp*," he growled. Maclean didn't appear to have heard Alec's offer, and if he had, he'd chosen to ignore him.

That mattered not though. What did was that the laird of Moy Castle now had his back to him.

Alec didn't hesitate.

In one swift move, he'd drawn his knife from his boot, and the next, he was behind Maclean, the blade angling for his throat.

But, somehow, the bastard sensed him.

Leod Maclean turned with a speed that belied his size, his shoulder barreling into Alec's chest. The two men hurtled sideways, crashing against the wall, and the laird whipped out his dirk.

"She hasn't sent MacDonald, has she?" he snarled. "She sent *ye*."

"Aye," Alec grunted. "Think of me as her avenging angel." He shoved Maclean back and then pitched himself forward, headbutting him.

The laird staggered yet righted himself fast. A moment later, his dirk slashed at Alec. "What did the bitch promise ye?"

He didn't answer. Instead, he dodged the blade easily and kicked his opponent savagely in the knee. "Apart from the pleasure of killing ye?"

Maclean cursed, staggering once more. "I swear, ye'll never get yer filthy hands on my coin." His dagger struck again, this time tearing Alec's sleeve. A sting followed, warning that he'd drawn blood. The pain spurred him on, and his knife slashed down Maclean's left side, crimson blooming upon his dun-colored lèine.

"Whoreson!" Maclean grunted, coming for Alec again, driving in with a lethal strike.

But Alec anticipated him, darting to one side so that the dirk-blade scraped against stone.

Leod Maclean was an aggressive fighter, preferring the offensive to the defensive. Rage had also turned him vicious. Alec's style was cannier. He'd grown up on the docks of Oban and learned how to fight with a blade at a young age. The best fighters kept moving and turned the exchange into a dance. However, Maclean was like a maddened bull, charging at him repeatedly.

Alec ducked under his next frenzied stab and drove his blade into the chieftain's thigh.

Maclean roared, swiping at him, but Alec was faster.

Yanking the blade free, he drove it up under the laird's ribs and twisted. He then stepped in, his free hand clamping around Maclean's wrist.

The dirk slipped from the laird's fingers, clattering onto the floor.

His opponent's face had blanched, his mouth working as Alec leaned in, bringing their faces close. "This is for Liza," he murmured. "Ye never deserved her."

Fury flared in Maclean's peat-dark eyes, despite the agony he was in, although when Alec twisted the blade once more, his face froze.

His big body sagged then, and Alec released him, letting him fall.

Sprawled on the floor, his blood pooling over the wooden planks, Maclean glared up at his attacker. "Baseborn bastard," he rasped. "Ye won't get away with this."

Alec favored him with a thin smile. "Maybe not … but ye won't be here to find out."

He stood over the laird, watching as his eyes fluttered shut, as the life drained from him.

A chill settled over Alec then, one that made the hair on the back of his arms prickle. Some acts forever changed the course of a man's life. Aye, he'd just killed one of Loch Maclean's chieftains. Would this turn the clan-chief against him? It all depended on the view Loch took of Leod Macleod's attempt to kill his wife.

The throbbing in his left arm drew his attention then, and he glanced down to see that the linen sleeve was ripped and stained crimson. The cut was deeper than he'd thought, and it would need seeing to. Not yet though.

First, he had a castle to take.

Untying the sash from around his waist, he stepped over Maclean's prone form and crossed to the window. He then waved it, leaning forward and letting the wind catch the bright fabric like a flag.

Cory, Gunn, and the others would have been blind not to see it.

Turning from the window, he ripped off a length of the sash and bound his forearm with it to staunch the bleeding. He was just securing the bandage when shouting reached him, followed by the clang of blades clashing, echoing up from the barmkin below.

A smile tugged at his mouth then, his uneasiness of moments earlier forgotten. The lads had seen him and had rushed the gates.

They were raising hell.

Liza paced the railing, her gaze trained north. "Where are they?"

"The captain will be on his way soon enough," Rabbie assured her. The lad sat on a coil of rope, lanky legs stretched out in front of him. He was whitling a piece of rosewood with a thin knife, seemingly unworried that noon had long passed. The sun was sinking toward the west now, and there was no sign of Rankin or his crew.

Liza's breathing grew shallow, and she halted, wrapping her fingers around the polished wooden railing. "It's taking too long." Suddenly, all she could think about was Craeg. What if he'd gotten caught up in Rankin's attack? What if he'd been maimed—or worse?

"Storming a castle isn't the work of a few moments, Lady Maclean," Egan pointed out, yanking her out of her spiraling thoughts. The pirate was washing the deck with a dirty mop. "It'll take time to secure it."

"Aye, and the captain won't send word unless it's safe for us to join them," Rabbie added.

Turning, Liza leaned her back against the railing and tried to calm the anxiety that now danced in her belly.

So much depended on the outcome of today. It was hard not to imagine the worst. She couldn't keep thinking about it, keep worrying. She needed to distract herself.

Her gaze drifted to the piece of wood Rabbie was whittling. His long freckled fingers worked nimbly. "What are ye making?"

The lad's lips stretched into a lopsided smile. "It's a dog."

"Ye are fond of dogs then?" Rabbie's earnestness made her return the smile. It helped distract her from the worry that gnawed at her belly.

He nodded. "Aye … wolfhounds especially."

Egan snorted behind him, sloshing his mop into a bucket of oily water. "It's always a hound, lad. Do ye whittle anything else?"

Rabbie flashed the older man a wounded look. "I like dogs."

"Aye, but how about something different? A fish. A cat." Egan leered at him. "Or a naked lass."

Rabbie flushed scarlet, and despite herself, Liza swallowed a smile.

"Aye," Egan continued, warming to his subject. "Make me a naked woman, Rabbie … one with huge—"

Rabbie leaped to his feet, cutting the older pirate off. "I've seen something."

"Oh, aye?" Casting aside his mop, Egan swaggered to the railing and peered north.

Liza swiftly turned, her gaze following his. "Where?"

"There." His thick finger pointed to the right, where the sparkling water merged with the hazy mainland.

Liza blinked, even as her pulse quickened. Her eyesight wasn't as sharp as Rabbie's or Egan's. She couldn't see anything.

However, as the moments passed, and she squinted, a tiny shape hove into view.

The rowboat.

Her heart kicked against her ribs. "Is it them?"

Egan flashed her a grin, revealing more gum than tooth. "We'll see soon enough."

The three of them waited at the railing, watching as the boat gradually inched closer. And as it neared *The Blood Reiver*, Liza counted just four men aboard, all of them rowing.

To her relief, they were all pirates. However, Alec Rankin wasn't among them.

Her belly clenched. This didn't bode well.

"Is it done?" Egan shouted down to them as they brought the boat alongside the cog.

"Aye!" One of the men called back, a wide smile upon his blood-splattered face. "The castle is ours, lads. The captain wants us to bring *The Reiver* in."

Stepping out of the rowboat, her slippered feet slipping on loose stones, Liza realized she was shaking.

Time had passed in a blur ever since Rankin's crew returned with the news.

The Moy Guard had apparently put up quite a fight, but taken unawares, they'd eventually been bested. Only ten of them had survived the attack though, and they'd all been taken captive—for her to deal with.

Heart thumping in her ears, Liza wiped her damp palms on her surcote and glanced over her shoulder.

The Blood Reiver bobbed there, south of Eilean Mòr—the largest of the isles in the loch, and one that connected to the mainland at low tide. The pirate cog was far enough back from the shore that she'd remain in the water, even when the tide drew out.

The bloody flag fluttered from her mast.

Liza's skin prickled.

She'd been bloodthirsty earlier that morning, when she'd watched Rankin and his men depart, full of revenge and desperation. But her courage was starting to falter now. She'd done the unthinkable—had made a pact with pirates. She'd happily hand over the coin she'd promised Rankin, but would he honor their agreement? Or would the lure of *all* the coin in the chieftain's strongroom be too much temptation for him and his crew? Rankin had surprised her the night before—and heat flushed across her chest whenever she thought about what they'd done together—but she didn't know him at all.

And if he did decide to help himself to everything in the strongroom, she wouldn't be able to stop them.

Trying to ignore the foreboding that had settled in her gut, she picked up her skirts and made her way up to the path leading to the tower house. As often, her gaze traced the crumbling walls. Moy was a faded beauty these days, but it had become home.

She tightened her jaw then, her spine straightening.

I'll repair it.

Aye, Leod's miserly ways had taken their toll on this castle and the village of Lochbuie beyond. Ever since arriving here, she'd itched to restore Moy to its former glory and also help the locals prosper.

And now she could.

She hadn't been happy here, but all the same, she'd grown fond of this castle with its views south over Loch Buie and its fertile farmland. Moy sat in a cradle, nestled between land and sea, with the rocky slopes of Ben Buie rising to the north, and the rugged outline of the Druim Fada range stretching south.

Usually, she spied sentries on the walls as she approached, but not this afternoon.

The castle was eerily quiet.

14: HOLDING BACK THE TIDE

ENTERING THE BARMKIN, Liza halted, her gaze sweeping over familiar surroundings—the stables and byre to the right, the bakehouse and kitchen to the left, and the great stone well that sat in the heart of the cobbled space.

The bodies of the dead guards sprawled on the ground, many of them still clutching their dirks and swords. And among them was a big man with wild red hair. Captain Alasdair MacCormick. The leader of the Moy Guard had stood by and watched as Leod dragged Liza down to the rowboat. They all had. Nonetheless, the sight of his body made queasiness churn in her belly.

The iron tang of blood lay heavy in the air.

Liza breathed shallowly, a chill settling over her. *Ye ordered this.*

Usually, the barmkin would be bustling with activity at this hour. But it was deserted now. The servants of Moy had either fled or were cowering somewhere.

Liza's heart leaped into a canter.

Or they're dead. Where is Craeg?

At that moment, figures emerged from the shadows around her.

Men in bloodstained braies and lèines, their hair disheveled, and victorious smiles upon their faces. Pirates.

"My son?" she said, wishing her voice didn't sound so panicked. "Where is he?"

"Safe," Cory assured her. *The Blood Reiver's* first mate approached in loose strides, a bloody dirk still gripped in his right hand. "He's hiding with the servants in the cellar."

Relief washed over Liza, and her legs wobbled under her. Drawing in a deep, steadying breath, she met his eye. "And Rankin?"

Cory's mouth quirked, his chin kicking toward the tower house. "Speak of the devil."

She turned, watching as the pirate captain emerged. Like his men, Rankin's clothing was torn and bloodied. His left forearm had been bound, and he walked with a slight limp.

Halting on the top step, Rankin's gaze met hers. He then favored her with a nod. "Welcome back to Moy, Lady Maclean."

Their gazes held a long moment before she cleared her throat. "Is it done?"

"Yer husband is dead in his solar … if ye want to see for yerself."

Dread dragged through Liza's stomach. Seeing the bodies of the Moy Guard scattered across the barmkin had unnerved her. But her husband was a different matter.

Aye, she hated Leod Maclean—and had hired someone to kill him—but he was the father of her child. Once, she'd dreamed of winning his affections, had hoped he might grow to love her. But she'd given up a while back. No, she had to remain steadfast, for her biggest challenges were likely yet to come.

Lifting her chin, she held Rankin's eye and took a step forward. "I shall go up now."

"Ma!" A cry brought her to a swift halt.

Behind Rankin, a small figure burst from the doorway. Her son hurtled down the steps, legs flying, and across the distance separating them.

And when Craeg launched himself into Liza's arms, she choked back a sob. They clung to each other for a few moments before she lowered herself to her knees in front of him and drew back, her gaze roaming over his tearstained face.

God help her, she'd gut Rankin if he or any of the other pirates had harmed her son. "Are ye hurt, love?"

"No … just scared."

She swallowed, her throat suddenly tight. "All is well, love. I'm here."

"Da said ye'd gone away forever" —Craeg's dark eyes were huge on his pale face, filled with hurt and confusion— "that ye didn't want us anymore."

Fire ignited in her veins at these words, a red veil dropping over her vision. Suddenly, any regret for what she'd done lifted like morning mist.

The bastard.

Killing his wife wasn't enough; he'd tried to poison their son against her as well.

"I'd *never* leave ye, Craeg," she whispered, squeezing his thin shoulders firmly. "I swear." She swallowed then, to try and loosen the tightness in her throat. "Yer father sent me away for a few days … that's all … but I'm back now."

Oh, how she wanted to tell him what a monster Leod was, yet something checked her. She wasn't like him. She wouldn't poison Craeg. Their son was too small to understand the complexities of adult relationships, but when he was ready, he'd learn what his father had done—and he could make up his own mind about whether to hate him.

Weariness swept over her then, pressing down upon her shoulders like two heavy hands. It was over. Leod was dead, and Craeg was safe. For the past few days, she'd been cast adrift in a violent storm, and now she'd finally reached a safe haven.

All she wished to do was crawl into a soft warm bed and pull the blankets over her head, but she couldn't. Not yet.

"But why was everyone fighting?" Craeg whispered, his attention shifting to the corpses scattered around him. "Why are all those men sleeping?"

Sleeping? Liza's throat started to ache. The Saints forgive her, she'd wanted to spare Craeg this, spare him the ugliness of life. Leod had accused her of coddling the lad, of making him soft, but she'd only wanted to protect her son, to let him believe the world wasn't a harsh, violent place, if only for a short while.

But it was like holding back the tide.

"Hold still, I'm nearly done."

Brow furrowed, Liza dug the bone needle into Rankin's arm once more, drawing the lips of the wound on his forearm together and making her last stitch. She then cut the catgut and tied it off.

The captain let out a slow, relieved breath, peering down at her work. "Ye have done a neat job."

She gave a soft snort before reaching for the bottle of strong wine she'd asked a servant to bring up from the cellar. "Aye, the women in my family are all skilled with a needle and thread." Taking hold of his forearm, she then doused the sewn wound with wine.

Rankin's hiss of pain filled the solar.

He sat upon the table, while she worked with the light of the setting sun filtering through the window.

They were alone. Her husband's body had been carried away, yet a dark stain still covered the floorboards. She'd ask one of the maids to deal with it shortly—to scrub away all evidence of what had happened in this chamber.

Ignoring the pirate's reaction, Liza reached for a cloth and gently patted his arm dry. She then picked up a length of clean linen and began to wrap the wound. Focusing on this task made being in this man's presence easier, made the queasiness that had lodged in her throat ever since stepping inside the barmkin earlier settle a little.

"How does it feel then?"

She glanced up from her task. "What?"

"To be laird of Moy Castle."

She pulled a face. "To be honest, it hasn't quite sunk in yet."

"I assured ye, my men and I would remain here for a few days … to ensure ye are safe," he replied, holding her eye. "And we will."

Liza stared back at him, uneasiness fluttering in her belly. "I appreciate that," she murmured. And she did; she wasn't sure how she'd cope without assistance, for she didn't yet know if the servants were on her side. Not only that, but the surviving ten warriors of the Guard were waiting for her in the dungeon pit.

Would they swear to follow her when she freed them?

Aye, as much as this man's presence unsettled her, she was relying on him at present.

"In the meantime, I will organize yer payment," she answered, cutting her gaze away while she secured the bandage with a neat knot. "We shall go down to Leod's strongroom first thing tomorrow."

"Thank ye, Liza."

Heat flushed across her chest. She wished he wouldn't address her so informally. Aye, they were alone now, but he still took liberties. He clearly thought the intimacy they'd shared gave him the right.

Heat washed over her then as she remembered her boldness the night before.

What madness had possessed her?

The situation had addled her wits, but now that she was back home, sanity had returned. She couldn't let Rankin think they'd ever lie together again.

She had to put some distance, some formality, between them.

As he'd just reminded her, she was laird now—and she needed to start acting as such.

Putting the items she'd used to tend to his arm back into her healing basket, she favored him with a level look, even as her pulse skittered. "We had an agreement, Captain Rankin," she said cooly. "And I shall uphold my end of it."

15: A PIRATE TAKES HIS PLUNDER

NIGHT SETTLED OVER Moy in a gentle blanket, a swathe of stars coming out to play above. Standing upon the walls, Alec tilted his head to watch them. He knew all their names. There was the North Star, of course, a sailor's compass, for it never changed position in the sky. His gaze slid to the Dog Star then, glittering brightly against the black curtain of night, before following the sparkling expanse of Orion's belt.

Whenever life was in turmoil, he took solace in the stars.

They were old friends.

Ye should leave soon, he counseled himself. *Ye don't belong here.*

Alec's mouth thinned. It wouldn't take long for word to spread that Lady Maclean had hired pirates to storm the castle, killing the laird and half the Guard. And soon enough, the clan-chief would hear of it.

Loch would want answers, and Alec would be wise to depart before the Maclean clan-chief came calling. But he wouldn't.

He'd assured Liza he'd make sure she was safe, and at present, she wasn't. He would stay on at Moy until she found her feet.

She was putting up a brave front. Nonetheless, he sensed her worry.

Liza was too proud to admit it, but they both knew the truth. She didn't know where to start with taking over from her husband. She needed guidance, and although Alec didn't have experience running a castle, he understood how to command others.

Once she has the folk of Moy onboard, I shall move on, he promised himself.

His injured forearm twinged then, reminding him of how well Liza had tended to him. She had a healer's touch.

Shaking himself free of his thoughts, Alec moved along the wall—still favoring the knee Camron MacDonald had injured, and his fight with Leod had aggravated—to where Cory stood keeping watch. His first mate was a lean shape silhouetted against the night.

"All's well?" he greeted him.

"Aye," the pirate replied, turning to him. His eyes glinted in the light of the brazier burning nearby. "For now."

"Do ye think one of the villagers will have set off for Croggan or Duart … to raise the alarm?"

Cory harrumphed. "Most likely."

"Lady Maclean will need to talk to the prisoners tomorrow then … find out who's loyal and who isn't."

"Surely, that doesn't matter to us?" Cory murmured. "We should just take our coin and leave."

Alec flashed his first mate an arch look. "And we will … once the dust settles."

Cory made another sound in the back of his throat, an exasperated one. "I thought ye wanted the crew to think ye are a ruthless wretch?"

"And I've been successful … don't ye think?"

His first mate eyed him. "Ye have … but lingering at Moy and holding the new laird's hand doesn't make ye look like a villain. A pirate takes his plunder and sails away."

Alec snorted, even as irritation speared his chest. It was unlike Cory to question him, but there was no mistaking the challenge in his eyes this evening.

His first instinct was to snarl at his friend, to remind him who was captain here. However, he checked himself.

As much as Alec hated to admit it, Cory was merely pointing out the truth.

"This way, Rankin."

Holding a lantern aloft, Liza descended the damp stone steps to the cellar beneath Moy Castle. Behind her, she heard the scuff of the captain's boots.

As promised, as soon as she'd broken her fast with fresh bannock, butter, and honey with Craeg, she'd called for him.

Best to get this over with.

Keys jangled at her waist as she reached the cellar—chatelaine keys. She'd always carried these, although there was one key her husband had never trusted her with, and she'd retrieved it from his desk in the solar. Reaching for the heavy iron ring, she selected the newest of the keys, making her way to the back of the cellar, past stacks of musty-smelling barrels, to a trap door.

Then, dropping to a crouch, she put down her lamp and unlocked the chain that secured the door.

"That's quite a chain," Rankin observed, stopping next to her.

"Aye, well … my husband didn't trust his servants not to help themselves to his coin," she replied. "No one but him has ever been down here."

"Not even ye?"

She stiffened at his question, aware that when they'd been on board *The Blood Reiver*, she'd told him she knew what her husband had in his strongroom. It was time for some honesty. "*Especially*, not me."

The lock gave way with a grinding noise, and she pulled the chain free. She then opened the door and rose to her feet, glancing the captain's way.

To Liza's surprise, Rankin wasn't looking down at the open door, but at her.

There was a gleam in his eye that she didn't trust.

"How is yer arm this morning?" she asked cooly.

His mouth curved. "On the mend."

"Aye, well, I should take a look at it again later … just to make sure it isn't souring."

She stepped back from him then and jerked her chin downward. It was time to get back to business. "After ye."

To her ire, his smile widened.

Without another word, he took the lantern she passed him and moved past her, lowering himself into the darkness.

A few moments later, Liza followed.

In truth, she was curious to see Leod's strongroom. Over the past six years, she'd occasionally seen boxes of coin carried down here, yet she wanted to know just how much wealth the laird had accumulated. He collected taxes, not just for his own coffers, but for the clan-chief too, and Lochbuie had a thriving wool trade.

Reaching the bottom of the ladder, she surveyed the chamber that had been dug out of the rock. Her gaze widened as it slid along shelving that reached from floor to ceiling. Both sides of the strongroom were packed with wooden boxes and heavy bags of coin, and a large table that sat against the far wall groaned under the weight of a bulky iron chest.

Rankin gave a low whistle. "Christ's teeth, I'd wager *Loch Maclean* himself doesn't have as much wealth as this."

"No," Liza murmured, discomfort feathering through her. Aye, Leod had been a pinchpenny, but the wealth around her was shocking. The man had let his stronghold crumble around his ears while amassing enough wealth to build a fortress to rival Duart Castle. "How does a chieftain who makes most of his coin from wool amass so much?"

Rankin made a non-committal sound in the back of his throat before moving over to a shelf and opening the nearest of the boxes. Bronze, silver, and gold coins gleamed in the lantern light. "How much do ye know about yer husband's affairs?"

She swallowed, heat flushing across her chest and creeping up her neck. She was glad the dim light in the strongroom hid her embarrassment. "Very little," she whispered. "As ye might have guessed."

The pirate opened another of the boxes on the shelf, and then another. Each was filled to the brim with coin. "There's a fortune here," he murmured.

Liza folded her arms across her chest, suppressing a shiver. "Aye, well … half of it's yers."

Rankin turned to her. The shadows in the strongroom highlighted his high cheekbones and the proud beauty of his face. "Are ye sure, Liza?"

She nodded, clenching her jaw once more at his overly familiar manner. She realized then how close they were standing. The scent of him—salt and leather, with that spicy hint of mint—made her pulse quicken, and her body's response to the pirate unnerved her. Once again, it reminded her of their night together aboard *The Blood Reiver*, of how much pleasure he'd given her. "I'm sure."

Stop it, she chastised herself as she gestured to the row of shelves they stood beside. "Take this entire side."

He nodded, his gaze searching her face. "I'll get the lads down here then."

"Do that." She took a step back, desperate to put some air between them.

However, Rankin's gaze never left her face. "Aren't ye curious to know how yer husband accumulated all this coin?"

"Aye," she admitted, looking away from him to take in the laden shelves surrounding them once more. And she was. Leod was a man with secrets, it seemed. "I think it's time I took a look at the ledgers in his solar." She paused then, her attention returning to the captain once more. "However, there are a few things I must take care of first. Once ye have helped yerself to the coin, can ye bring the prisoners up from the pit? I want to speak to them."

16: OUT OF HER DEPTH

STANDING IN THE BARMKIN, a salt-laced breeze tugging at her loosely braided hair, Liza viewed the ten warriors the pirates had dragged from the dungeon pit and brought before her.

They were a bloodied lot—they hadn't given up without a fight, it seemed—and most of them glowered at her. She knew she must present quite a sight, standing before them, her husband's dirk buckled around her hips.

She wouldn't go anywhere without it now.

The dagger bolstered her confidence. No one would know how fast her heart was beating, or that sweat trickled down between her shoulder blades. Her skin prickled under such hostile glares, although she did her best to ignore them. She hadn't expected this to be easy. Of course, it didn't help that the pirates had hauled the captive guards out here, or that Alec Rankin stood a few feet behind her now. Her new bodyguard.

Squaring her shoulders, she decided it was best to get to the point.

"I don't expect any of ye to be happy about this," she began, her gaze sweeping over their faces. "But it was necessary."

The man nearest muttered a curse under his breath and spat on the ground.

Liza ignored him, even as her pulse started to hammer in her ears. His aggressive manner reminded her of Leod.

Hold fast, Liza, she counseled herself. *Pretend ye are a woman to be reckoned with … like Makenna.* Indeed, her younger sister would face down any man, with a gimlet stare. And if a glare didn't do the trick, she wasn't averse to a bit of violence. However, Liza wasn't like her sister, and although she'd stood up for herself over the years, there was a part of her that feared men.

"What would ye do, if yer spouse trussed ye up like a Yuletide goose and left ye to die on a rock at sea?" she asked, grateful her voice remained steady. "If they stole yer son from ye?"

Silence followed these questions, although a few of the guards looked uncomfortable now. One or two stared down at their boots, their jaws tightening.

"Aye, ye know what Leod Maclean did … but none of ye stopped him." Heat kindled in her belly as she remembered how she'd screamed, pleaded, for help on that fateful day. They'd all turned their backs on her. "Aye, he was a vicious bastard," she continued, her voice catching. "I wasn't the only one he bullied." She drew in a deep breath then before letting it out slowly. "And that is why I shall spare yer lives."

The guards exchanged wary glances. Some of them were sweating now as if they expected her to play a cruel trick on them.

But she wasn't Leod. Liza's father had brought her up to be firm but fair and to speak plainly. All the same, she could have done with her father's solid, reassuring, presence by her side at present. "I offer ye a choice. Kneel before me now and swear yer fealty to the new laird of Moy … if not, ye are free to go." She paused then, her heart lurching as some of the men's gazes narrowed, before forcing herself to continue. "However, ye will no longer be welcome on my lands."

"*Yer* lands," the warrior who'd spat—a hatched-faced man named Mal, whom she'd never liked—growled. "Listen to ye." His hazel eyes glittered. "I'll not take orders from a pirate's *whore*."

The men around Mal shifted uncomfortably. One or two even stepped back, as if distancing themselves from his words.

Mal glanced around him. "It's true. I heard one of the pirates boasting last night," he told his audience. "Rankin made bedding her part of the deal."

Cold washed over Liza in an icy tide. *Mother Mary, no.*

She should have realized the pirates wouldn't keep their mouths shut. Of course, Rankin likely hadn't told them to. How would she be able to command respect here now?

Sensing her panic, Mal's mouth twisted. "Aye, everyone knows what a *slut* ye are now."

Behind her, she heard the rasp of steel against leather as Rankin drew his dirk. "Insult the lady again, and I'll kill ye," he said softly.

The chill drilled into Liza's bones, panic cleaving her tongue to the roof of her mouth. She didn't know how to respond, how to drag herself out of the hole Mal had just thrown her into. By the saints, she was out of her depth.

The warrior glared back at Rankin, a nerve flickering in his cheek.

Liza deliberately didn't look the pirate captain's way. She felt sick to her stomach, and as the coldness ebbed away, hot shame kindled deep in her chest. She noted that Rankin didn't put them right; not that anyone here would believe him anyway. Of course, he couldn't reveal his ruse before his crew, or he'd likely have a mutiny on his hands when he returned to *The Blood Reiver*.

When she didn't speak, Rankin moved forward, his boots scuffing on cobbles. "Elizabetta Maclean is laird of Moy now … and if ye aren't happy with that, ye can leave." He paused then, his voice hardening as he continued. "Make yer choice … the offer won't be repeated."

Another silence followed before Rankin cleared his throat. "What do ye wish us to do, Lady Maclean?"

Steeling herself, Liza turned her head and met his eye. The steadiness of his gaze calmed her racing heart, and she swallowed. "Order yer men to untie their wrists."

The captain shifted his focus to the pirates encircling the prisoners. "Do as she says."

Casting her sidelong glances, as if they weren't sure what game she was playing, the men complied. Moments later, the ropes were removed.

"Those who swear to follow the new laird of Moy shall now kneel," Rankin announced. Liza's belly clenched. She should be saying these things, yet her mind had suddenly gone blank. "And those who don't can leave."

A heavy silence fell in the barmkin, the wind sending dust devils dancing across the cobbles. A crowd had gathered around them, pale-faced kitchen assistants, servants, and maids emerging from the bakehouse and tower house to watch the scene unfold.

Liza couldn't meet any of their gazes. All she could think about was that everyone knew she'd spent the night with Captain Rankin. They all thought she'd bartered her body for his help. The fire in her chest expanded then, heat climbing up her neck to her face.

The devil take her, all of Mull would know soon enough—including the Maclean clan-chief.

Moments passed, and like everyone else in the barmkin, she waited, watching as five of the guards slowly lowered themselves to one knee and bowed their heads. However, the remaining five—Mal among them—did not.

Instead, the warrior's face twisted, and he spat on the cobbles between them once more. He minded his tongue this time though, his gaze flicking to Rankin. The pirate hadn't yet sheathed his dirk.

Wordlessly, those who hadn't knelt shifted back toward the gates. Their faces were taut, and they glanced around as if expecting the gathered pirates, who watched them hungrily, to pounce.

But Rankin's crew let them leave unmolested.

And when they'd departed, Liza surreptitiously wiped her damp palms on her surcote. Heart still pounding, she turned back to Rankin. He was watching her expectantly.

"Give them back their dirks," she ordered, wishing her voice didn't sound so shaky.

The captain raised a tawny eyebrow. "Are ye sure?"

She nodded, even as her mouth went dry. She wasn't certain at all, but she had to do something or the servants and guards looking on would think a lackwit had taken over this castle.

Rankin glanced over at his men. "Ye heard the lady. Do as she bids."

The pirates obeyed, handing the warriors their dirk belts.

Liza waited while, still kneeling in front of her, they strapped them around their hips, before speaking once more. "Draw yer dirks."

The scrape of steel rang across the barmkin as they complied. "Raise yer gazes."

They did, and Liza's skin prickled under their stares. As a bairn, she'd seen men sink to their knees and swear oaths to the MacGregor clan-chief. She'd never forgotten how proud she'd felt to have such a strong, powerful father. Now, she desperately grasped for some of his gravitas. "Do ye swear by yer own blades, to give me yer fealty and pledge yer loyalty to the new laird of Moy?" she asked huskily. "Do ye swear that, if yer hand shall ever be raised against me in rebellion, the steel ye carry shall pierce yer heart?"

A heartbeat of silence followed before a gruff chorus of 'ayes' answered her.

Liza cleared her throat, forcing herself to finish. "And I, Liza Maclean, laird of Moy, accept yer oath."

"How are ye bearing up?"

Liza glanced up from where she was sitting at the window in the chieftain's solar, a heavy ledger on her knee. The noon meal had just ended, and she'd settled herself here while Craeg played with wooden blocks by the fire.

But Alec Rankin's arrival shattered her peace.

Stiffening, she cut him a frown. "Don't ye know how to knock, Rankin?"

He responded with a shrug. "The door was open … I thought ye were accepting visitors."

Meanwhile, Craeg had put down his blocks and was regarding the pirate curiously.

Liza pursed her lips, waiting for Rankin to remember his manners and leave. But as the moments passed, he didn't.

Instead, his sea-green eyes fixed upon her. "I'm sorry about earlier … my crew have big mouths."

Her jaw tightened. "I thought ye might tell them to keep their tongues leashed."

He shrugged. "I couldn't without making them doubt me."

Anger ignited in her belly, followed by the urge to lash out at him. After all, if he hadn't been trying to fool his men into believing he'd coerced her into being bedded, she wouldn't have ended up humiliated this morning.

But nor would she have had the most revealing, wild night of her life.

Cease this, immediately. She swiftly slapped away the traitorous thoughts that made her lower belly clench.

"Aye, well … thanks to them spreading gossip like fishwives, I've lost the respect of everyone in this castle … not to mention the nearby village." A heavy weight settled across her shoulders at this admission. Suddenly, the task she'd set herself seemed overwhelming.

He snorted at this. "Ye don't know that." His gaze narrowed then. "Respect is earned, Liza … *show* them what a strong laird ye are."

Liza swallowed hard. "I'm not doing a grand job of it so far. Lord knows what would have happened if ye hadn't stepped in earlier"—she broke off as the humiliating scene revisited her—

"and with a Guard of just five men, I can't even protect my own castle."

Rankin's brow furrowed. His gaze slid to the ledger upon her knee then. "Any luck discovering where all that coin came from?"

She shook her head, grateful for the change of subject. "No … just the inventory I'd expect." She motioned to the desk in the corner, where a stack of leather-bound volumes sat. "I've still got a few to work my way through."

"Of course, Leod might not keep a ledger detailing secrets out in the open," Alec pointed out. "Ye may want to try his bedchamber."

Liza considered this. Curse him, he had a point. "I'll have a look," she replied, snapping the ledger shut. "Did yer visit this afternoon have a purpose?"

His mouth curved, letting her know that her blunt tone didn't bother him. "Aye … I wanted to let ye know I've sent some of my men back, with the coin, to *The Reiver.* However, six of us will remain for the time being."

She nodded, even as anxiety clutched at her chest.

"As ye pointed out, five guards aren't enough," he continued smoothly. "Ye will need to hire more. Shall I ask around in the village for ye?"

Liza stilled. Part of her wished to tell him that she would take care of the defenses of this castle. Nonetheless, today had knocked the confidence out of her. She was new to being laird, new to commanding men. She could learn much from Rankin before he departed and would be wise to do so. "Aye, I'd appreciate that," she replied grudgingly.

"Nettie says ye are the captain of a pirate cog," Craeg spoke up then. "Is that true?"

Rankin glanced over at the lad, who still crouched by the fire, staring up at him.

Discomfort shifted in Liza's stomach. She didn't like the awe upon her son's face. Like most lads his age, he was looking for a hero—but he wouldn't find one in Rankin.

"Aye, lad," the captain replied with a smile. "She's called *The Blood Reiver.*"

Craeg's eyes gleamed with interest. "Is she fast?"

"Aye, she's outrun many a clan-chief's birlinn."

Liza ground her teeth. *Braggart.*

"What color is her sail?"

"Emerald. Would ye like to see her?"

Craeg leaped up, wooden blocks scattering. "Aye!"

Liza set the ledger aside and pushed herself off the window seat. "Rankin," she said sharply. "I don't think—"

It was too late though, for the pirate had just swept her son into his arms. Then, balancing him on a hip, he carried him to the window. She noted he was no longer limping; the injury he'd sustained to his knee appeared to be on the mend. "There she is."

Craeg gasped, his eager gaze seizing upon where the cog floated, bathed by bright sunlight. Her green sail was currently furled, but the bloody flag fluttered in a stiff breeze. "Where do ye travel?"

"Wherever the mood takes me."

"To England?"

"Sometimes … I sailed the coast of northern France a few years ago."

"And have ye been in many battles?"

Rankin laughed. "A few."

"Come, Craeg." Liza moved forward and took her son. However, she had to pry him off the captain, for Craeg clung to him like a barnacle. "Captain Rankin is very busy … we mustn't hold him up."

She marked his wince as he handed Craeg back to her. Aye, she'd need to dress his forearm later as she'd promised.

"I always have time for ye, Liza," Rankin replied, his cheek dimpling then as he grinned.

Liza shot him a warning look. She didn't want this man talking to her son or influencing him in any way. A pirate could fill a bairn's head with nonsense.

"All the same, we shall let ye get on with yer day," she said, her tone cooling. "Ye have men to recruit on my behalf, have ye not?"

17: LET THIS BE

"WE'VE GOT VISITORS."

Liza turned from where she'd been instructing the cook—a belligerent man who'd been giving her more trouble than usual of late—her brow furrowing as her gaze settled upon Captain Rankin.

"Who?"

"From the looks of the banners, it's the Maclean clan-chief. A party is riding in from the north. They'll be here soon."

Liza's belly flipped over.

The clan-chief.

Rankin didn't look happy about this development either. Instead, his handsome face was almost stern. "Aye ... news travels fast, it seems."

Liza's lips compressed. Indeed, she'd wager that Mal and his friends had taken off at a run after she dismissed them, heading straight for Duart.

Loch had come to deal with her personally.

Liza's mouth went dry, her pulse fluttering. If only the clan-chief had given her more time. She'd spent the past week dealing with rebellious servants and sullen guards. She wasn't ready to receive the Maclean.

Mastering her nerves, and the thoughts of impending doom that accompanied them, she cut her gaze back to the cook, who was watching her, dark brows knitted together. "Ye and I will continue this discussion later, Murdo," she said firmly.

Murdo merely curled his lip in an expression that made her want to slap his face. She and the cook had often clashed in the past, but since her return to Moy, his disdain had been thinly veiled. Liza wouldn't let him intimidate her though, and as such had taken to visiting the dour bastard every morning.

Turning her back on Murdo, Liza left the kitchen and stepped out into the barmkin. After a spell of sunny weather, a blanket of grey cloud had descended. The air this morning was damp and heavy, and she sucked it deep into her lungs to steady herself.

Glancing up at the walls, she spied some new faces. Rankin had surprised her by recruiting twelve lads from the village. They were all green and unskilled with a blade, but he'd started training them. Nonetheless, Rankin could only do so much with limited time. Any day now, he and his crewmates would pack up and set sail, and when they did, she'd truly be put to the test. She'd see then what those who served her really thought of their new laird, and whether they'd follow a woman.

Her stomach twisted, for she was beginning to fear they wouldn't.

Glancing over at where Rankin had stepped up to her shoulder—while the thunder of approaching hoofbeats warned that the clan-chief was just moments from bursting into the barmkin—she met his eye.

"Courage, Liza," he murmured. "Loch is a fair man."

Her pulse jolted. Curse Rankin, somehow, he'd sensed her rising panic. The man paid too much attention to her. "Aye," she managed roughly. "But Lord knows what Mal and the others told him."

Rankin's gaze never wavered, even if she marked the shadow in it. "And ye will put him straight. Nothing happened between us, remember? Loch's spared ye a trip to Duart … for ye intended to speak to him anyway."

"I know, but—"

Their conversation was cut short then, by the sight of a powerful bay courser entering the barmkin. A broad-shouldered man with long dark hair and a beard trimmed close to his jaw rode it, a clan-sash—the red Maclean plaid—across the front of his padded gambeson.

Loch Maclean led his escort into the fortress. The clan-chief was a striking man; Liza could see why he'd turned his wife, Mairi's, head, but right now, his brow was marred by a deep scowl.

Her breathing grew rapid and shallow.

Hell's teeth, this wasn't going to end well for her.

A company of men clattered into the barmkin after the clan-chief and drew their horses up either side of him. Liza recognized one of them, a lean man with sharp features and mussed light-brown hair: Finn MacDonald, Captain of the Duart Guard. Like his clan-chief's, MacDonald's expression was grim this morning.

Meanwhile, Loch's gaze narrowed further as his attention settled on Liza. A heartbeat later, he shifted his focus to Rankin, and his mouth pursed. "What's this, Alec? Ye've taken to murdering my chieftains?"

Liza's stomach clenched. How typical. She was the laird here, and yet the clan-chief addressed the pirate first. A crowd gathered in the barmkin now as servants stopped work to get a look at the clan-chief. She could feel their gazes upon her, eagerly awaiting her humiliation.

Hot, prickling embarrassment swept over Liza, as she anticipated giving them another spectacle to gossip over, before something gave way inside her. She forgot her fear then, indignation rising in her breast. The past week had been a trial. She was tired of being sneered at and undermined.

"Go back to work." Her voice rang against stone as she swept her gaze over the gathering servants, daring them to defy her. A strained silence followed before they reluctantly obeyed, drifting away and leaving Liza and Alec to face the clan-chief alone.

Pulse thumping in her ears, she focused on Loch once more. She had his attention now, at least. He was staring at her, his dark brows knitted together. "He did it on my orders," she said, her voice louder than she'd intended. "We made an agreement … and he honored it."

Silence followed these words before the clan-chief swung down from the back of his courser. He then moved forward, stopping when they were only a couple of feet apart. He was a big man, looming over her. "Aye," he growled. "I've heard all about the *arrangement* ye made with Rankin."

Standing before the hearth in the laird's solar, Liza eyed the three men who'd accompanied her upstairs.

She'd surprised herself again outdoors by raising her chin—even as her heart slammed against her ribs—and holding Loch's eye. "This isn't the place to talk about such things, Maclean," she'd replied, relieved that her nerve held. "I shall wait for ye upstairs."

Then, before Loch could reply, she'd turned on her heel and stalked back into the tower house. Her own audacity had astounded her, yet here they were, a short while later—alone. Although she'd sent the guards, servants, and stable lads back to work earlier, she still didn't want to have this conversation out in the barmkin where they risked being overheard.

Unfortunately, though, Loch Maclean didn't look any happier than before. His brow furrowed as he leaned against the window ledge and regarded her.

Folding her arms across her chest, she held his eye. "Ye know what Leod did to me, I assume?" Loch's expression tightened at this, his dark-brown eyes shadowing as she continued, "He tied me up and left me to die on that rock."

"Ye should have come to me," he shot back. "I'd have dealt out justice."

Liza's pulse fluttered. Swallowing hard, she tilted her chin higher. She wouldn't look away. "I didn't think ye would," she replied, her voice catching. "I thought ye'd take yer chieftain's word over mine … that he'd tell ye I was a madwoman, and ye'd believe him."

A muscle feathered in his jaw.

"Deny it," she said roughly. "Men always stick together, don't they?"

A few feet from the clan-chief, MacDonald murmured an oath under his breath.

Eventually, Loch answered. "Ye have been ill-treated … I see that."

Liza didn't respond, even as her throat grew tight, and her eyes began to burn. No, she wouldn't humiliate herself by weeping. She needed to stay strong. For her people. For her son. Upon re-entering the tower house, she'd bidden Nettie to take Craeg into the lady's solar and play with him for a while, for she didn't want her son to overhear this conversation. "I took my revenge on a man who wronged me," she pushed on, clenching her hands at her sides. "Will ye punish me for it?"

There wasn't any point in avoiding this subject. She had to know.

Rankin had told her to set the clan-chief straight about the fact he hadn't coerced her into lying with him, but something inside her quailed at telling Loch so. Instead, she focused on the real issue: the fact she'd had her husband murdered and taken his place as laird.

Loch continued to stare at her for a moment longer before muttering a curse. "Ye deserve punishment, Liza. I can't have pirates storming my castles and putting my chieftains to the sword … or forcing women into their beds." His attention snapped to where Rankin stood by the closed door to the solar. "What's wrong, Alec … have ye lost yer tongue?"

The pirate captain's mouth curved into a tight smile that didn't reach his eyes. "No … I was letting the lady speak for herself," he replied. "But since she hasn't enlightened ye, I shall." He paused then, his gaze narrowing, while Liza's pulse took off at a canter. *Lord, here we go.* "The rumors that reached ye were wrong. I didn't coerce Lady Maclean into lying with me. It was nothing but a ruse."

Loch's dark eyes glinted. "Ye expect me to believe this?"

"It's the truth." The words rushed out of Liza. "As soon as we were alone together, Rankin assured me he wouldn't touch me."

"I've been having trouble with my crew," the pirate added. "Ever since I allied myself with ye." He paused then, grimacing. "Pirates are fickle bastards … I needed to do something to get them back on side."

Loch's mouth pursed once more, an expression he seemed to make whenever something vexed him. His hard gaze, still fixed upon Rankin, made it clear he wasn't impressed. "Whether or not ye forced Lady Maclean into yer bed, the fact remains that ye have ruined her reputation," he growled.

Liza couldn't help it, she snorted. Her reaction made Loch's attention snap her way, but she didn't let his withering glare cow her. "I've just had my husband murdered," she pointed out. "Whether or not everyone on this isle thinks I'm a pirate's wench matters not now, does it?"

A surprised silence followed these words.

Rankin broke it, his mouth curving into a rueful smile. "I did ye a favor in getting rid of Leod Maclean." He nodded to Liza then. "We both know his wife will make a far better laird."

"That's not yer decision to make," Loch shot back, his temper fraying. "Ye took advantage of a desperate woman."

Rankin shrugged, even as his sea-blue eyes narrowed. Suddenly, the air inside the solar turned charged, as if a storm were just about to break overhead. "The lady offered me a job, and I took it."

Loch pushed himself up off the window ledge. His hand then strayed to the hilt of his dirk, and he took a menacing step toward the pirate captain. "Aye, so ye could line yer own pockets." Violence sparked in his eyes. "Now, ye shall pay."

Rankin moved forward to face him, as he reached for his own weapon.

Without thinking, Liza stepped in between them. She raised her hand then, placing it upon Loch's chest. "Stop," she gasped. "This was entirely my choice, Loch … he wanted to take me to ye, but I refused."

Loch's gaze jerked to her. "Christ's blood, woman. Ye'd defend him?"

Liza's pulse beat a tattoo against her breastbone. "I don't want any more blood spilled because of me," she whispered while she kept her palm pressed against his chest. "*Please*, Loch. Let this be."

Moments slid by, and then Loch's face twisted in disgust, and he stepped back. Liza's hand fell away, and she moved aside. She could feel Rankin's gaze boring into her, yet she refused to meet his eye.

"Ye are a fool to have lingered here." Loch turned his attention to the pirate captain once more. "Ye should have taken yer blood-soaked coin and sailed off."

"Lady Maclean couldn't hold this castle without help," Rankin replied, his tone wintry now. "I promised her I'd stay until she found her feet."

Liza did glance his way then. There was a coiled tension in his body. His hand still rested upon the grip of his dirk. "Rankin has helped me," she admitted, focusing on Loch again. "He's recruited men to my Guard and has started training them. His pirates stand watch over Moy's walls at night."

Loch's glower didn't soften at these words, and Liza's pulse fluttered. "Aye, yer chieftain is dead … but I'm to blame," she pushed on, a little shakily now as she clung to her courage. "And what's more, I'm not sorry. Leod tried to kill me, and I paid him back."

"Ye took justice into yer own hands, woman," Loch ground out. "I should string ye up by yer neck from the walls as a warning to others."

Liza's bowels cramped at this threat, her bravery crumbling. Loch Maclean's wrath was terrifying to behold.

Another silence fell in the solar, and she clenched her fists by her sides, waiting for the clan-chief to sentence her.

I'm sorry, Craeg. She started to sweat as she imagined her son's stricken face at the sight of his mother's corpse hanging from the castle walls. *I've failed ye.*

"Leod Maclean was a secretive bastard," Rankin spoke up then. His tone was veiled, yet reassuringly calm. He'd been angry earlier, but Loch's threats didn't appear to have scared him as they had Liza. "Ye didn't know him as well as ye think … and his widow has some news regarding his affairs that might interest ye."

Loch folded his arms across his chest. "Oh, aye?"

18: TURNING THE TABLES

A DEEP SILENCE settled in the chieftain's solar while Loch Maclean sat at the desk and went through the ledger. Finn MacDonald stood at his shoulder, reading, his brow furrowed. Liza and Rankin waited together by the hearth.

Liza's belly churned.

Indeed, as Rankin had suggested, she'd searched her dead husband's bedchamber and discovered a ledger under his bed. And within, a list of income that had nothing to do with the wool he sold or the taxes he collected.

"He's taken care not to label the source of these takings," Loch said eventually, as he turned the final page of inventory. Liza was relieved to note that the anger had cooled in his voice. He hadn't spoken again about executing her either.

"Aye," MacDonald muttered. "He's just used a series of initials ... they could mean anything."

"There's a pattern to them though," Rankin replied. "Most of them are in late spring and autumn ... with a break during winter and high summer."

Loch nodded. "And they started three years ago … a couple of months after our victory over the Mackinnons."

"Leod wasn't happy about how that all ended," the pirate pointed out then. "Do ye recall?"

The clan-chief frowned, pushing himself up from the desk and striding over to the open window. "Aye … but I doubt this has any connection."

"No?" A challenge crept into Rankin's voice then. "The chieftain of Moy was vexed that ye spared Bran Mackinnon's life … angry enough to conduct secret business and fill his strongroom full of coin he never shared with ye, if ye ask me."

The words were blunt, and Loch's spine stiffened.

Meanwhile, Liza's pulse quickened. The last thing she wanted was for Rankin to vex the clan-chief again.

"Alec has a point," MacDonald replied. He bent over the ledger then, his gaze narrowing as he leafed back through the entries. "How was he getting his hands on so much coin?"

Loch scowled. "Smuggling?"

"Perhaps." MacDonald shook his head, clearly unconvinced. "But what?"

"I haven't seen any goods being transported here," Liza said. She cast her mind back over the past three years, trying to pick out a variation in her husband's routine, something that might give them a clue. "However, over the past two years at least, he's had a regular visitor."

The clan-chief's gaze fastened on her. "Who?"

"That's the strange thing," she murmured, recalling the rare occasions she'd glimpsed the man. "Usually, Leod hosted guests in his hall, and I'd pour wine for them … but not with this one. He met with him in here … and I was never invited to join them. I never heard his name."

Loch's jaw flexed. "Did ye get a look at him?"

Liza nodded. "A big man with wild dark hair, a beard, and heavy features. He dressed in worn leathers."

MacDonald cursed. "That could describe half the men on this isle."

Liza grimaced. "That's all I remember, sorry."

"Aye, well … I shall investigate this," Loch replied, lowering himself onto the window seat. "In the meantime, I need to decide what to do about Moy Castle's future … and *ye*, Liza."

Dizziness swept over her. "Will ye hang me?" she asked huskily.

Loch huffed a sigh before sharing a look with his captain. A heavy pause followed, and then he swore under his breath. "I should."

Her belly started to churn, and her mouth went dry. However, she held her tongue. *Ye knew there was a risk of this*, she reminded herself, even as her legs began to tremble. *But ye didn't care.*

No, she hadn't. All that had mattered was avenging herself on Leod and returning home to her son. She'd brushed worries of any consequences aside. But now, here they were, staring her in the face.

Fool, she railed at herself. *Leod taught ye how men in power behave.*

The silence swelled before Loch dragged a hand through his hair. "But I won't."

Liza's breath whooshed out of her. She reached out then, steadying herself against the mantelpiece, for her legs had gone as weak as a newborn foal's. She couldn't believe it—maybe Loch wasn't like her husband, after all. "In that case, I wish to remain here as laird."

The clan-chief stared back at her, his dark eyes widening at her audacity.

Liza didn't blame him. She'd shocked herself as well. The man had just spared her life, and here she was already making demands on him. However, the words slipped from her tongue before she could stop them. "I know lady lairds aren't common … but I shall serve ye well, if ye put yer trust in me."

His lip curled. "I'm not sure ye are worthy of my trust."

"I *am*," she gasped, panic bubbling up once more. "Give me six months, Loch. Let me prove to ye I'm fit to rule Moy."

His expression didn't soften as he stared back at her. "And how do I benefit from such an arrangement?"

Liza dragged in a deep breath. "Leod has no brothers or cousins … there's only his son to inherit. And as soon as Craeg comes of age, I am happy to step aside."

"Aye … but that's years away. I could easily find someone to act as steward until yer son is old enough."

"Ye could … but the people here know me." She didn't admit that most of them viewed her with a jaundiced eye these days. "And I have plans to use some of that coin Leod hoarded to make Moy and Lochbuie thrive once more." She paused then, aware that she was sweating heavily now. So much depended on this. "Ye have seen the poor state of the castle walls, the neglected crofts in the village. I swear to ye, I will see it all repaired."

A crease etched between his eyebrows, although she marked the gleam of interest in his eyes. "And what of yer Guard, Liza? Even with yer recruits from the village, it's sparse."

"It will grow. I have sent word to nearby villages. More men will come. By summer's end, we'll have a full Guard once more."

"But do ye have the stomach to lead them?" Loch countered, his voice hardening. "To rule requires difficult choices. Could ye order a man to be flogged or hanged, if necessary?"

Liza held his eye, even as her pulse went wild. "I paid a pirate to kill my husband. What do *ye* think?"

To her surprise, Loch Maclean snorted a humorless laugh. "God's bones, woman." He gave a rueful shake of his head. "Ye have a sharp tongue on ye."

Liza frowned. She wasn't sure whether the clan-chief was mocking her or not, and now braced herself for his scorn.

"Ye are no fazart, I'll give ye that," Loch continued then. "But ye're still vulnerable here." His chin jerked in Rankin's direction. "He'll be gone soon. Most men don't like the idea of being ruled by a woman. Ye can't trust yer local recruits not to turn on ye the moment the pirates raise anchor."

"Ye could send someone ye trust?" she asked, her breathing growing shallow. Loch was considering letting her stay on, but she could feel him wavering. "Someone to ensure my men stay loyal."

Loch weighed up her request then, his brow furrowing. "Very well," he said finally. "But I will give ye just *four* months to prove yer worth." *Four months?* Liza's heart kicked against her ribcage at this announcement. How the devil would she achieve anything in that time? However, Loch plowed on. "And in the meantime, I will—"

"There's no need to send anyone," Rankin cut Loch off, his tone brusque. "I'll do it."

All gazes turned to him, and Alec gave himself a swift kick. *What have ye done?*

Couldn't he have kept his gob shut? Liza was doing an excellent job of negotiating her position with the clan-chief. All he had to do was let her secure the help she needed from Loch. He'd be off the hook then, free to sail away from Moy Castle without a backward glance.

But instead, he'd offered up his own services.

Loch's piercing gaze bored into him. "Ye'll do *what*, exactly?"

Alec stared him down. "I'll stay at Moy Castle. I will captain the Guard … for as long as Lady Maclean needs me."

His attention shifted to Liza then. She was staring at him, stunned.

"Why?" she whispered.

Alec's heart started to pound. The devil's turds, he'd just dug a great hole for himself. In truth, he wasn't sure what had made him blurt the words out—only that he'd started to feel personally responsible for Liza Maclean. He couldn't admit such a thing though. "Ye gave up much to take this castle," he replied, wishing his voice wasn't so rough. "Including yer reputation. I shall help ye regain it."

Loch snorted.

Heat washed over Alec. He couldn't blame Loch for deriding him. In his place, he'd have done the same.

"Christ's teeth," MacDonald murmured. "I do believe yer conscience is bothering ye, Rankin."

Alec made a dismissive sound in the back of his throat, not looking Finn's way. "The reason doesn't matter … it's the offer that does." He met Loch's eye once more. "See this as my way of mending our relationship." It struck him then that despite the animosity that had sparked between them during this meeting, Loch Maclean's good opinion still mattered to him.

However, Loch pulled a face, making it clear that Alec would have to do better than that to regain his trust or respect.

"What about *The Blood Reiver?*" Finn pointed out then.

Alec's stomach clenched. "She'll set sail without me."

"Ye would walk away from yer crew?" A deep groove had etched itself between Liza's finely shaped brows. Her lovely brown eyes were still clouded with confusion. "I don't understand ye, Rankin."

He shrugged, wishing she'd change the subject. "They'll survive just fine without me."

Liza's words back on *The Reiver* revisited him then. *Ye will leave no legacy behind ye … nothing permanent to be remembered by.* His gut hardened. He'd scoffed at the time—for his name as a notorious spùinneadair-mara would surely survive after him— yet something about her words had needled him ever since. And in the past week, the restlessness he'd been suffering for a while now had intensified. He felt strange, as if he'd just drawn in a deep breath and was still waiting to exhale. He was about to walk a different path, and it rattled him slightly.

But Liza was right. Maybe he did want to be remembered for something good—something besides piracy.

Loch cleared his throat. "Aye, well, ye could stand in for a while, I suppose," he replied, his tone grudging. "The Ghost Raiders hit Craignure a few days ago … and I need all my men at present."

Alec stiffened at this news. Craignure was a busy port village, a stone's throw from Duart Castle. It was a bold target. "And are they demons aboard a phantom ship, as folk say?"

"I wasn't there to witness the attack," Loch replied frowning. "It took place on a foggy eve, so no one saw the cog approach. Its crew were all garbed in black hooded cloaks, horned sheep's skulls covering their faces. However, demons or not, they ransacked the village … and carried off all the coin they got their hands on."

"Since when do demons need earthly riches?" Alec asked.

"Exactly."

"Even so, they killed the men who tried to stop them," Finn added. "The villagers are still frightened … and the fishermen are refusing to go out."

The clan-chief's features tightened at his. Aye, it seemed that Loch did have his hands full. He glanced Liza's way then. She stood there, still and pale, a muscle working in her clenched jaw.

"If ye wish to keep Rankin on to captain yer Guard for the time being, I'll permit it," Loch said then. "But the choice is yers."

Silence fell once more in the solar. However, this time, the attention wasn't upon Alec but on Liza.

To Alec's surprise, he realized he was sweating.

Cods. He couldn't help but think he'd just made a gesture that would merely end in his humiliation. He didn't like how swiftly the tables had turned. Until now, he'd enjoyed a position of power, knowing that Liza relied upon his assistance.

Now though, she could throw it back in his face.

He couldn't get angry at her for that though—he was the idiot who'd made the offer. As such, he braced himself to be spurned.

Liza favored Loch with a stiff nod before her gaze settled upon Alec.

He started to sweat under the hard look she was giving him. "Very well, Rankin," she murmured finally. "Ye can stay on."

19: BETTER THE DEVIL YE KNOW

MACLEAN AND HIS men departed in the misty dawn, ghostly shapes passing under the stone arch.

Liza and Rankin stood together in the barmkin watching them go.

And as the hoofbeats faded, Liza slowly turned to the man who now led her Guard.

"That went better than I expected." Rankin's tone was light, although his expression was difficult to read. Nonetheless, she sensed his tension this morning. Since he'd accepted her offer, they'd barely spoken. She'd been taken up by the clan-chief anyway, and ensuring his needs were met.

In response, she gave a soft snort. "Aye, well … I did my best to smooth Loch's ruffled feathers yestereve."

Indeed, she'd put on a special supper for him, quite a feat at short notice, yet Murdo and his assistants managed it. The grumpy cook didn't dare complain about having to prepare a feast for Loch. He'd dug dried sausage and tangy goat's cheese out of the spence, which his lads served with braised onions and platters of boiled spring greens, alongside cobs of oaten bread.

Rankin eyed her. "Ye two appeared to have much to discuss during supper?"

"Aye," she replied. "He wished to detail my responsibilities to him, as clan-chief. His bailiff will collect levies twice yearly, and I must provide Duart with a quota of wool every summer."

Rankin nodded. "Did he take yer husband's ledger with him?"

"Aye … he promises to find out what Leod was up to."

Liza drew in a deep breath then. The conversation at supper had been challenging, although they hadn't spoken of Leod again, or of what Liza had done. Nor did Loch visit the former chieftain's grave, on the fringes of the kirkyard in Lochbuie village. It was clear he condemned her husband's act.

"He also reminded me that my position here isn't secure," she admitted after a pause, lowering her voice. "In fact, he'll be sending someone to 'check up on me' and report back to him. Then in four months' time, he'll let me know his decision."

"Aye, well … it could have been worse," Rankin replied.

It certainly could have been—which was why Liza had accepted all of it with a nod. Even so, her belly twisted. Four turns of the moon would pass in the blink of an eye. And in that time, she'd have to prove herself and earn the respect of the locals. She couldn't waste time and would now get to work. Even so, her dealings with the clan-chief surprised her. Her time with Leod had sown distrust of men, but although Loch Maclean was arrogant and forthright, he hadn't treated her cruelly—and he was giving her a chance.

"Did ye show him the strongroom?" Rankin asked, drawing her out of her thoughts.

"Aye … I took him down there before we retired for the eve." She pulled a face then, recalling Loch's scowl as he viewed the heavy bags and crates of coin stacked upon the shelves from floor to ceiling. "Even half-emptied, the room still holds considerable wealth. I suggested he took some … but he refused."

Silence fell after these words, and Liza mulled over the ramifications of Loch's visit. She'd put the clan-chief up in Leod's bedchamber overnight. Since taking Moy Castle as her own, she'd decided to remain in the small chamber she'd made hers over the years. She didn't want to sleep in her husband's bed. His room would be for guests from now on.

The night before, she'd slept fitfully. In truth, she regretted agreeing to let Rankin stay on. It was best for everyone if he set sail and left her to get on with things. But his offer had thrown Liza, and as much as it galled her to admit it, she needed his help.

Of course, Loch would have sent someone from Duart. But the man would likely be a stranger. Curse it, she'd gotten used to having Rankin around.

Aye, the arrangement unsettled her. If they were going to work together, she had to make a few things clear.

"A private word, if ye please, Rankin," she said then, jerking her chin to the armory to their left—a long, narrow, and windowless building squashed in between the stables and the outer wall. She could have called him up to the laird's solar, but she didn't want to draw this conversation out. She had a busy day ahead, after all, and while the clan-chief had been in residence, she'd barely seen her son. She'd seek Craeg out now, and ensure all was well with him, before she drew herself up a plan of how to achieve the things she'd promised the clan-chief.

Rankin inclined his head. "Ye wish to speak to me in the armory?"

"Aye," she said crisply. Most of the servants had returned to their chores now that the clan-chief had departed, but Liza's conversation with her captain was about to take a different turn, and she couldn't risk being overheard.

He nodded, curiosity lighting in his eyes. He then set off wordlessly across the barmkin. Drawing open the wattle door, he allowed Liza to enter first.

She did, with a purposeful stride.

Inside, the dim interior, lit by a single lantern hanging from the rafters, smelled of leather and iron. Rows of axes, pikes, and fighting daggers hung neatly from the walls, while stacks of iron helmets lined a narrow bench along one side.

Liza was pleased to see that Rankin had instructed the guards to tidy this place up. Leod's approach to such things had always been slovenly. In the past week, Liza had done her best to bring order to the castle. Two days earlier, she'd had lads out sweeping and scrubbing the cobbles in the barmkin. In the past, Leod had always forbidden her from giving such instructions.

She wouldn't praise her captain just yet though. She hadn't called Rankin in here to stroke his already inflated male pride.

"Close the door," she instructed, turning to face him.

Rankin did as bid, his lips lifting at the corners. "Interesting place for a chat, Liza," he murmured.

Her jaw tightened, and irritation flared. "I can see I need to make a couple of things clear," she replied stiffly. "The first is that from now on, ye are to address me as 'Lady Maclean' … both when we are surrounded by others *and* when we are alone."

He inclined his head, acknowledging her command. "And the second?"

Liza folded her arms across her chest. "I want to know the *real* reason ye offered to captain my Guard."

"I told ye yesterday."

"Aye, some blether about feeling responsible for me … and wanting to repair things with Loch." She stared him down then. "Frankly, I don't believe ye."

His mouth quirked. "A lady in distress has always been my weakness."

She made a rude noise in the back of her throat.

He shrugged. "Let's just say, I didn't like the idea of Loch sending someone ye didn't know … or trust … here. Ye are vulnerable at present."

The fire in her belly started to pulse. "What makes ye think I trust *ye*?"

He flashed her a grin. "Better the devil ye know."

His flippant reply made her frown. "And will any of yer crew remain?"

His expression sobered. "I don't know. I told my men of my decision yestereve, and they didn't take the news well. It remains to be seen if any will stay on at Moy."

Her gaze roamed over his face, frustration tightening in her chest. By the Saints, she wished she could read his thoughts. "I don't understand ye, Rankin," she muttered.

"Ye don't need to … but ye have my word that I will serve ye well."

He was looking at her intensely now, and there was a heat in the depths of his eyes that made her feel flustered. She'd started this exchange in control, but she could feel the reins slipping between her fingers.

Her frown deepened to a scowl. "How easily promises glide off yer tongue," she replied, her manner stilted now. "We shall see if ye are worthy of my trust."

He took a step toward her, his own gaze narrowing. "Didn't I prove that to ye already … aboard *The Reiver?*"

Liza's pulse skittered. There was an intimacy to his voice that made her feel all hot and flustered. Aye, he was reminding her of how he'd made it clear he wouldn't touch her. Indeed, he'd gone to sleep—and then she'd woken him up and asked him to plow her.

Her breathing grew shallow then, humiliation flushing up her neck.

Hades, this conversation hadn't gone at all as she'd hoped. They'd strayed into dangerous waters now, and she needed him to leave.

Turning abruptly away, so he wouldn't see her glowing face, she cleared her throat. "That's all, Rankin," she said as she tried to pull herself together. "Ye can return to yer duties now."

Silence fell in the armory, and she waited for the creak of the wattle door.

Instead, she heard the scuff of his boots moving toward her. Liza's pulse took off like a bolting pony. What was he doing?

"I'll leave ye soon enough, Lady Maclean." She jolted as his breath feathered her ear. He was right behind her, so close the warmth of his body enveloped her as if she were standing next to a furnace. "But first, let me ask *ye* a question … why did ye defend me to the clan-chief yesterday?"

"I wish I hadn't," she gasped, grabbing hold of the edge of the bench to steady herself. She should turn around and shove him in the chest, should jump to one side. But she didn't. Instead, she sucked his fresh scent deep into her lungs.

"I've never had a woman put herself between me and an adversary before," he murmured, his breath tickling the shell of her ear once more. A shiver rippled through her as her body responded. Suddenly, they were back on *The Blood Reiver*, and he was whispering wicked things in her ear as he took her from behind in slow, deep thrusts. Her knees trembled at the torrid memory, lust igniting low in her belly.

"I didn't want to see blood spilled," she ground out.

"Perhaps." He stepped in closer then, their bodies touching now. "But I was flattered all the same."

She swallowed hard. "Don't be." Lord, she wished the words didn't gust out of her as if she was panting. "It meant nothing."

"It did to me." He leaned in further. "And when ye put yer hand on Loch's chest, I wanted to draw my dirk and kill him."

Her breathing caught. "Jealous, Rankin?"

"Aye."

Liza bit down on her lower lip. Even with the layers of her kirtle and surcote, she felt him, hot and hard, pressing into the cleft between her buttocks. Her fingernails dug into the wooden bench, even as her quim started to ache.

Mother Mary, this situation was spiraling. She had to claw back control before she humiliated herself. The urge to push back against his erection, to grind herself against it, was overwhelming, but she wouldn't give in to it. She wasn't aboard *The Blood Reiver* anymore. That night had been a stolen moment in time, but now she was home and laird of Moy Castle. She couldn't let base lust rule her—she couldn't give the servants reason to whisper behind her back.

Satan smite her, she shouldn't even be alone with him in the armory.

Loch had barely departed, and she was already making poor decisions.

"Ye have no cause for jealousy," she managed throatily, clawing back her wits. "I'm not yer woman … and from now on, our relationship will remain strictly professional."

Rankin's body tensed against hers. He drew back then so that they were no longer touching. That was better. She could think again. Her heart was pounding so fast now, she wouldn't be surprised if he could hear it too.

All the same, his silence made her uneasy.

"Ye should go," she added, wishing she didn't sound so breathless. She still didn't turn to face him. Coward that she was, she didn't want to see the hunger on his face, to meet his burning gaze.

"Aye," he replied roughly. "I should."

Silence followed as he moved away. A moment later, she heard his boots on the wooden floor, followed by the thud of the armory door closing behind him.

20: A BED OF NAILS

ALEC'S CREW WAS waiting for him on the shore. And as he approached, he marked the scowls on their faces. Behind them, *The Reiver* was a phantom shape in the mist. The sun was burning the fog off though; it wouldn't be long before the sky was clear.

No, his men weren't happy, and he didn't blame them.

Right now, he wanted nothing more than to return to his ship, raise the anchor, and set sail.

But he wouldn't be leaving. He'd made a promise—not only to the new laird of Moy, but to the Maclean clan-chief as well. He wouldn't go back on it.

Nonetheless, after that encounter in the armory, things would be awkward between him and Liza now.

Had he taken leave of his wits? What had possessed him to approach her like that, to rub himself up against her like an animal? His groin still ached, and his rod was as hard as wood in his braies. Walking had chafed him, yet he'd clenched his jaw and willed his erection to subside.

Heat washed over him as he recalled the things he'd said to her—things he hadn't even admitted to himself. That he'd been pleased she defended him, and that he'd been jealous when she touched Loch.

Understandably, she hadn't responded well, and humiliation now burned like a lump of peat in his gut.

"Lads," he greeted his crew.

Grunts and glowers answered him.

Stopping before the group of hard men dressed in salt-stained braies, lèines, and worn leather vests, he surveyed them. A pressure rose under his breastbone then. He couldn't believe he was abandoning them. "I'm sorry to let ye down," he said, folding his arms across his chest.

Cory frowned. "So, ye haven't changed yer mind then?"

Alec shook his head.

Next to him, Gunn cracked his scarred knuckles. "Ye'll regret this."

I already do.

"*The Reiver* is yers, Cory," he said, focusing on his first mate once more. "May she bear ye as fast and safely as she has me all these years." Christ's blood, the pressure in his chest had turned to an ache now. Trying to ignore it, he let his gaze travel over the faces of the rest of the crew. "Yesterday, I asked if any of ye would remain at Moy with me … to take up a new role as a warrior in my Guard." He paused then, raising an eyebrow. "Do I have any takers?"

Silence followed.

A stone settled on Alec's chest, even as he forced a smile. "I thought as much," he said, careful to keep his voice emotionless. "Ye are all sea dogs through and through … I'd expect no less from ye."

"Ye used to be just like us," Cory replied, stroking his wispy beard as he eyed him. "It's *her*, isn't it?"

Alec stilled.

"Ye don't even know if Elizabetta Maclean will remain laird here." Cory shook his head, huffing a deep sigh. "She's bewitched ye."

"Ye shouldn't have made that deal with the woman," Gunn said then, scowling. "The coin would have been enough."

"Aye, ye shouldn't have stuck yer prick in her," Egan growled from behind Gunn, his round face florid with anger. "Ye haven't been yerself ever since."

"Careful," Alec murmured, his voice lowering in warning. "Mind yer tongue, Egan."

The pirate glared back yet heeded him.

Meanwhile, despite the mild morning, a chill enveloped Alec, seeping deep into his bones. He'd played a high-stakes game, believing he was in control of the outcome, but he wasn't. Not any longer.

It was time to be honest with them.

"It was all mummery, lads," he said after a heavy pause. "As soon as I was alone with Liza, I assured her I wouldn't touch her." They stared back at him, their faces stiffening with surprise as Alec added firmly. "I still draw the line at rape … and I always will."

Egan snorted. "But ye plowed the woman … we all heard!" This comment brought nods and mutters from some of the other crewmates.

Alec's gaze narrowed. "Whatever happened between Lady Maclean and me … it's *our* business … not yers."

Glowers followed this comment, yet none of them argued with him.

"Why did ye lie to us?" Gunn asked roughly. Next to him, Cory remained silent, his gaze shuttered.

"It matters not," Alec replied. Gunn wasn't the brightest of men, although judging from the glint in the eyes of the other crewmates, most of them had guessed the reason. They'd fill him in later. And of course, Cory had always known. Alec wouldn't betray him though.

A brittle silence fell then. Alec let it lie. He had nothing else to say.

Eventually, Gunn growled a curse, spun on his heel, and lumbered down to one of the two boats waiting on the tideline.

The others departed moments later, although not without muttered oaths and dark looks. Alec watched them cramming themselves into the boats. They then rowed out to the cog, the splash of oars carrying through the still morning.

He lingered on the pebbly beach. He should really return to the castle, for he had more men to recruit and green warriors to train. However, his feet wouldn't move.

The pirates were climbing up the cog's rigging now and preparing for departure.

Christ's bones, he longed to go with them. He was a fool to think he could live any other life. His soul was only ever at peace at sea, yet he'd just turned his back on it.

Out of a misguided protective streak, restlessness, and a desire to make his life count for something.

"Well, that's it," he murmured. "Ye have made yer bed, now ye'll just have to lie in it." He grimaced then. Pity it was a bed of nails.

"When is Da coming home?"

Craeg's question made Liza freeze. She'd been about to take a spoonful of mutton stew, yet her appetite now deserted her.

Her son was watching her from across the table, worry shadowing his dark eyes.

Aye, he was young, too wee to fully understand death, but he knew something unpleasant had befallen his father.

They sat in the laird's solar having supper together. On this, her first evening of officially being the laird of Moy—since the clan-chief had given her his temporary blessing—Liza had wanted to enjoy a meal alone with her son. She was still shaken from her encounter with Rankin in the armory and just wanted to end the day peacefully and retire early.

But her son, as young as he was, wanted an answer.

She drew in a deep breath. Initially, she'd told him that there had been a fight, and his Da had gone away afterward. But under Craeg's disarming gaze, she couldn't lie to him again.

"He won't be," she whispered.

"Why?"

"Because" —Liza swallowed hard— "he's dead."

Craeg stiffened, confusion clouding his face. "Has he gone to live with the angels now?"

Liza nodded. *More like in the fiery pits of hell.* "He's buried in Lochbuie kirkyard … I shall take ye to see his grave tomorrow," she replied gently. Hades, she wasn't any good at this—but there was no way to say such things easily.

Craeg's eyes filled with tears, and Liza's heart lurched. Rising from her seat, she circled the table and lowered herself into a crouch next to him. "I'm so sorry, love."

Lord forgive her, she wasn't, but for him, she'd pretend. His father had shown his son little softness or warmth, although Craeg was too young to resent him for it. Maybe he would one day. For now, though, his love for his father was unconditional. His heart was still pure, still untainted by disappointment and bitterness.

Unlike hers.

Aye, she'd started off hopeful, her head full of fanciful ideas, but Leod had quickly crushed her dreams underfoot. He'd made it clear early on that their union was one of convenience. He needed an heir, and she'd provide one.

She enfolded Craeg in her arms and let him weep against her shoulder. And when his sobbing had passed, and he lifted his tear-stained face to hers, her heart nearly broke. When she'd been filled with hate and vengeful fury toward her husband, she never considered what killing him might do to their son.

She'd told herself he'd be both happier and safer without Leod, and he was.

However, at that moment, she despised herself for what she'd done. And one day, when Craeg learned the truth, maybe he'd hate her too.

Vengeance came at a price, it seemed.

Her son's gaze searched her face, looking for answers he was too young to hear.

Her own eyes filled with tears then, not for Leod—she'd never weep over the cruel bastard—but for Craeg, and for herself. For broken dreams, and the happiness that had always eluded her.

21: THE LAIRD OF GAMHNACH MHÒR

LIZA WAS CROSSING the barmkin when the visitor arrived.

She'd just left the kitchen, where she'd locked horns with Murdo again. She'd bested the cantankerous cook in the end, and they'd planned the coming week's meals together. All the same, it was a relief to be out of that hot, smoky place. She was enjoying the feel of the sun on her face when a feather-footed cob passed under the stone archway.

Liza pulled up short, her gaze going to where two of the Guard stepped out to block his way. Her gaze narrowed then. She recognized the man astride the horse. He was big with a heavy brow and a mane of dark hair. A thick beard covered his jaw. He was the individual she'd told Loch about—the mysterious visitor Leod received sometimes.

And as the newcomer drew up his horse, Rankin descended from the walls to greet him.

Liza's pulse quickened at the sight of the Captain of the Guard. A fortnight had passed since that incident in the armory, since Loch had departed leaving her in charge of Moy—for the moment at least—and in that time, things between her and Rankin had been tense.

Reaching the cobbled barmkin, the captain strode across to the newcomer.

Liza's gaze tracked him. He no longer looked like a pirate captain these days. Instead, he wore leather braies and a padded gambeson, and his long fair hair was pulled back from his face and secured at the nape of his neck.

"What's yer business here, stranger?" Rankin greeted the man astride the cob.

The man didn't answer immediately, for he was surveying the stonemasons on the eastern wall, who were rebuilding a section. It was the most urgent of the repairs, for that wall had started to crumble in places. However, the newcomer's brow furrowed at the sight. "Maclean's been busy," he muttered. "It looked as if half of Lochbuie village were repairing their roofs as I rode in."

"Aye," Rankin replied. "There's plenty of work to be done here."

The man's gaze swung back to Rankin, his frown deepening. "Where's MacCormick?"

"He's dead. I'm the Captain of the Guard now."

The stranger stiffened. "And ye are?"

"Captain Rankin. Now, ye answer *my* question."

"I'm here to see the laird," the man growled. "And our business doesn't concern ye."

"I think ye'll find it does," Liza spoke up then, moving across the barmkin toward them. "Whatever ye have to tell me, ye can share with the captain of my Guard."

The stranger's gaze snapped to her, his dark eyes widening. "Get yer husband, woman … I'm not talking to ye."

"Leod's dead," she replied, halting next to Rankin. "I'm in charge here."

A thrill went through her as she spoke those words. The past fortnight hadn't been easy. She'd dealt with more than her share of sullen servants, wary villagers, and sneering guards, but after her victory over Murdo this morning, her confidence had been bolstered. She certainly wouldn't let this man humiliate her the way Mal had.

A heartbeat of silence followed this admission before the man's mouth twisted. "Lying bitch."

"Lady Maclean speaks the truth," Rankin answered, his hand straying to the hilt of his dirk. "Disrespect her again and ye shall taste steel."

The stranger's heavy-featured face tightened, and he glanced around, taking in the faces of the other guards now surrounding them. He likely didn't recognize many of them, although his gaze lingered upon where four men had turned from their posts on the wall to watch. "What happened here?" he finally rasped, cutting his attention back to Liza.

"Leod made a mistake that cost him his life," she answered, putting her hands on her hips. "I'm a busy woman. Tell me yer name."

The stranger's lips flattened. "Ross Macbeth ... I'm laird of Gamhnach Mhòr."

Liza frowned. Gamhnach Mhòr was a small island off the south coast of Mull, a short distance from Carsaig, a village to the west of Moy. "I didn't think anyone lived on Gamhnach Mhòr."

"Aye, well, Leod gave it to me," Macbeth replied, his tone surly.

Liza inclined her head. "How curious." Indeed, this was the first she'd heard of any such arrangement, not that she should have been surprised. Leod had shared little with her. "So, what brings ye to Moy, Macbeth?"

His eyes narrowed. "My business is with Leod, not with ye."

"Well, unless ye can talk to the dead, ye are out of luck," Rankin replied, a warning in his voice.

Macbeth remained mutinously silent. Meanwhile, Liza's gaze swept over him and his horse, marking the bulging leather satchels strapped behind his saddle.

"I'm in charge of these lands now," she said finally, lifting her chin to eyeball him. It was impossible to warm to this bullish, mannerless man. Her response was aggressive, but something about him made her hackles rise. "What are ye carrying in those fat saddlebags?"

A muscle flexed in his jaw, visible even under his thick beard. His big hands clenched upon the reins. Macbeth's gaze shifted then, going to the tower house behind Liza. Something unpleasant flickered in his dark eyes.

Without thinking, Liza's hand strayed to the hilt of the dirk she'd taken to wearing of late. Fortunately, Makenna had taught her how to defend herself with one of these—a skill she'd never thought she'd need.

However, a lady laird might.

A flush crept over Macbeth's face then as he struggled with his anger. "Nothing," he snarled. Then, muttering a curse under his breath, he reined his cob around and kicked it into a canter, leaving as swiftly as he'd arrived.

As the thud of hoofbeats receded, Liza turned to Rankin. "That was the man I told ye and the Maclean about … Leod's visitor."

"Really?" A groove etched between the captain's eyebrows at this news. "He was certainly a shifty bastard."

"Aye." She exhaled sharply then, realizing that she'd been breathing shallowly. Her welcome had sent Macbeth on his way, yet she couldn't help feeling as if she'd failed. His reaction to the news she was laird stung—a reminder that some men refused to treat with women.

"I wonder what he had in those satchels?" she mused.

"Something he was anxious ye didn't see," Rankin replied. He turned to his men then, who'd gathered close, curiosity gleaming in their eyes. "Spectacle's over, lads," he said gruffly. "Back to yer posts."

Liza's chest constricted. *I should have detained him.* Aye, maybe—although his abrupt departure had caught her by surprise.

The guards went swiftly and obediently, leaving the laird and captain standing together alone in the center of the barmkin.

Rankin swiveled back to Liza then, his gaze spearing hers.

Liza stilled. Mother Mary, she wished her pulse wouldn't spike every time this man looked her way; it was starting to vex her.

"I'd say Leod's mysterious friend definitely has something to do with that strongroom full of coin," he said quietly.

Liza's gaze widened at these words. *Cods.* "In that case, Loch will be interested to learn about Ross Macbeth of Gamhnach Mhòr," she replied. "Can ye spare one of yer warriors?"

He nodded.

"Good." She stepped back from him, eager to put some distance between them once more. "I shall write the Maclean a missive now."

She was about to turn and make for the entrance to the tower house when howling rang through the barmkin, the noise echoing off stone.

Rankin murmured an oath, glancing around him.

And then, an instant later, a lad of around seven winters ran out into the cobbled space, blood streaming from his nose. "Da! Where's my Da?" he bawled.

Halfway across the barmkin, the lad tripped, falling flat on his face. His howls grew louder still. A moment later, Rankin scooped him up before glancing up at the walls. "Fergus, is this yer lad?"

A wiry warrior with thinning red hair appeared, his gaze going to the weeping boy in the captain's arms. "Davy? What happened to ye, lad?"

"Craeg hit me!"

Liza stiffened. That made no sense at all. Her son was two winters younger than Davy and a gentle soul.

Rankin set the boy down, allowing him to clamber up the stairs and throw his arms around his father's legs. Meanwhile, Liza had turned, her gaze shifting to the gap between the kitchen and the bakehouse, where Davy had burst from moments earlier.

She then headed toward it.

She was vaguely aware of Rankin following her yet ignored him. Her focus was on locating her son.

Liza found him sitting in the narrow passage between the bakehouse and the wall. He'd scrunched himself up into a ball, his head buried against his knees, and his shoulders were shaking.

"Craeg!" She rushed to him, sinking to her knees at his side. "Are ye hurt?"

He raised his head, his face flushed, his cheeks wet with tears, and she recoiled to see anger in his night-brown eyes. "Davy Black is a liar!"

Liza's breathing grew shallow. "What did he say, love?"

Her son's thin throat bobbed. "That ye killed Da!"

Cold washed over Liza. She'd hoped to keep the truth from her son for a while yet, until he was old enough to understand. But she should have realized that others living within these walls wouldn't be so cautious—especially bairns who listened in to whispered adult conversations.

A scuff of boots behind Liza warned her that Rankin had arrived.

Still ignoring the captain, she drew a deep breath and held her son's eye. Lord, she didn't want to speak of this to Craeg. However, she was now backed into a corner.

"Yer Ma didn't kill yer father," Rankin said then, his voice gentler than she'd ever heard it. "I did."

Liza's heart kicked against her ribs, her lips parting. She should be angry he'd interrupted, and yet relief washed over her.

Craeg's attention shifted to beyond her shoulder, his gaze fixing on the captain, and a tremor shuddered through him. His small hands clutched at her arm, clinging on. She too glanced Rankin's way, to see that he'd lowered himself to a crouch so that he wasn't looming over them.

Liza swallowed then, as her throat tightened. "Don't be afraid, lad," she whispered, focusing on her son once more. "Captain Rankin won't hurt ye. He did it for me … I asked him to." Craeg's face was a picture of confusion, and so she plowed on. "Yer Da tried to kill me … and failed. The only way I could return to ye was to attack this castle."

His bottom lip started to tremble, his eyes gleaming. He understood now though what the shouting had been about on that morning he'd hidden in the cellar with the servants—and that those men he'd seen in the barmkin hadn't been sleeping.

"Da tried to kill ye?" he finally asked, his voice weak, lost.

"Aye." Liza hauled him into her arms, crushing him in a firm embrace. "But he failed." Her eyes started to burn then, tears sliding down her cheeks.

I'm an awful mother.

She was supposed to be a protector, to shield her bairn from what she'd done. But she'd failed. Her gaze met Rankin's then. His blue eyes were shadowed, his handsome face strained. She wagered he'd never told a bairn he'd killed his father before. Aye, their bargain had benefited each of them, although it had come at a great cost to Craeg.

It was a sobering moment—for them both.

22: AT MY SHOULDER

A KNOCK AT the door dragged Liza from her brooding.

She was sitting at the open window. It was getting late. The sky outdoors had turned indigo, and a crisp breeze had sprung up. Nonetheless, she was loath to lower the sacking.

She'd sat here for a while, staring out at Loch Buie.

"Aye," she called huskily, turning toward the door, imagining that her handmaid, Nettie, had come up to ask if she wanted anything.

Although it wasn't the shy lass with silky blonde hair who opened the door, but Alec Rankin.

Liza stiffened.

Her soul was bruised and sore this evening. She didn't have the strength to deal with this man. "What is it?" she greeted him, her voice flat and weary.

Rankin stepped inside and halted; his gaze then swept over her. "I thought I'd look in on ye, Lady Maclean."

Liza rose from the window seat and turned from him, undoing the sacking and lowering it. "There was no need."

"How is Craeg faring?" he asked, ignoring her cool response.

She glanced over her shoulder. The question surprised her, although she noted the concern in his eyes. "He wept all afternoon," she replied huskily as her throat started to ache, "and is in bed now."

Liza shifted away from the window then, moving to the sideboard where a row of pewter goblets and a ewer sat. "Wine?"

She didn't want him to linger, but her mother hadn't brought her up to pour herself refreshment without offering any to others.

"Aye, thank ye," he murmured.

She poured the plum wine, noting the way her hands trembled as she did so. Clenching her jaw, she tried to pull herself together. She was the laird now; there was no room for weakness, especially in front of Rankin.

"How fares yer arm these days?" she asked lightly, struggling to find something to say.

"Almost healed … thanks to ye."

She cut him a sharp look but found no teasing light in his eyes.

Passing the captain his drink, she retreated to the fireside, where a large log smoldered. She then sank into one of the high-backed chairs flanking it.

Rankin didn't take a seat opposite, however. Instead, he remained where he was, cradling the goblet in one hand, his gaze upon her. "He'll recover, ye know?" he said after a lengthy pause. "Bairns are accepting of things."

Liza's chin jerked up. "Will he?" Her fingers tightened around the goblet's stem. "He's barely said a word to me since … and when he looks at me, I swear I see fear in his eyes."

"He doesn't fear ye. He's confused … that's all."

Rankin did move to the vacant chair then and sank down onto it. "I was the same age as Craeg when my Ma died … and I too struggled to understand what that meant."

Liza lifted the goblet she grasped to her lips and took a sip, welcoming the heat that pooled in her belly afterward, melting the lump of ice that had settled there ever since Craeg had learned the truth. "Aye, and look at what it did to ye."

Rankin stiffened, his gaze narrowing.

"Our first experience of death leaves a deeper scar than ye think," she explained. "It likely made ye into the man ye are today."

"And what sort of man is that?"

Her pulse quickened as she witnessed the challenge spark in his eyes.

"A pirate, of course."

He gave a soft, dismissive snort. "I was no helpless victim of fate, Liza. I chose my path because it suited me."

Taking another sip of wine, she bit back the urge to reprimand him for not addressing her formally. A heaviness pulled at her limbs, and she sank back in her chair. She truly didn't have the strength to duel with him this eve. Couldn't he just leave?

But he didn't. Instead, he settled himself in his chair and crossed one booted ankle over his knee. "And when did death first touch *ye*?" he asked finally.

Liza sighed. She didn't want to talk about herself. Nonetheless, the sharpness in his gaze goaded her, and so she considered his question. "I remember feeling sad that my grandfather died," she admitted. "I couldn't accept that he'd never visit us again." She glanced away then, lost in the past for the moment, watching the flames dance in the hearth.

Silence fell then, and neither of them rushed to fill the void. Despite that it was late spring now—Bealtunn was just over a moon away—the evening air held a sting. Even so, the fire threw out a warmth that wrapped itself around Liza like a hug.

She welcomed it. Nonetheless, the sense of well-being didn't last long. As always, these days, her mind couldn't rest. She had three and a half months to prove herself to Loch and couldn't help but feel she wasn't doing enough. Her gaze flicked to Rankin, to find him watching the fire, his expression introspective.

"Is my missive on its way?" she asked.

He blinked, coming out of his reverie and looking in her direction before nodding. "A rider left for Duart a few hours ago." He paused then. "Fear not, Loch will investigate Ross Macbeth." Rankin reached up then, scratching his chin. "I'd wager he'll take a birlinn down to Gamhnach Mhòr himself and ask the man some questions in person."

"I'd never heard of that isle having a laird."

"There's been a ruined broch on it for years … I've sailed by it many a time … but Macbeth must have repaired it."

Her brow furrowed. "But even if he and Leod were up to something together, that still doesn't explain how they got their hands on all that coin."

"No … that'll be why Loch shall speak to him," he said firmly.

Her attention settled on him fully then, her gaze narrowing.

He inclined his head. "What?"

"Do ye find yerself hankering for yer life aboard *The Blood Reiver?*"

"Not yet," he replied, his expression giving nothing away. "It's still early days."

"I thought ye'd feel … *restricted* here," she pushed. Something in his tone made her doubt him.

He shrugged. "I've been too busy to give it much thought." He paused then, his blue eyes shadowing. "It's a different life at Moy though … I'll give ye that."

Liza continued to observe him, her frown deepening. "I don't understand yer loyalty to the Macleans … if I didn't know better, I'd think ye *respect* Loch."

"That's because I do," he replied, his mouth lifting at the corners. "But it was his father I owed a debt to."

"Aye?" Liza couldn't help it; she was intrigued now.

He nodded. "When I was a lad, I tried to steal Iain Maclean's coin purse on the docks in Oban. He caught me in the act, and I thought I was in for a whipping … but instead, he surprised me by handing me a silver penny." His lips quirked once more. "He also told me that I needed to look a man in the eye when I stole from him."

The faint smile upon her lips widened. For a moment, she imagined the ragged urchin this man had once been, his blond hair knotted, his face thin and grimy. "He left an impression upon ye then?"

"Aye … he was the first man to ever treat me like I was worth something. Ye don't forget something like that."

His candid response caught Liza by surprise. She was used to Rankin keeping things light, to deflecting personal questions. But she didn't know what to say now.

As if realizing he'd been too open, the captain set his empty goblet down by the hearth and rose to his feet. "I'd better check on the night watch," he said, his tone reserved now. "Make sure they aren't slacking."

"Can ye accompany me to Lochbuie tomorrow morning?" she asked, her tone equally polite. "I'm meeting the stonemasons and some locals there … about building a village wall … and I'd like yer opinion too."

"Of course," he replied without hesitation. "What time?"

"Early … as soon as I've broken my fast."

He nodded. "I shall await ye in the barmkin tomorrow morning then."

Liza watched as he turned and made for the door. He'd almost reached it when she cleared her throat. "Captain."

He halted, half-turning to her. "Aye, Lady Maclean."

"I appreciated yer assistance today … with Macbeth … and with Craeg." She halted then, swallowing as her throat tightened. She couldn't believe she was admitting this, yet it needed to be said. "My new role is harder than I thought it would be. There's so much to learn about being laird, and I'm terrified that Craeg will resent me now … but it's good to know I have ye at my shoulder." Her cheeks warmed. Hades, she'd said too much and would earn herself a smirk and an arrogant comment that would curdle her stomach.

However, Rankin surprised her, yet again. His lips curved into a warm smile that made her pulse stutter. "And I will remain at yer shoulder," he replied softly. "For as long as ye need me."

23: UNFETTERED

"SEND UP TWO dozen eggs to the castle." Liza flashed the man before her a smile. "Murdo has already started preparing for Bealtunn. We shall have honey-cakes this year." She glanced down at Craeg then, ruffling his hair. "What do ye think about that, mo laochain?"

To her relief, her son grinned. He usually enjoyed being called her 'little hero'. "I love honey-cakes!"

"Aye … they're my favorite too." The farmer admitted with a smile, while his wife picked up a basket and started filling it. "Lorna will take the eggs up to the castle kitchen now, Lady Maclean."

"Thank ye, Harris," Liza replied. The egg vendor didn't realize it, but he'd just given her another small victory. Her first trips to Lochbuie's weekly market after taking over as laird had been uncomfortable experiences. Few of the locals had favored her with friendly looks, let alone smiles. But these days, they were warming up.

Three weeks had passed since Ross Macbeth's mysterious visit to Moy, and since Craeg had learned the truth about his father. In the days following, Liza had set about bringing in more stonemasons to repair the castle walls and the crumbling cottages in the village. She'd also organized to have a wall built around the village itself—something the locals had requested a while back from Leod, to keep the mountain hares from their gardens. In addition, she'd set up a weekly audience in her hall so that the folk of Lochbuie could bring any grievances they had to her. This was also something Leod had ignored, preferring instead to leave such matters for his overworked bailiff.

And now that the villagers could see the effort that she was making to serve them properly, she was starting to earn a few smiles.

Warmth suffused Liza's chest then. Aye, she'd turned a corner. Finally, she was no longer floundering in her new role. If things continued like this, there would be no reason for Loch to deny her lairdship of Moy.

Handing Harris two silver pennies, she moved on, weaving through the stalls. The village was small, consisting of little more than a scattering of squat bothies with thatched roofs along one street. She walked with Nettie—her maid carried a large wicker basket over one arm and a cloth bag over her other shoulder—as well as an escort of three guards.

One of them was Alec Rankin. He and his men followed a few respectful yards behind, their gazes watchful as they surveyed the crowded market.

Their presence made the glow of pride that warmed Liza's chest moments earlier subside, especially when she marked the looks some of the marketgoers were now exchanging. She knew what they were thinking.

A male laird wouldn't need armed guards shadowing him everywhere.

Aye, that was the truth of it.

She'd tried to tell Rankin she didn't require an escort for market day, but he insisted. Nonetheless, he'd been supportive of her over the past weeks, offering her advice whenever she asked for it, and attending the weekly audience she gave, just in case any of the locals got pushy. They also met each afternoon on the walls, where he'd tell her about anything that needed to be discussed, and she'd give him the necessary instructions. Rankin joined Liza and Craeg in the hall for the noon meal too, seated to her right at the laird's table. It was usually a tense affair though, for Craeg eyed Rankin warily, as if trying to decide whether to hate him or not.

Liza gave herself a mental shake then. What did it matter if she never went anywhere without her bodyguards? The important thing was that she was winning at this. And with the treats she was preparing for the locals for Bealtunn, she'd soon have everyone on her side.

"We need honey, Ma," Craeg chirped then, gripping her hand and towing her toward a nearby stall.

"Aye, we do," she agreed. "Which one is best for baking?" Liza asked the woman sitting behind a selection of earthen jars.

"Ye'll be wanting something mild ... like clover or blossom."

"Aye," Nettie piped up. "Heather is too strong for honey-cakes."

Liza tasted both, and had decided on the blossom, when murmurs to her left drew her attention. The marketgoers were pointing to the hill behind the village, where four horses were descending the path.

Gaze narrowing, she wished—not for the first time—that her eyesight were better.

"They aren't wearing clan-sashes, Lady Maclean." Captain Rankin's voice, right behind her, made her startle. She hadn't realized he'd approached. "And it looks as if two of the riders are women."

Liza squinted at the newcomers once more. "Ye have eyes like a sea eagle," she murmured.

Even so, he'd piqued her curiosity. Over the years, Moy had received few female visitors.

Meanwhile, the honey vendor had just finished wrapping two pots, which she handed over to Nettie. Nodding her thanks, Liza paid the woman, turned away, and waited for the riders to make their way down the hill into Lochbuie. If they were heading to the castle, they'd have to travel through the village first.

The crowd parted to let them through. And as they approached, she saw the two riders out front rode upon garrons, heavyset ponies with feathered feet.

Rankin stepped up next to her then before murmuring. "One of the women is armed."

Liza cut him a questioning look. "Aye?"

"Aye … she has a dirk strapped to one hip and longsword upon the other … and there's a quiver of arrows on her back."

Her pulse quickened then. She'd only ever met one lass who carried weapons so boldly.

Makenna.

For a moment, she froze.

Christ's bones, what is she doing here?

She hadn't been in contact with either Kylie or Makenna, not since she'd canceled her trip back to visit her family at Meggernie Castle the past autumn. Makenna hadn't responded to her hastily scribbled missive, with its flimsy excuse, and Liza had wondered if she'd been upset with her.

And as the women drew closer, Liza's gaze narrowed. *She's brought Kylie.*

Heart racing, she moved forward, just as the women brought their ponies to a halt.

"Liza!" Kylie swung down from her garron and hurried toward her. Her elder sister appeared travel-worn; her plum surcote was dusty and stained around the hem, although her braided hair, wrapped tightly around the crown of her head, didn't have a strand out of place.

"Kylie," Liza responded stiffly, forcing a smile. "This is … unexpected."

Not answering, her sister enveloped her in a crushing hug. The gesture was surprising, for Kylie wasn't usually given to such demonstrative behavior.

Drawing back slightly, Kylie's gaze dropped to the lad who stood at his mother's side, eyes wide. "This must be Craeg," she said, her mouth curving.

"Aye … Craeg, greet yer Auntie Kylie and Auntie Makenna."

"Hello," he said solemnly.

"Good day, Craeg," Kylie replied. "My goodness, ye are tall."

"Greetings, nephew," Makenna called as she handed her pony over to one of the two warriors who'd accompanied them. She then flicked her long unbound hair over her shoulder— she'd braided the front of her thick mane in thin braids, so it didn't fall in her face—before flashing Craeg a grin. The lad merely gaped at her, clearly unsure what to make of this auntie. Winking at Craeg, she strode forward and nudged Kylie out of the way. Her green eyes narrowed as she met Liza's gaze. "Why did ye never organize another date to visit us?"

"Sorry," Liza admitted, guilt darting through her. "I meant to … it's just been … difficult."

Makenna's expression shadowed at this admission before she too pulled Liza into her arms. Like Kylie, she wore a finely made yet travel-worn surcote, although her clothing had been altered to make it more practical. Her skirts were slitted at the sides, so she could stride out properly, and she wore long boots and thick cloth chausses. She smelled of roses and sunshine, a scent that reminded Liza of their mother.

Liza's throat constricted then. "It's good to see ye both." And it was. By the saints, she'd missed these two over the years. All the same, she wasn't ready to see her sisters, or to tell them what had befallen her. Everything was still raw, and she didn't want her parents to find out just yet, or to worry about her.

Drawing back from the hug, Makenna folded her arms across her chest, eyeing her older sister. Of all the five MacGregor sisters, she was the one who favored their father the most. The rest of them bore traces of their mother's looks to varying degrees—her dark hair and eyes, and golden-skin—but Makenna was pale with freckles and brown hair threaded with gold and red, and eyes the color of moss. "Is Craeg fully recovered from his illness?"

Liza swallowed, even as her stomach twisted. "He was never unwell, Makenna," she whispered. "I lied."

Both her sisters frowned at this. She was suddenly aware of the stares they were attracting from the surrounding villagers. She glanced over at Rankin then, who stood patiently with his men a few feet away. Meeting her eye, he raised an eyebrow. Aye, this wasn't a conversation she could have out here.

Clearing her throat, Liza favored her sisters with a reassuring smile. "Come … I will explain everything once we get back to the castle."

Silence fell in the solar once Liza concluded her tale. Both her sisters wore grave expressions when she shifted her attention back to them.

She'd started from the beginning—right from when Leod had forbidden her from visiting her kin, to the clan-chief's reluctant agreement to trial her as laird for the time being. Aye, they knew the entire gut-wrenching story. She'd left nothing out, except for the fact that she'd spent a torrid night with the man who now captained her Guard. Some things were best kept secret.

It took a while for either of her sisters to answer, but when Kylie did, she was visibly shaken. "I can't believe he'd try to murder ye." She crossed herself then, a shudder rippling through her.

"When ye canceled yer journey to Meggernie, I knew in my bones that something was wrong," Makenna replied, her eyebrows knitting together in a frown. She paused then, a muscle flexing in her jaw. "Filthy whoreson … I hope Rankin made him suffer before he ended him."

Liza flinched at her sister's bloodthirsty words, grateful that she'd sent Craeg to his bedchamber upon their return to the tower house, to play with Nettie. The noon meal was looming, and he'd be able to spend some time with his aunties soon enough.

Her sister's reaction was also a reminder of her own thirst for vengeance, and how it had tasted like ashes in her mouth when she'd witnessed Craeg's grief.

"Ye don't both think less of me now then?" she asked softly. "After what I did."

Kylie's oak-brown eyes, the same hue as her hair, shadowed before she shook her head. "No," she said huskily. "Although yer methods have been … unusual."

"He got what he deserved," Makenna said, her tone cool. "The bastard gave ye little choice but to fight back." Her green eyes glinted. "I always knew ye had it in ye."

Liza favored Makenna with a wan smile. "Did ye?"

Makenna gave a firm nod.

"I bring ill-tidings of my own, Liza," Kylie spoke up once more. Her strong-featured face, so much like their mother's, wore a strained expression now. "Errol died two moons ago."

Liza stared back at her. Kylie was widowed? "Ye never sent word," she whispered, even as her chest tightened. She was no better, for she hadn't let any of her family know that Leod was dead.

Her sister glanced away. "No," she replied, her voice roughening. "I wanted to tell ye … in person."

Liza rose from her chair by the hearth and moved to where Kylie sat opposite. She then lowered herself to her knees before her and reached out, taking her hands. "I'm sorry, Kylie."

"Thank ye." Her sister managed a half-smile. Her throat bobbed then. "I'm bearing up well enough. Errol and I weren't happy together … but I never wished him dead."

Liza squeezed her hands. "Of course, ye didn't."

"Och," Makenna made a noise in the back of her throat. "It's a relief to see ye both unfettered. It'll be like old times … like when we were lassies."

Liza glanced over her shoulder, raising an eyebrow at where her younger sister perched on the window seat. "If only that were true," she replied with a shake of her head. "But none of us are lassies any longer."

Makenna snorted, and Liza's gaze narrowed. "Ye haven't updated me on *yer* situation," she said. "Has Da set a wedding date yet?"

Makenna rolled her eyes. "No … and I'd thank ye never to remind him." She paused then, her sharp features tightening further. "He still hasn't let Bran Mackinnon know he won't be getting his eldest daughter's hand in marriage … but his *youngest.*"

Kylie muttered something under her breath at this, while Liza's lips thinned.

Makenna shrugged off their reactions. "I'm hoping Mackinnon will refuse to honor the agreement. He didn't make it, anyway … his father did … and he's dead."

Liza gave her head a rueful shake. Bran had recently taken over from his father, Kendric, as clan-chief of the Mackinnons of Dùn Ara. The latter had met his end at the Battle of Dounarwyse three years earlier.

"Da doesn't like to be reminded of that defeat against the Macleans," Kylie replied, her brow furrowing. "But he still intends to make Bran Mackinnon honor his father's promise."

Makenna scowled back at Kylie, her lips parting to answer. However, a swift knock at the door interrupted their conversation.

"Aye?" Liza called out.

The door creaked open, and Rankin stood there. Tall and leather-clad, his fair hair spilling over his shoulders, he drew the eye of all three sisters. Curse him, the man was dangerously attractive and oozed a masculinity that would have made an abbess's heart flutter.

"Apologies for the intrusion, Lady Maclean," he said, nodding to her sisters before meeting her eye across the room. His mouth then curved. "But today is one for visitors, it seems. The chieftain of Dounarwyse has just arrived."

24: THE EMISSARY

"LOCH WISHES ME to stay here until after Bealtunn," Rae Maclean announced as he took his seat in the hall. "I shall stop off at Duart Castle on the way home and report back to him on yer progress."

Liza nodded in response and forced a smile, even as her stomach clenched.

God's blood, he wasn't wasting any time checking up on her. She'd thought Loch would wait until she'd been laird a couple of months, at least. "I'm surprised the clan-chief would bother *ye* with such a task." It was hard not to let resentment creep into her tone. How could she find her feet here with Loch and his chieftain breathing down her neck?

"It's no bother at all," Rae assured her. "In truth, it's been a while since I paid Moy a visit." His brow furrowed then. "Ever since we fought the Mackinnons, Leod had little to do with me."

Around them, the noon meal was being served, and men, women, and bairns were taking their places at the trestle tables.

Meanwhile, Rankin, Kylie, and Makenna had joined Liza and her guest at the laird's table.

Liza's fingers tightened around the goblet of wine Kylie had just poured. Her sister was graciously making her way around the table, offering wine to everyone present. "I wondered why we hadn't seen ye in a while," she admitted.

Rae sighed before rubbing his clean-shaven chin. "Aye, well … he turned bitter after that battle … although, in honesty, he was never easy to deal with."

Despite that she didn't want Rae here, Liza found herself studying him. She hadn't seen the laird of Dounarwyse in over four years. His broch lay on Mull's eastern coast, not far from the port village of Craignure.

The years had altered Rae. He was as tall and broad-shouldered as she recalled, yet there was a severity to his face she didn't remember from their last meeting. She guessed he was around five and thirty, although the stern set of his features made him look older, as did the severe cut of his auburn hair, cropped close to his scalp.

"I heard of yer loss, Rae," she said after a pause. She didn't want to appear churlish; it wouldn't help her case. "And I'm sorry."

The chieftain nodded, his expression shuttering. "Thank ye … these past two years have had their trials."

Although Leod had shared little with Liza over the years, news still reached her of the goings-on upon Mull. She listened to servants' gossip and the chatter of villagers at market. She'd heard through them that Loch had become a father for the second time—and that Rae Maclean's wife had died.

A brittle silence fell across the table before Rae cleared his throat. "I noted the building work on the way in," he said then, swiftly changing the subject. He inclined his head in thanks as Kylie filled his goblet. "What repairs have ye done since taking over from Leod?"

Irritation stabbed through Liza once more. They hadn't even eaten, and the man was getting down to business. Once more, she was reminded that it was a man's world. Loch would never have sent an emissary if a male laird now ruled Moy.

"The eastern wall is close to being shored up," she replied stiffly. "And I've employed more stonemasons … they're currently doing some work in the village and building a much-needed wall around Lochbuie's perimeter." She paused then before adding. "After that, the masons will make some repairs to the village kirk."

Rae nodded, his expression still giving little away. He then took a sip of wine, his gaze holding hers. "And what of the Moy Guard?"

"We started with only five warriors from the original Guard. But Captain Rankin has recruited fifteen more. He's training them up."

"Aye?" Rae's gaze flicked to Rankin then, his brow furrowing. "No offense, Alec … but ye have no experience in defending a castle."

Liza thought Rankin might have bristled at this—for she found herself tensing at Rae's dismissive tone—yet he merely inclined his head. "On the contrary, I've found it to be much like captaining a ship's crew … only, the lads I command now have better manners."

Rae snorted. "I'm sure."

Servants were bringing out tureens of thick mutton stew and dumplings, the rich aroma filtering through the hall.

Liza cleared her throat then, drawing the chieftain's gaze once more. Enough of the interrogations, she wanted some of her own questions answered. "Has Loch done any investigation into Ross Macbeth?"

Rae's brow furrowed. "Aye … he traveled by birlinn to Gamhnach Mhòr, only to find the broch abandoned."

"Interesting," Rankin spoke up once more. "The man did have something to hide, it seems."

"Aye," Rae answered, although his focus remained upon Liza. "So, ye had no idea of the riches yer husband was amassing?"

Liza's pulse skittered. Did she imagine it, or was there suspicion in Rae's green eyes? "No … he never let me into his strongroom."

Their gazes held a moment before Rae scowled. "What the devil were he and Macbeth up to?"

"We were hoping Loch would have some answers by now," Alec replied, deliberately letting a challenge creep into his voice.

That got the chieftain's attention. Rae's gaze snapped his way. "Macbeth has disappeared," he answered, his tone cooling. "We both have men out looking for him."

Staring back at the chieftain, Alec swallowed his own irritation. He'd had no quarrel with the laird of Dounarwyse in the past, but his arrival here—and his questioning—were starting to get on Alec's nerves.

Of course, Rae had come at the clan-chief's behest, but his comments still felt undermining. Liza had made great strides of late, and her confidence was increasing with each passing day, while Alec was doing his best to train the lads he'd recruited into the Guard. The last thing Liza needed was Rae Maclean lingering here, observing—and judging—every decision before reporting his findings to Loch.

"Bealtunn is still a few days away," Alec said after a pause. "Aren't ye needed at Dounarwyse?"

Rae raised an eyebrow as he helped himself to some stew. "My brother will look after things while I'm here."

"I'm sure yer bairns will miss ye though," Liza added, as if sensing the point Alec was making.

Rae's expression tightened just a little at this comment. "I suppose so."

"How many children do ye have, Maclean?" Kylie asked politely. She'd now finished pouring the wine and taken a seat next to Makenna at the other end of the table.

Rae glanced her way, his fingers tightening around his spoon. "Two lads," he replied. "Ailean is a little older than Craeg … and Lyle is around a year younger."

"Ye must bring them on yer next visit," Kylie said, smiling. "I'm sure Craeg would love to meet them."

An awkward silence fell at the table, although Alec ignored the discomfort on Rae's face. Instead, he took the opportunity to observe Liza's sisters. Like her, they were well-built and bonnie, but Kylie, the elder of the two, was prim and self-contained, while Makenna appeared a plucky lass with a wild edge to her.

Eventually, Rae cleared his throat. "Perhaps," he replied with a strained smile. He shifted uncomfortably on the bench seat before taking the basket of bread Makenna passed him. "How have the locals been treating ye, Liza?" he asked, deftly changing the subject once more.

"Well enough," she answered. "They're warming to me now."

"Was Leod popular with the villagers?"

She pulled a face, giving him his answer. "He ignored them most of the time … and over the past years had ceased his monthly audiences." She paused then. "At present, I meet with the locals every week to settle disputes and sort out any problems."

Rae nodded at this, and he managed a grudging smile. "Good."

Alec made his way out of the tower house and into the barmkin beyond. The noon meal had dragged on—while Rae continued to throw questions at both him and Liza. It was a relief to return to his duties. As much as it vexed him to admit it, the chieftain of Dounarwyse's arrival was unsettling. It was a reminder that his four newest recruits were far from battle-ready.

Outdoors, an overcast sky hung overhead, and the air was sticky with the promise of rain. Ignoring the weather, Alec gathered the most inexperienced members of the Guard for training. Unfortunately, these lads were so green they risked impaling themselves on their own swords in a fight. As such, he took them through a series of simple drills, to practice feinting and parrying an attack. The recruits, all of them from Lochbuie village, were eager to learn. Nonetheless, their fumbling attempts were painful to watch.

"Stand yer ground!" he shouted as two of the recruits cowered under the onslaught of wooden blades. "Block and strike! Block and strike!" Christ's blood, even young Rabbie onboard *The Reiver* had more natural ability than these lads. They were all in awe of him and hurriedly obeyed every order. There was no banter like he'd had with his crew—no cursing, boasting, and ribbing.

A sudden wave of wistfulness caught him by surprise.

Where was *The Reiver* now? Terrorizing the northern coast of Mull, most likely.

Aye, he'd chosen to step away from his old life, yet suddenly, he wished he were standing at the bow of his cog again, the salty wind whipping his hair in his eyes. He'd loved the freedom of that life, but today, he felt confined. Frustrated. But more than that, he felt as if he didn't belong here.

"These four couldn't defend themselves from kittens." A woman's low voice, laced with wry amusement, intruded upon Alec's brooding then. He turned to see that Makenna stood behind him.

He eyed her, taking in the lass's fashionable surcote and kirtle, both split at the side for ease of movement. Underneath, she wore cloth chausses and fine leather boots. Makenna MacGregor carried herself with the calm assurance of someone who knew her own worth.

"They'll improve," he replied, his tone cool. "With time."

"Back at Meggernie, we practice with real swords. Nothing makes a warrior improve faster."

Alec pulled a face. "There's also no quicker way to lose limbs."

"Care to give them a demonstration on how to handle themselves properly with a blade?" Makenna's moss-green eyes glinted as she nodded at the spare wooden practice swords leaning up against the nearby armory.

Alec stilled before raising an eyebrow. "Ye want to fight me?"

She smiled, causing her cheek to dimple. "Aye … unless ye're afraid I might show ye up?"

Alec snorted. "Not likely." He turned to the recruits then. Luckily for her, he could never resist a challenge. "Halt yer practice for a moment, lads," he called out. "Let the laird's sister show ye how it's done."

This brought smirks to their faces.

Makenna, however, merely went to retrieve the wooden swords.

They circled each other, and Alec found himself studying her face. She was certainly confident; there wasn't a glimmer of uncertainty in her eyes.

Clack. Clack.

Their blades collided.

Aye, and she had swift reflexes too. Makenna wasn't a big woman, yet she was sturdily built, and with enough strength in her arms to parry even his harder strikes. And as they fought, Alec's irritation lifted, his mood improving. Soon he was grinning. For the first time since taking up residence at Moy, he was truly at ease. They continued to circle each other, attacking and feinting. It was a dance Alec knew well, one he enjoyed, and Makenna was a worthy opponent.

"Ye fight well," he admitted, as she swiftly side-stepped a deft cut. "Who taught ye?"

"The Meggernie Guard. I joined when I was sixteen."

"And how is it, yer father would allow his daughter such liberties?"

She lunged so swiftly that he had to take a step back to avoid a blade slamming into his ribs. "I'm the youngest of five sisters," she answered, pressing her advantage. "And when my mother's womb never quickened with any more bairns, Da realized he'd never get the son he craved." Her mouth quirked. "So, he indulged his strong-willed daughter instead."

They fought on, and Alec let her think she was on the cusp of beating him. Then, as Makenna attempted to sweep under his guard, he dodged her strike and kicked her feet out from under her.

The lass landed on her back, her breath whooshing out of her lungs.

"That was a dirty trick, pirate," she wheezed, her brow furrowing as he placed the tip of his wooden blade at her throat.

Alec laughed. "Didn't yer father's men teach ye any?"

Her green eyes narrowed. "Captain Walker told me a warrior should fight fair."

He snorted. "Honor will only get ye so far in life, lass. Such moves could save yer life."

Withdrawing his blade, he then leaned down and offered her his hand. Ignoring it, Makenna rolled to her feet and dusted her fine clothing off.

Alec glanced up then, his gaze alighting upon a figure standing on the walls. An instant later, his smile—and his buoyant mood—faded.

Rae Maclean was there, watching them. Earlier, the chieftain had worn a serious expression. However, mirth now sparkled in his eyes.

Alec stiffened. He wasn't sure what to make of Rae's reaction.

"Can I fight?"

A hesitant young voice behind Alec drew his attention then. He turned to find a small lad with mussed dark hair gripping a wooden sword.

Unbeknown to Alec and Makenna, it hadn't just been the recruits and Rae who'd been watching their fight. Craeg had been too.

25: AN OVERSIGHT

DELIGHTED SQUEALS OF laughter drifted in through the open window of the solar, making Liza look up from the ledger she'd been writing in. Moy had just had two wagonloads of grain delivered—oats and barley—and she was making note of the number of sacks they'd carried into the granary, and the coin she'd paid. In truth, Rae's arrival had flustered her, but she was determined that he wouldn't find anything lacking in her lairdship.

"There's nothing like the sound of a happy bairn," Kylie said, her lips lifting at the corners wistfully. Her sister sat by the fire, mending one of Craeg's tunics. It was a chore that Liza usually did, but ever since stepping into her new role, she didn't have the time. Indeed, she'd barely set foot inside her lady's solar—a smaller chamber next to this one, where she'd once whiled away many hours sewing or at embroidery or weaving.

"I agree." Liza got up, stepped away from her desk, and crossed the chamber to the window. "Let's see what they're up to."

Peering out, she saw the grey clouds that had been gathering all afternoon were now overhead. The air was warm yet charged, and thunder rumbled in the distance. However, those in the barmkin below paid no attention to it.

A group of the Guard looked on, cheering as a tall fair-haired man parried with a wee lad. They both gripped wooden swords, and every time the man lunged at him, the boy gave a squeal and smacked at his blade with his own. In response, the man grinned, his eyes alight with joy.

Liza stilled, the smile upon her lips freezing.

Rankin and Craeg.

She then breathed a curse under her breath.

"What is it?" Kylie asked, no doubt marking her reaction.

"How dare he?" Liza growled, turning on her heel and stalking toward the doorway.

"Who?"

Liza didn't answer. She was already flinging open the door and crossing the landing. Then, picking up her skirts in one hand, she descended the stone steps two at a time.

Emerging into the barmkin a short while later, she found Rankin on his back upon the cobbles with Craeg sitting on his chest. The lad was waving his toy sword in the captain's face.

Rankin was laughing, the rich sound drifting across the barmkin.

"Mercy!" Rankin cried out, while the men surrounding them grinned. "I surrender!"

Vaguely aware that Makenna was amongst the crowd, and that she too was smiling, Liza strode across the yard toward the group.

"What do ye think ye are doing, Rankin?" Her angry voice cut through the humid air.

Both the captain's and Craeg's gazes snapped her way, surprise flickering across their faces.

"Liza," Rankin murmured, his smile fading. "Is something amiss?"

"Aye." She halted before them. Leaning down, she hauled Craeg off his chest. Her son's body went rigid in her arms, yet she was too busy glaring at Rankin to focus upon him right now. "Ye have no right to take such liberties with my son." she ground out.

Rankin cocked an eyebrow and rolled to his feet. "Liberties? We were just play fighting."

"I don't care what ye thought ye were doing … ye will not lay a hand upon my son again. Is that clear?"

Rankin's face tightened, his gaze shadowing.

"He wasn't hurting Craeg," Makenna stepped forward then, her expression wary. "They were only—"

"Ye should have put a stop to it immediately," Liza turned on her sister.

Makenna's lips thinned at her venom.

Liza's heart was slamming hard against her ribs now, even as something clenched deep inside her chest. They were all acting as if she was making something out of nothing. None of them understood what she and Craeg had been through.

"Liza." Rankin's voice was surprisingly soft, yet his familiarity—one she'd already warned him about—just made her ire rise further. "I didn't mean any harm."

"Of course, ye didn't," she snarled back. "*Men* never do … until it's too late."

Liza caught sight of Rae Maclean's tall figure then, standing on the walls, and she froze. Rae's brow furrowed as he watched her. An instant later, a lump of ice settled in the pit of her belly. Christ's teeth, he'd just witnessed her loss of control.

Nausea rolled over her. *What have I done?*

She was supposed to be demonstrating her leadership qualities and proving that she was a worthy laird. But instead, she'd just made a spectacle of herself. Loch wouldn't want her staying on as laird after this.

A sob caught in her throat then. Turning on her heel, and still clutching a rigid and teary-eyed Craeg in her arms, she ran indoors.

Craeg started to cry as they entered the tower house, soft sobs as if he was afraid of how she might react if he made a noise.

Her throat began to ache. Of course, Leod had taken to cuffing his son around the ear if he wept. He was scared she might do the same.

She wouldn't.

Instead, she felt like smacking herself around the face. For frightening her son. For acting like a hysteric out there, in full view of *everyone.*

"I'm sorry, love," she murmured as she carried Craeg up the stairs. "I'm not angry at ye."

"Captain Rankin didn't scare me, Ma." His voice was small, cowed, and it cut her to the bone.

"I know … I know," she replied, her voice soothing now.

The damage had been done though—it was too late for her to repair it.

Aye, it had been obvious it was nothing but innocent play fighting. She should have been pleased to see her son so happy, so comfortable with adult men. But instead, panic seized her.

Rae Maclean's arrival had put her on edge—but she couldn't blame him for her reaction. Suddenly, she hadn't been in the present, but in the turbulent past, facing off against her husband after he'd just snarled at their son, or raised a hand to him. She'd been Craeg's protector for so long, it was an old pattern. Ingrained. Hard to break.

Her vision blurred then, and her throat started to ache.

Curse ye, Leod. Her husband might be dead and buried, but his shade still dogged her steps.

"Someone has tried to break into the strongroom!"

The news, delivered by a breathless kitchen assistant, made Liza turn from where she'd been talking to a shepherd. It was two days after Rae Maclean's arrival, and she'd taken him into the village to show him the wall she was having built.

The chieftain of Dounarwyse had been listening as she agreed to build a winter enclosure for the shepherd's sheep. Lochbuie gained most of its income from the wool trade. As such, they needed to ensure their sheep were well looked after during the colder months.

Captain Rankin had been standing a few yards back, observing the meeting with a shuttered expression. But upon hearing Dougal's announcement, he stepped forward. "Did they steal anything?"

The lad shook his head, his chest rising and falling sharply. "No," he gasped. "Murdo sent two of us down to the cellar to fetch some cider … and we heard the rattle of a chain. But when we went to investigate, whoever it was had fled." He paused then, his gaze shifting to Liza. "They left behind a pair of blacksmith's pliers."

Liza's belly clenched. "God's blood," she muttered. "I can't believe we have a thief inside the castle."

"It's not that surprising," Rae rumbled. "News of Leod's hoard will have spread … and some folk can't resist the lure of coin."

Liza nodded, even as her pulse quickened. He was right of course. Even so, she'd had to force herself to meet the chieftain's eye. She'd largely avoided him after the scene in the barmkin—as she had Rankin too—taking her meals in her solar and making excuses to avoid any meetings. But she couldn't stay away from either man forever.

On the way down to the village, she'd made light conversation with Rae, but all the while, she'd felt Rankin's gaze upon her back.

Aye, sooner or later, she'd have to talk to him. However, she couldn't face it today. Right now, she had other problems to deal with.

"I'd better get back to the castle." She gave the shepherd an apologetic nod, gathered her woolen cloak about her—for it was unseasonably cold this morning—and headed east down the path that would take her back to Moy.

Inside the cellar, they found the abandoned pliers next to the trap door.

Liza watched as Rankin hunkered down beside it and examined the chain. "There are a few nicks out of the iron," he observed. "But it's secure."

She let out a sigh. "That's a relief."

Meanwhile, Rae was glancing around the shadowy space, brow furrowed. "Ye will need to post guards down here from now on." He paused then. "In truth, ye should have done so before now."

Liza tensed, her gaze cutting to Rae, only to find him looking at Rankin.

Her pulse started to thud in her ears, and she cleared her throat. "*I* make such decisions, not Captain Rankin."

"But the Captain of the Guard needs to take the initiative," Rae replied cooly, shifting his attention to her.

"He's right." Rankin's voice was uncharacteristically gruff. "It was an oversight on my part." His gaze flicked to Liza. "I shall ensure a guard is posted down here at all times from now on, Lady Maclean."

Their eyes met, for the first time since she'd railed at him over Craeg in the barmkin, and heat flushed over Liza. Rankin's expression was stern, his jaw set. She didn't like that he'd shouldered the blame for this—or that Rae likely saw them *both* as incompetent.

26: A LONELY PATH

IT GREW LATE. All the inhabitants of Moy Castle were abed, save for the Watch.

And for the laird.

It was the night before Bealtunn—the last day of spring. Rain battered against the thick stone walls of the tower house and pushed against the heavy sacking covering the window.

Seated before the flickering hearth, her fingers curled around a cup of wine she'd barely touched, Liza listened to the gusting wind and the hiss of the rain.

Nature was venting its spleen tonight. She hoped the locals had thought to cover the huge mound of twigs and branches they'd spent the past few days amassing—the Bealtunn fire—with sacking. Otherwise, the following night's celebrations would be damp indeed.

Liza had been looking forward to Bealtunn—and had organized plentiful food and drink for the locals, but this evening, nervousness fluttered in her belly.

Ever since the failed robbery of the strongroom, she'd done her best to reassure Rae Maclean that she was up to the job. Nonetheless, she worried he'd go to Duart and tell Loch otherwise. Rae's presence here was exhausting; everywhere she went, the chieftain shadowed her. Earlier that day, he'd looked on while she opened her hall to locals. She'd done her best to settle a bitter dispute between two neighbors and allegations of swine stealing—but in the end, Rankin and his men had been forced to turf the rowdy men out of the castle.

And all the while, she imagined Rae's judgment.

Did he think she lacked the gravitas a man would have in such a situation?

A knock at the door made her spine stiffen.

It was nearing midnight. Both her sisters would be asleep, as would Craeg.

Was something wrong? Rising to her feet, she cleared her throat. "Aye?"

The door creaked open, and Alec Rankin stood there. He was wearing a dripping oilskin cloak. He'd pushed the hood down, and his hair clung to his wet cheeks. "Sorry to bother ye, Lady Maclean," he greeted her, his expression guarded. "But I was just up on the walls and saw a glow from yer window." He paused then, discomfort flickering across his handsome features—an expression she'd never seen him make before. "It's late … I just wanted to check that all was well."

"Aye," she replied stiffly, even as heat rose to her cheeks. Rankin was the last person she wanted to see at present. Ever since the incident with Craeg, she'd continued to avoid him where she could. It was cowardly, but she was ashamed. "I'll be retiring shortly."

He nodded, his gaze roaming her face as if he were trying to read her thoughts. Lifting a hand, he raked it through his wet hair, pulling it back from his face.

"Very well." He took a step back. "Good night then."

Liza watched him move toward the door before she spoke once more. "Alec."

He turned, his gaze widening in surprise, for it was the first time she'd ever addressed him by his given name. The informality caught her off-guard, and her breathing grew shallow. "I just wanted to apologize," she said, her cheeks burning now. "I know ye didn't mean any harm … with Craeg."

And she was in earnest. She trusted that he would never raise a hand to her son. Or to her.

Rankin stared back at her before clearing his throat. "I'm sorry too, Liza … I didn't mean to give offense … or to overstep."

She nodded, wishing her throat didn't feel so tight, and that the backs of her eyes weren't prickling. Turning from him, she placed her barely touched cup of wine on the mantelpiece. She closed her eyes then and attempted to pull herself together.

"Yer husband left scars, didn't he?" Rankin asked after a pause.

"Aye," she whispered, still not looking his way. "I could weather his cruelty when it was directed at me. But when he turned it upon Craeg, I crumbled." She halted there as painful memories resurfaced. "If Craeg ever made the mistake of wanting to play with his father … Leod would turn it into a real fight." She swallowed to try and ease her tight throat. "Once, he put a hand over his mouth to frighten him. Craeg turned blue before I managed to rescue him."

Her pulse raced now, for talking about such things made her feel sick to her stomach. But Rankin's presence just a few feet away was steadying. Aye, she could be honest with him. "Craeg was gasping for air, and weeping … and all his father could do was curl his lip and tell him to toughen up."

"He was a bully," Rankin replied softly. "I know the type … for my father was the same."

Liza nodded, squeezing her eyes tightly as a hot tear escaped and slid down her cheek. "I wanted to be strong enough to defend Craeg against him … but I wasn't."

"Neither was my mother." His voice was closer now, and she realized he'd crossed the solar and was standing before the hearth. His scent—the smell of wet leather, and the freshness of rain—enveloped her. "But I never blamed her. Da was stronger than all of us … and he wielded his strength as a weapon."

Drawing in a deep breath, Liza opened her eyes and turned to him.

Rankin was staring down at her. Concern shadowed his eyes, and something else—an emotion she couldn't quite identify. Understanding settled between them.

"I don't like to see ye weep," he murmured.

Liza sniffed and knuckled away the tears from her cheeks. "Pay me no mind. I'm a foolish woman who … in an attempt to rescue her son from imagined danger … only upset him. Not only that, but Rae Maclean now believes I'm a foolish hysteric."

"No, he doesn't." Rankin's mouth quirked. "And Craeg will forgive ye." He reached up, his fingertips brushing a tear that had reached her chin. "The important thing … is that ye forgive yerself." He stepped closer then, and a wave of dizziness swept over her. "Aye, ye've made mistakes … and in the years to come, ye shall make plenty more. Some ye'll learn from, and some ye won't … but that's just life."

"But some mistakes have dire consequences," she answered, her voice catching. "Today was another example. What will I do, if Loch decides I can't stay on as laird?"

"Ye shall rally … just as ye always have, for ye are strong."

His words wrapped themselves around her, drawing her in.

"I wanted to give Craeg the perfect childhood," she whispered. "To make up for everything he's suffered so far … but since my return to Moy, I've only hurt him."

Rankin made a sound in the back of his throat, even as his fingers slid along her jawline, and he cupped her cheek. "Nothing in this world is meant to be perfect."

Liza's breathing grew shallow. Suddenly, the air between them shivered, as if the storm that raged outdoors had blown aside the sacking and now swirled around them.

But it hadn't.

They stared at each other for a few moments before he leaned in, his lips brushing across hers. Liza froze, all thoughts escaping her, like leaves scattered by a gust of wind.

And when he repeated the move, allowing the softness of his lips to caress hers, another sigh escaped her.

"Liza," he whispered against her mouth, cupping her face with both hands now. The tip of his tongue traced the seam of her lips, and before she knew what she was doing, she opened for him. He kissed her gently, thoroughly, his tongue exploring her mouth, his teeth grazing her lips.

And when he sucked her tongue, she groaned.

Heavens, he tasted good, and a thrill shivered through her.

She kissed him back, their tongues entwining now. Their embrace became more urgent then, fevered. The wetness and heat of his mouth made hunger twist in her belly. Her already muddled mind grew hazier still, and she leaned in, craving more.

Answering her, Rankin drew her into his arms. His hands slid down to her shoulders—as his mouth devoured hers now—and then traveled down the curve of her back. And when his hands cupped her backside, squeezing tight, she gasped, heat igniting between her thighs.

Rankin's lips left hers then, and he worked his way along her jaw to her throat.

Trembling now, Liza let her head fall back.

The Virgin forgive her, his mouth felt so good, as did his hands on her. She wanted nothing more than to let him take her, here, for him to strip her naked before the fire and plow her on the sheepskins. She'd welcome every hard thrust.

But amongst the haze of desire, common sense pricked at her.

What are ye doing? If ye are to remain the laird of this castle … protector and ruler of the folk of Moy and Lochbuie … ye can't let yerself fall prey to base lust.

That did it.

The fog drew back, cold reality rushing in like an icy slap of wind to the face.

Heart racing, her breathing ragged now, Liza put her hand on Rankin's chest. His gambeson was damp, and through it, she could feel the pounding of his heart. The intimacy of the gesture made her knees tremble, yet she held fast.

"Alec," she breathed. "We can't do this."

He drew back instantly, leaving the brand of his lips on her neck.

Liza started to tremble. His mouth had been moments from dipping to the neckline of her kirtle—a dangerous progression indeed. If things went any further, she'd lose her wits completely; she'd be beyond rational thought.

Sea-blue eyes questioning, he placed his hands on her shoulders, even as his chest rose and fell sharply. "Apologies," he said huskily. "I got carried away."

She swallowed. "We both did … but it can't happen again."

He stilled at these words, although she shook her head, resolve hardening within her. Dropping her hand from his chest, she took a step back so that he too removed his hands from her shoulders. This would be easier if they weren't touching.

"My son has my loyalty now," she continued, the words tumbling out of her, "as do my people … there's no room for anyone else."

Rankin favored her with a tight smile. "That's a lonely path ye have chosen."

"Aye … but it is mine to take."

His gaze narrowed. "A *man* wouldn't martyr himself like this."

She huffed a humorless laugh. "No, he wouldn't … but I'm a lady laird and the world judges us more harshly." Her voice hardened as she added. "I'll not give Loch another reason to deny me."

Rankin's jaw tightened. He looked like he wished to argue with her, yet Liza stared him down. Aye, he knew she was right. Moments passed, and, eventually, he nodded, his gaze veiling. "As ye wish."

Alec reached the ground level of the tower house and pulled up the hood of his oil-skin cloak, readying himself to go outside into the driving rain once more.

It was then he marked the slight tremor in his hand.

"Christ's blood," he growled. "What has she done to me?"

This was his doing. He'd overstepped. Again.

The incident a few days ago with Craeg had bothered him far more than he cared to admit. Liza's response had been extreme, yet he'd known its cause, and he'd been worried about her. He'd ruminated over it ever since, and this evening—as a stormy dusk settled over Moy, and he prowled the castle walls—he'd let instinct get the better of him.

Going to see her had been unwise—as had approaching her when she'd wept.

But it had been pure idiocy to kiss her.

Ye fool. He couldn't be surprised that she'd reacted as she had. Even so, his gut churned now.

Yanking up his hood, he hauled open the heavy oaken door and let himself out into the wild night. The wind and rain were so violent that they had extinguished most of the flaming torches that hung from chains off the walls in the barmkin. The braziers lining the castle walls smoked and guttered as well.

Alec stood in the barmkin for a few moments—as the wind howled like a banshee, ripping at his cloak and stinging his face—and let his vision adjust to the darkness. It also permitted him to gather his wits.

A short while later, he climbed the steps, perilously slick with rain, up to the walls, and made his way to the first of the sentries keeping watch. "All is well, Beathan?"

The warrior, one of the five from the original Guard who'd stayed on at Moy, blinked and turned to him, water running off his iron helmet. "Aye," he muttered. "Only the Blue Men of Minch would be out and about on a foul night like this."

Alec snorted, peering out into the murk. He could hear the crash of the surf against the pebbly shore over the whine of the wind. "Keep yer eye out, nonetheless."

Beathan studied him in the weak glow of the brazier, his grizzled face wary. "Are ye expecting trouble, Captain?"

Alec flashed the man a grin, falling into a role he was comfortable with. "I *always* look out for trouble … that's why I'm still alive."

Beathan continued to watch him, his expression thoughtful now. "I didn't think ye'd last longer than a few days, Captain."

Alec held onto his grin, with effort this time. "Aye?"

"Me and the lads thought ye'd get fidgety."

Alec pulled a face. "I have been at times," he admitted. "It takes a while for a pirate to get used to living on land again." He didn't add that he'd begun to feel more settled at Moy of late—or he had before he overstepped with Liza.

"Still restless, are ye?" Beathan asked.

"Only for this vile weather to pass." Alec clapped him on the shoulder and moved past the guard, making it clear the conversation was over. Beathan wasn't a bad sort, but he could tell the warrior was in a bold mood, and he didn't feel like indulging him.

Moving on, Alec made his way to the eastern ramparts, stopping at a spot between two merlons. There, he halted once more and stared out at the darkness. Fortunately, there wasn't anyone posted here to question him.

However, as he stood there, alone with his thoughts and battered by the storm, a boulder settled in his gut.

27: AS YE WISH

THE MORN OF Bealtunn dawned dark, wet, and misty.

The murky weather matched Liza's mood. She'd awoken out of sorts. Nonetheless, she put it all aside and greeted her sisters and Craeg with a warm smile when they joined her in the laird's solar to break their fasts.

They ate wedges of bannock, fresh off the griddle, smeared with butter and heather honey, and drank cups of warm milk.

"Are ye well, Liza?" Kylie asked, her brow furrowing.

"Aye, thank ye," she replied briskly. "I slept badly last night, that's all."

"Ye are as pale as a bucket of whey," Makenna added.

"Don't fuss," Liza replied, dismissing both her sisters' concerns with an airy wave. She then glanced over at where Craeg was eating bannock, all the while watching his mother warily. Ever since the incident with Rankin, he'd been slightly withdrawn, nervous even.

And marking the worry in his eyes, Liza's chest constricted. Her fingers then tightened around her butter knife. "Are ye looking forward to seeing the Bealtunn fire, mo laochain?" she asked softly.

He nodded. "Will it rain?"

Liza sighed, glancing out of the window, where the mist wreathed like smoke. "Hopefully not … and a bit of fog won't stop us from lighting the fire." She paused then, favoring him with a reassuring smile. "Or eating cakes dripping with butter and honey."

To her relief, her son's mouth curved, excitement sparking in his eyes.

"Aye, and there will be music … and dancing," Kylie said. "Will ye do a lively step dance with me, Craeg?"

"Aye!" he cried.

"Och, who cares about dancing," Makenna replied with a snort. "What I'm looking forward to is a large cup of hot caudle."

Caught up by his aunts' enthusiasm, Craeg squealed, and something unfurled inside Liza's chest. Her sisters' arrival had been ill-timed, but there was no doubt that Craeg loved having his aunts here. Fortunately, Kylie and Makenna had both respected her time, allowing her to attend to daily business without making demands on her. Their only crime was their tendency to fuss like two over-protective mother hens.

Buttering her piece of bannock, she then helped herself to some honey and took a bite. As usual, the griddle scone was crumbly and delicious. However, despite that she'd just reassured Craeg, Liza's appetite was poor this morning.

And she knew the reason.

Alec.

She pulled herself up sharply then. No. He had to remain 'Rankin' to her. She had to stay strong. The trouble was, she'd grown to genuinely like and trust him—aye, she admitted it. After Leod, she'd thought she'd never let another man in—but it would be so easy to fall for the pirate, to lose herself in him.

But she couldn't, not if she hoped for Loch to take her seriously. Vulnerability was a dangerous thing for a woman in her position.

After breaking their fasts, Liza suggested the four of them take a walk together. Mist still wreathed around Moy, but she was eager to stretch her legs and clear her mind. She had to pull herself out of the mire of her own thoughts. The past days had been a flurry of activity—and with Rae Maclean following her around, she'd spent too little time with her family.

Makenna especially was enthused about the idea. Her sister was restless by nature and used to spending her days working in the Meggernie Guard.

Donning cloaks, lest the mist should deteriorate into rain, the three sisters and Craeg exited the tower house. They were crossing the barmkin when Liza spied Captain Rankin talking to one of the guards by the gate.

Her belly betrayed her by going into a steep dive at the sight of him. Irritation knifed her a moment later, and she clenched her hands by her sides. Just a glimpse of him made her feel as if she were teetering on the edge of a precipice, but she couldn't have it.

"Lady Maclean," he acknowledged her before nodding to Liza's sisters. "Off for a stroll?"

"Aye," she replied briskly.

"I shall join ye with some of my men."

"There's no need, Captain … we have Makenna with us." Indeed, her sister carried a longsword at her side and a dirk at her hip. "And fear not … we won't stray far."

Rankin's mouth quirked at this, although his gaze remained unreadable. "As ye wish."

Her breathing grew shallow, longing twisting deep in her chest. They were the same words he'd said before leaving the solar the night before.

As ye wish.

Lord, what she truly wished for was to go to him, to have him enfold her in his arms as he'd done before the hearth. His whispered words had soothed her bruised soul, and his kiss had made her yearn for closeness.

No. She yanked herself up short. *Hold fast.*

Taking hold of Craeg's small hand, she swept him away, trying to ignore the look of awe on her son's face as he stared up at Rankin. It seemed that their play fight—far from cowing him—had merely stoked his fascination with the Captain of the Guard.

Outside the castle, Liza slowed, for Craeg's wee legs were having trouble keeping pace with her. Her sisters easily caught up with them, and she let go of Craeg's hand, as he wished to go to Makenna. Watching the way he capered and squealed as her sister tried to catch him made a smile tug at Liza's mouth.

He'd miss his aunties when they went. And she would too.

She fell in step with Kylie then, and the two of them drew slightly ahead on the path that led east on the edge of the pebbly shore. Mist swirled across the dark waters of Loch Buie. It was a beautiful, yet eerie, sight.

Eventually, Kylie broke the companionable silence between them. "Do ye wish to speak about it?"

Liza cut her a look. "About what?"

"Ye and Rankin."

Heat flushed over Liza. "I don't know what ye mean," she replied, even as her voice caught.

Kylie gave a soft snort. "Liar. I've seen the way he looks at ye sometimes … and the way ye watch him when ye think no one's looking."

Liza stumbled. Righting herself, she flashed her sister a scowl, even as her pulse bolted. Mother Mary, had Kylie been listening to servants' gossip? Pushing this disturbing thought aside, she met Kylie's eye. "Don't worry … nothing will come of it."

Her sister gave an approving nod. "A wise choice … having an affair with the Captain of the Guard would undermine ye."

"I've made it clear there can never be anything between us," Liza assured her. "I can't let anything … or anyone … put my lairdship at risk." She pulled a face. "Rae Maclean is looking for a reason to damn me, I'm sure."

Kylie considered her words, her brow furrowing. "Rae doesn't seem the malicious sort."

"Maybe not … but the clan-chief wants him to assess my ability to lead … and I'm worried I'm not doing a good enough job."

Kylie snorted. "Nonsense. Since we arrived here, ye have been tireless. Rae will have noted how generous ye have been with the villagers, and the repair work ye have undertaken."

"Aye … but is it enough?"

"I hope so … ye deserve some happiness, dear sister."

Kylie's words made Liza's throat constrict, and when she noted tears glittering in her sister's oak-colored eyes, she linked her arm through hers and squeezed gently. "I have neglected ye and Makenna since yer arrival here … and I'm sorry."

"Ye have been busy."

"Aye, but yer life hasn't been easy either."

"No," Kylie admitted softly. "It hasn't."

Liza viewed her sister closely then, noting the tension in her face, the shadow in her gaze. "Were ye and Errol really so unhappy together?" she murmured.

Kylie's throat bobbed. "We were strangers by the end."

"Really?"

"He resented me for being barren." A nerve flickered in her cheek. "And it didn't help that he sired three bastards in the local village … and everyone knew it."

Anger knotted in Liza's gut at these words. "Don't ye dare blame yerself for his behavior," she muttered. "The man wasn't worthy of ye."

Kylie's eyes gleamed at her fierce words, and she blinked rapidly. "Thank ye," she whispered. "It helps to hear that." Her cheeks had flushed; she still looked on the verge of weeping. Liza wished they were alone so she could wrap her arms around her elder sister, to comfort her.

She was about to say something else when her gaze caught upon something up ahead, and she slowed her pace. "What's that?"

Kylie's step faltered as she peered into the wreathing mist. "It's a man pushing a rowboat into the water."

Indeed, it was. And as they drew nearer, Liza's pulse quickened. Even with her poor eyesight, she recognized the burly figure with his unruly mane of dark hair and beard. He hadn't seen them as he clambered into the boat and started to row away from shore.

"Ross Macbeth," she whispered. "What's he doing here?"

"Who?"

Liza didn't reply. Her gaze shifted back to shore, to where another figure, long and lanky, clambered up the bank and disappeared into a hazel thicket. She drew to a halt then, the fine hair on the back of her arms prickling.

"Liza?" Concern laced Kylie's voice. "What is it?"

"I'm not sure," Liza answered, swiveling to meet her sister's gaze. "But we must return to the castle … immediately."

Alec's gaze narrowed as he listened to Liza's breathless words. He hadn't expected her back so soon, but here she was, her cheeks flushed from racing up the path into the castle.

"Are ye sure it was Macbeth?"

"Aye," she assured him. "But I didn't get a good look at the other man. He was tall and lean though."

Alec's frown deepened. Unfortunately, many of the men who lived around Moy and Lochbuie were lanky.

"Did ye see Macbeth talk to anyone from the castle or village when he was here last?" Rae spoke up then, a groove etched between his dark-auburn eyebrows. The chieftain of Dounarwyse stood next to Alec, while the Highland collie he'd brought with him sat faithfully at his side.

"No," Alec replied, casting his mind back. "Although he took an interest in the repairs to the east wall."

"Aye," Liza agreed. Her expression turned thoughtful. "And I caught him looking up at the guards."

"Maybe he knows one of them," Rae suggested.

Alec frowned. "If he does, none have let on." Uneasiness shifted in his gut then. Of course, he hadn't captained the Moy Guard for long. He didn't know any of the men he led well, and most of them were new. What if Macbeth had friends locally? What if one of the Guard was behind that failed attempt at gaining entry to the strongroom?

Liza must have been thinking along similar lines, for her lovely features tightened. "He's up to something." She reached down to take Craeg's hand as he joined her. "We must be vigilant over the next few days, Captain."

"I will start asking a few discreet questions amongst my men," Alec assured her. "And will double the watch on the walls tonight, just to be safe." The lads would complain, for tonight was Bealtunn, and many of them were keen to join the revelers at the bonfire and enjoy the food and drink the lady laird was putting on for the folk of Moy and Lochbuie. However, it had to be done.

"In the meantime, I will take a stroll down the shore and see if there's anyone else lurking in the mist," Rae announced curtly, heading toward the gate. His dog trotted after him.

Irritation speared Alec's guts. Curse Maclean, he'd been about to suggest that.

"I'll come with ye, Maclean," Makenna said, her gaze glinting as she moved toward Rae.

"As will I," Alec muttered. Nodding to Liza, he followed Rae and Makenna out of the castle.

28: WILL YE DO AS I ASK?

LIZA TOOK A bite of cake, sighing at the rich flavor of honey and butter that exploded on her tongue. She'd eaten little all day, yet her appetite had returned the moment the aroma of freshly baked cakes drifted through the misty air.

Murdo had done her proud. Not only had the cook provided baskets of honey-cakes, but he and his assistants had baked mutton pies, apple tarts, and an array of other treats that were being passed around amongst the excited revelers. Liza had also sent down a wagon with barrels of Leod's finest wines, mead, and ale—which the locals were now lining up for.

Licking the honey off her fingers, Liza surveyed the crowd gathered before the Bealtunn bonfire. Murdo was amongst them too, his cheeks flushed with ale, his eyes sparkling with pride. He was currently making half-hearted protests as his wife pulled him toward the dancers.

Liza smiled. It warmed her to see the residents of Moy and Lochbuie enjoying themselves. Leod hadn't bothered to attend fire festivals, let alone provide any refreshments. Despite the trials she'd had of late, she was still proud of what she'd achieved. The villagers were happier, and Moy Castle was looking worthy of its name once more. Surely, Rae couldn't fail to be impressed by it all?

As her gaze slid over the crowd, she spied Alec Rankin. Her smile faded. He was standing apart from the revelers, far enough back that the drifting fog that blanketed Lochbuie this eve almost swallowed him.

He didn't glance her way though, and a foolish part of her wished he would.

As she looked on, Rae Maclean approached him, and the two men began speaking.

Liza forced herself to tear her attention away then. It was best not to be caught staring at the Captain of the Guard, and she didn't want Alec to notice either—especially after she'd made their relationship clear the night before.

The delicious honey-cake she'd just eaten churned in her belly now, her enjoyment at attending the Bealtunn fire fading. A moment later, her chest started to ache.

Despite her best efforts to tell herself otherwise, she wanted Alec. Curse her, she did. She'd never met anyone like him. He'd given up his life as a pirate to stand at her side, had shown her that some men were worthy of her trust.

Liza swallowed hard. Kylie was right—giving in to her desire for the man who now worked for her was ill-advised. No, she had to fight this.

"There's nothing like a Bealtunn fire."

She turned to find Makenna standing at her shoulder, a half-smile curving her lips. The ruddy light of the bonfire that burned a few yards away softened her sister's face and deepened the green of her moss-colored eyes.

"Aye," Liza replied, trying and failing to rouse a smile of her own. "It certainly illuminates this dreary eve."

Makenna's gaze roamed her face. "Is something amiss?"

Liza shook her head. "Nothing a large cup of hot caudle wouldn't cure."

Makenna snorted. "Is that a request?"

"Aye, if ye wouldn't mind."

"Well, lucky for ye, I've a hankering for a cup as well."

She let out a slow, relieved breath as Makenna moved away, walking in determined strides toward where two older women were ladling out caudle into cups from a large iron pot. A queue had formed, so her sister would have to wait a while.

Liza grimaced then. The request had been a ruse to stop Makenna from questioning her. In truth, she found thick oaten caudle, mixed with butter and sweetened with honey, cloying. Nonetheless, she knew her younger sister loved it. She felt too brittle this evening to fend off an interrogation.

Kylie was thankfully occupied at present too, chatting with two women from the village. Her sister, clad in a smoke-grey cloak, her brown hair tightly braided in two coils above each ear, was nodding earnestly at something one of the women had just said.

A few yards away, Craeg was play fighting with one of the lads from the village, while the boy's father and Liza's handmaid kept an eye on them. Liza's lips lifted into a wistful smile. With his face already sticky with honey, and his cheeks flushed from the bonfire's heat, her son looked the happiest she'd seen him in a long while.

"Can I ask something of ye, Maclean?"

The chieftain inclined his head at Alec's question before taking a sip of ale. "It depends," he replied. "On what it is."

"When ye go to Loch … ask him to send someone here to replace me as Captain of the Moy Guard."

Rae's eyes widened. "Ye are moving on?"

Alec nodded.

"Ye seemed to be settling into yer role well."

He had—but after his encounter with Liza the night before, he couldn't stay here now. "Aye, well … appearances are deceiving."

An awkward silence followed these words before Rae asked, "Does Liza know?"

"Not yet." He paused. "I will tell her … after Bealtunn."

Rae gave a slow nod, although his gaze turned searching.

Alec tensed; he didn't enjoy being scrutinized by the man.

"I thought ye had committed to yer new position?" Rae said finally.

"Aye, well, things change."

Rae lifted an eyebrow.

Alec sighed. He didn't want to go into this. "So, will ye do as I ask?"

Rae didn't answer immediately. Instead, he glanced over at where Liza stood alone while Makenna fetched her something to drink. Alec's gaze followed his. The lady laird of Moy looked like a goddess in her wine-red fur-trimmed cloak, her dark wavy hair pulled back from her face and tumbling down her back. The firelight kissed her golden skin and made her eyes luminous.

Alec's breathing grew shallow. She was a reminder of what he could never have.

"It's a pity," the chieftain said after a pause. "For ye are doing a good job here."

Alec inclined his head, acknowledging his compliment, yet didn't reply.

After a moment, Rae shrugged. "Very well, I shall let Loch know."

Liza watched Makenna take hot cups of caudle from the ladies standing at the cauldron and weave her way through a group of lads and lasses who danced in a ring around the crackling fire.

"Have ye got yerself two?" Liza asked, noting that her sister carried *three* wooden cups.

"This extra one isn't for me," Makenna replied airily. "But for Captain Rankin."

Liza stiffened, taking the cup her sister offered her. "Aye?"

Makenna flashed Liza a wry smile. "He looks like he needs one."

They both glanced over at where the man in question still stood apart from others. Rae had moved on and was now conversing with Kylie. Indeed, Alec wore an uncharacteristically stern expression as he stared at the fire.

Not waiting for her sister's response, Makenna walked off, circuiting the edge of the bonfire as she made her way toward the Captain of the Moy Guard.

Liza watched her go, her lips pursing. Ever since Makenna had sparred with Alec, she'd developed a fascination of sorts for him.

She took a sip of her caudle and pulled a face. Aye, it was as rich and sweet as ever. Her gaze flicked back to where Makenna had almost reached Alec, and an unwelcome shaft of jealousy pierced her breast.

Goose, she chided herself, ripping her attention away. *The man doesn't belong to ye ... he can talk to any woman he wishes.*

"Caudle, Rankin?"

Makenna thrust the cup at him, making it clear the drink she'd brought wasn't to be refused.

Alec wasn't overly fond of caudle and would have preferred a cool ale instead. Nonetheless, he took the cup and favored Makenna with a nod of thanks. "Thoughtful of ye, Lady MacGregor."

She made an irritated sound in the back of her throat. "My *mother* is 'Lady MacGregor' ... just call me Makenna."

His mouth quirked—and Makenna grinned back. "Finally ... I was wondering if ye'd forgotten how to smile."

He grimaced. "I've a few things on my mind."

Makenna's gaze narrowed as she surveyed him. "I imagine it's difficult to adjust to a life on land after so many years at sea."

"It has its challenges," he replied cautiously.

"Ye have a restless soul," she noted before sighing. "Something I understand."

Her expression was earnest, so he bit back a cynical comment. "Ye do?"

"Aye ... back at Meggernie, I'm always busy. Here, I find myself getting up before dawn every morning and pacing the walls, just to give myself something to do."

"Aye," he replied. "I've seen ye."

"Don't get me wrong," she went on with a shrug. "I needed to make this trip ... to reassure myself that Liza was well ... but I'm at my happiest helping defend my father's castle."

"I still can't believe he lets ye fight with his men."

He hadn't bothered to hide his incredulity, and a groove formed between Makenna's eyebrows. "Really? I'd have thought ye more open-minded about such things … since ye take orders from a woman." There was no mistaking the challenge in her tone.

Alec swallowed a sigh. He wasn't in the mood to lock horns with anyone this evening. He'd only intended to attend the festivities for a short while. He'd wanted to show his face, but he wasn't comfortable staying away—he should really get back to the castle and check on his men.

Unfortunately, though, Makenna had more to say. "I enjoyed fighting with ye the other day."

Alec snorted. "Aye?"

She nodded.

"So, ye appreciated my dirty trick in the end?"

"I've been thinking about that actually."

"Ye have?"

"Aye … Kylie and I will be off soon, but before we go, I'd like to spar with ye again. I want ye to teach me how to fight dirty … like a pirate."

Her request took him aback for a moment, and he was wondering how to answer when a woman's scream pierced the night, cleaving like an ax blade through the revelry. Alec turned around, his gaze sweeping the mist that swirled around the confines of the grassy field just outside Lochbuie village. He could just make out the dark shapes of the squat bothies on the fringes of the hamlet. A glow became visible through the fog then, steadily growing brighter as Alec looked on.

His brow furrowed. *What the devil is that?*

Another scream followed, and the laughter and dancing around the fireside stopped—as did the piper who'd been playing a merry jig.

"The village!" A man bellowed. "It's under attack!"

CURSING, ALEC TOSSED away the cup of caudle and drew his dirk. "Rory! Mac! Gilroy!" he shouted. "With me!"

An instant later, his men broke off from the swirling crowd and rushed toward him, the Bealtunn revelry forgotten. He led the way over to where Liza had just scooped Craeg into her arms, Nettie by her side. Rae and Kylie also approached.

"Ye need to get back to the castle, Lady Maclean," Alec greeted her. "Come with us."

"Makenna and Rae will see to that," she shot back, shaking her head. "Ye deal with whoever's attacking the village."

Alec stilled, heat flushing across his chest at her refusal to heed him. "Ye can't—"

"Don't question me, Rankin." Their gazes fused, and the stubborn glint in her eye was unmistakable. "Go!"

Swallowing down the urge to insist, Alec nodded stiffly. He then turned to where both Rae and Makenna had drawn weapons. "Don't take the shore path back to the castle," he instructed tersely. "The one that takes ye up the hill is safer."

Fortunately, neither of them argued with him.

"Aye," Rae replied, his gaze sweeping the fog and smoke wreathing around them. The shouts from the village were growing louder. "Mind how ye go … I'd wager the Ghost Raiders have paid Lochbuie a visit … it's their way to sail in when there's fog, although they've never attacked during Bealtunn before."

Alec's gaze narrowed at this warning. Of course, Dounarwyse's location on the eastern coast of Mull, facing out onto the channel between the isle and the mainland, left its nearby villages exposed to raiding parties. He'd heed Rae's words.

They all departed then, Liza, Craeg, Nettie, and Kylie hurrying up the hill flanked by Makenna and Rae, while Alec and his men skirted the edge of the fire and headed toward the ever-brightening glow in the direction of the village.

A few moments earlier, there had been a crowd of revelers around the bonfire, but they'd all disappeared. Some of the men had raced into the village to confront the attackers, whereas most of the other villagers had wisely slipped away into the mist like wraiths.

More of Alec's men joined him now, and they strode into Lochbuie village, weapons at the ready.

As soon as they made their way down the single street that bisected the village, the acrid tang of smoke caught in Alec's throat. It wasn't the smell of the bonfire behind them though, but the heavier, oiler smell of burning cottages.

Flames licked the mist, and up ahead, Alec made out dark shapes struggling together. Men fighting.

Alec broke into a run, and his men followed.

The attackers were a fearsome sight. Tall, broad-shouldered figures swathed in black hooded cloaks, surrounded by smoke and snaking mist, they looked as if they'd clawed their way straight up from hell. They wore mailed gloves that glinted in the firelight and fought with heavy claidheamh-mòrs—great broadswords. But the most disquieting thing about them was the horned sheep skulls that covered their faces.

Alec could see why folk thought them demons, for they all fought as if possessed, fending off the plucky villagers—armed with hoes, pitchforks, and rakes—who tried to defend their homes from them.

The warriors of the Moy Guard descended upon the Ghost Raiders like howling wolves. The counterattack took them by surprise. However, they rallied swiftly, and the ring of steel blades echoed through the night. Alec dived under the guard of his first opponent and drove his dirk-blade up, through his black cloak, and under the raider's ribs.

His blade met flesh and bone.

Aye, this was no demon.

The raider grunted, twisting away as Alec yanked his blade free.

The Moy Guard all fought with dirks rather than broadswords. As such, they employed the same tactics as their leader, moving in aggressively to avoid the lethal reach of the claidheamh-mòrs. In close quarters, a dirk-blade was far more effective.

Unfortunately, the thick smoke and mist, and the searing heat from the burning bothies, hampered them.

The raiders, realizing they were now under attack from more than just angry villagers, withdrew, taking with them the spoils they'd already hauled from the homes, cloth bags slung across their shoulders. The Guard had injured a few, yet they staggered off, disappearing like shades into the mist.

A lass screamed piteously as one of the attackers hauled her away.

Alec dove after them, cutting his dirk into the back of the raider's knees. The warrior crumpled, and the lass rolled to the ground. She scrambled to her feet and ran off. Meanwhile, the raider whipped around, his dirk slashing up. But Alec was faster, his blade slicing open his opponent's throat. Pushing himself off the ground, he shouted to his men, "After them!"

"Bar the gates behind us!" Rae shouted as he strode into the barmkin at Liza's side.

The guards eyed the chieftain of Dounarwyse dubiously, not moving to do his bidding immediately.

"The village is under attack," Liza panted, out of breath from her sprint up the hill, while carrying Craeg on her hip. "Do as he bids!"

The men leaped into action, and moments later, the gates rumbled closed, a heavy iron bar sliding into place.

"What about those still out there?" Makenna asked.

"Let our men in," Liza instructed the guards, "and any villagers who need help … but be wary." She paused then, surveying the night watch, who'd been left behind this evening to guard the walls. "It's difficult to tell the difference between friend and foe in the dark."

"Shall I put Craeg to bed, Lady Liza?" Nettie asked then. The lass was pale and trembling, yet her gaze was steady.

"Aye, thank ye," Liza replied with a tight smile. She then placed a kiss on her son's forehead and lowered him to the ground. "Ye go with Nettie … there's a good lad."

She'd expected Craeg to cling to her or start weeping, but he surprised her by stoically taking hold of Nettie's hand and letting her lead him away.

"Nettie will get ye some warm milk and honey," she called after them before turning her attention to the situation at hand. Climbing up to the walls, she looked west, hoping to see the village of Lochbuie.

On clear evenings, its home fires glowed. There was a full moon out, and the light would usually frost the world and gleam off the waters of the loch. But not tonight. On this Bealtunn, a thick blanket of fog obscured everything. She couldn't even see the bonfire they'd left or the burning bothies in the village. However, the tang of smoke hung heavily in the air, and as she waited, the faint sounds of shouting reached her. "What's happening down there," she muttered.

"Hopefully, Rankin and his warriors have dealt with the raiders," Rae replied.

Liza glanced sideways to see that he, Makenna, and Kylie had all followed her up onto the walls. Their faces were tense, their gazes shadowed in the light of the brazier that burned nearby.

"How can ye be sure it is the Ghost Raiders?" Liza asked. Indeed, hadn't she seen Ross Macbeth up to something earlier in the day?

"I can't," he answered with a shake of his head. "But the villages around Dounarwyse have suffered a couple of raids over the past two years … and they always sail in on a foggy night."

Liza swallowed, her gaze traveling south.

And as she looked on, the wreathing mist shifted, revealing the gleaming loch beyond. And there, its single mast piercing the fog, was the distinctive outline of a ship. "Look," she breathed.

"There she is," Rae murmured. "*The Night Plunderer.*"

"An apt choice of name," Kylie replied, her tone dry.

"Indeed," Rae answered with a snort.

"It looks like a pirate's cog," Liza said then, her gaze never leaving the ghostly silhouette.

Rae snorted. "Aye, well, that's what the Ghost Raiders really are … pirates in disguise."

She glanced his way once more. "So, ye don't believe they're demons then?"

"No."

The mist closed in then, shrouding *The Night Plunderer* from their gazes.

"If they're pirates, then why bother to use such a guise?" Makenna asked. She'd moved close to the edge of the wall, her brow furrowed as she glared down at the fog. Judging from the look on her sister's face, Liza sensed Makenna wanted to be down there, fighting with Alec and his men.

Liza was relieved she wasn't.

"To weave a cloak of fear and awe about them," Kylie spoke up after a pause. "Many folk will run screaming from their homes if they believe a horde of demons has sailed in on a ghost ship and attacked their village."

"Aye, men or wraiths, they're still dangerous," Rae agreed.

Liza's belly clenched then. She'd sent Alec off to deal with the raiders. The man knew how to handle himself, yet she suddenly feared for him—and his warriors. Some of them were seasoned fighters like their captain, while others were worryingly inexperienced.

A sickly sensation washed over her; she hoped she hadn't sent them off to their deaths.

They stayed up on the walls a while, listening and waiting, and eventually, shadowy figures emerged from the mist and headed toward the gates.

"Who goes there!" Liza shouted down.

"Yer Guard, Lady Maclean."

A relieved breath gusted out of her at the sound of Alec's voice. Her knees wobbled slightly then, and she caught hold of the wall to steady herself. Recovering, she cleared her throat and turned from the wall, calling to the guards standing in the barmkin below. "Open the gates!"

She then picked up her skirts and led the way down to meet the returning warriors.

Some of them limped into the barmkin, while others had cuts to their arms and scratches upon their faces. Alec appeared unharmed. Nonetheless, his face was the grimmest she'd ever seen it.

"What happened?" she asked, halting before him.

"It was the Ghost Raiders, all right," he confirmed. "We fought the bastards, injured some of them … and I killed one … but the rest of them got away." His eyes glinted then. "They sacked the village while everyone was at the Bealtunn fire … before torching homes."

"Did they *kill* anyone?" Liza asked, her pulse hammering in her ears now. Homes could be replaced, but lives couldn't.

"Two farmers died defending their bothies."

"Did ye track them to their cog?" Rae demanded. He'd followed Liza down from the walls and now stepped up to her side.

A muscle flexed in Alec's jaw, and he shook his head. "The smoke and fog are as thick as porridge down there, and the raiders took full advantage of it. They disappeared before we reached the water's edge."

Liza took all this in with a frown. The anger in her captain's voice was clear, although she'd not damn him for failing to apprehend the attackers. They'd been at a disadvantage from the start. "Ye did all ye could," she said after a pause. "Send some of yer men down to the village overnight though … just in case the raiders decide to return before dawn."

He nodded, his expression still thunderous. "I shall see it done."

"I'll go down too," Makenna offered, stepping forward.

Liza cut her sister a censorious look, but the bullish expression on Makenna's face warned her from arguing.

"I brought four seasoned warriors with me, and shall return to the village with them," Rae said then, meeting Rankin's eye. "If ye'd welcome our assistance?"

The captain favored him with a brusque nod. "I would."

30: NO CHOICE

IT WAS GETTING late when Liza left the solar and made her way to her bedchamber. Nettie would be waiting for her, to help her undress and prepare for bed. However, she wasn't tired.

The attack had left her on edge, restless.

She'd taken a cup of wine with Kylie, hoping it would ease the tension that coiled under her ribcage, but it hadn't. Her sister had retired a while earlier, while Liza had fought the urge to throw on a cloak, leave the tower house, and seek out Rankin.

She wanted to do something—anything—to help. Instead, she felt useless.

The folk of Lochbuie and Moy looked to her to protect them, but she hadn't. All the same, tonight's attack had come from nowhere.

Not entirely, a voice whispered in the back of her mind. *Macbeth was here today ... there could be a connection.*

Brooding, she let herself into her bedchamber.

A single lantern burned dimly by the canopied bed, casting most of the chamber into shadow. Nettie had a cot near the hearth, but she wasn't in it, and the brick of peat that sat there had gone out.

"Nettie?" Liza stepped forward, her gaze sweeping the darkened recesses of the chamber. "Are ye—"

A heavy hand slapped over her mouth, dragging her backward.

Liza jolted, grasping at her assailant. The hand over her mouth was gloved, and mail bit into her skin. She paid it no mind. Instead, she flailed and kicked. She tried to employ all the tricks Makenna had taught her: stomping on his foot, elbowing him the guts, and even arching back in an attempt to break his nose with the back of her head. However, all her attempts failed.

"A feisty one, aren't ye?" A rough male voice growled in her ear. "But I'd cease yer struggling, if I were ye ... or yer wee Nettie will have her throat cut."

His voice was slightly muffled, yet she felt a tickle of recognition all the same. Did she know him?

Before she had time to dwell on her discovery, Liza's attacker hauled her left then, to face the shadowy corner of the room. There, held fast in the arms of a cloaked and hooded figure, was her handmaid. Nettie's eyes were huge, glistening with tears. Her assailant had gagged her with a strip of linen and held a gleaming blade at her throat.

The sheep's skull that covered the man's face, with its curling horns, was an eerie sight indeed, and Liza imagined the raider who held her was wearing the same disguise.

She remembered Rae's words then. Aye, they were only men. But men could be just as dangerous as demons. She and Nettie were in grave trouble.

Liza stopped struggling; instead, her mind scrabbled.

How did they get in here?

Indeed, the gates had been closed and barred ever since the attack.

A chill washed over her. What if these two had entered the castle beforehand? What if the attack on the village had been a ruse to draw their eye?

Her heart started to kick like a mule against her breastbone. *Lord help us.*

"Good lass," the raider rasped in her ear. "Keep heeding me, mind … or Nettie dies."

Liza swallowed, her body taut as a drawn longbow now. The man who held her had an iron grip.

"Here's what ye shall do," the raider continued, frighteningly calm, as if he'd thought all of this through. "Ye shall take us down to yer husband's strongroom and unlock it for us."

Liza's breathing stilled.

So, this was their game. The Ghost Raiders wanted Leod's coin.

Keeping his hand firmly on her mouth, her arm twisted painfully behind her, the raider pushed her toward the door. "Let's go for a walk."

Liza was tempted to risk trying to escape once she got into the stairwell. But after a moment, she dismissed the idea. That other raider still had a blade at Nettie's throat, and Liza had no doubt he'd use it if she misbehaved. She had no choice but to obey, even if every step galled her. And as she led the two men and Nettie out of her bedchamber and across the landing to the stairs, anger smoldered in her gut.

She took them down to the ground level of the tower house, stepping into the darkened hall. The sound of snoring reverberated through the space, for some of the servants slept in here. But no one stirred while she crossed to the steps that led underground to the cellar.

Liza trembled now, not from fear though but from outrage. How dare these brutes rob her?

She remembered then that one of the Guard would be posted in the cellar, watching over the trap door.

Her pulse started to race. Mother Mary, she had to warn him.

In the damp cellar below, she made her way to the trap door, her eyes straining in the half-light for the man guarding the strongroom.

An instant later, she made out a tall, lanky figure. Tamhas, one of the original five men who'd stayed on.

Her heart gave a violent kick when her captor removed his mailed hand from her mouth and greeted him. "Good lad."

Tamhas grinned back, his teeth flashing white in the shadows. "Ye took yer time."

Liza's step faltered. "What—"

"Yer husband was a friend of ours, lass," the raider breathed in her ear. "We had a deal, Leod and I … *we* plundered, and *he* squirreled away our loot … after taking his cut of course." He paused then, his grip on her arm tightening. "Until ye ruined everything by giving half of our coin away to pirates … and wasting the rest on yer repairs."

Liza started to shiver. Leod had been in league with the Ghost Raiders? She was still taking the news in when the raider pushed her roughly to her knees in front of the trap door. "Unlock it," he ordered. "But do anything foolish and yer maid's blood will flow."

Liza could feel him right behind her.

Sweating now, she fumbled for the ring of keys at her belt.

Alec paced the castle walls. It was the witching hour, so silent that it felt as if the night were holding its breath. But he didn't trust the quiet.

Everything about tonight's raid seemed 'off' to him. The Ghost Raiders had left with a few bags of grain and produce—for the villagers had little else—but it seemed a lot of effort to go to for such meager takings. Alec couldn't escape the nagging feeling that he was missing something crucial.

Rae, Makenna, and the others were still patrolling the village. No doubt, they'd return soon, once it was clear the raiders wouldn't come back.

"Seen anything?" he asked Beathan, as he walked past the guard posted at the watchtower that looked southeast.

"Nothing," the warrior grunted in reply. "The world's gone to sleep, Captain … ye should too."

"I'll sleep when dawn breaks," he muttered, moving on. "And not before."

He walked down the newly repaired eastern wall then, his gaze traveling over the shadowed bulk of the tower house to his left. All the windows were dark; everyone was slumbering. He could retire too, as Beathan had suggested, yet the restlessness within him, the worry that clawed at his chest, wouldn't let him.

He passed another sentry, greeting him with a nod. Usually, at this point, Alec would swivel on his heel and pace back the way he'd come. But not this time. Instead, he took the wall right to the end, to where the crenellations met the edge of the tower house. Here, the shadows were deep. This part of the wall looked north, onto the wooded hillside that reared up behind the castle.

Alec halted, his instincts pricking.

Something wasn't right here. Moving forward, slowly now, he peered into the darkness. His eyesight at night had always been better than most. Cory had often joked that their captain was part owl, for he often spied things that the rest of the crew didn't. All the same, beyond the glow of the braziers and torches, there were many hidden corners up here that were too easy to ignore.

Alec stepped up to the wall and ran his hand along its surface. This north-facing wall was rough with lichen in places and slippery with moss in others. His fingertips skimmed across each battlement. He was halfway across the last of them when his hand hit something.

Bending close, his breathing caught.

A rope.

Someone had knotted it securely around the battlement, and a coil sat beneath, hidden by the deepest of the shadows.

Alec breathed a salty curse and stepped back, even as the fine hair on the back of his neck prickled.

The rope told him two things. The first was that someone inside the keep had betrayed them—for how else had the rope gotten here? And the second was that at least one intruder was likely inside Moy Castle.

Alec swiveled around, his gaze traveling to the rickety wooden ladder that led down to the barmkin just a few feet from where he stood. His men didn't use it often, preferring to take the stone steps on the southern wall.

Yet *someone* had likely used it this evening. It was the best way to get down from the walls to the barmkin without being seen. Turning swiftly on his heel, Alec sprinted back along the wall.

He had to find them.

"Hurry up, woman. My patience is thinning."

The raider's growl made Liza's heart stutter. God's blood, she couldn't delay any longer. She'd made a show of pretending not to know which of the keys opened the strongroom, of laboriously trying each one. But her time had run out.

All the same, slowing things down had allowed her to think.

In his eagerness to catch the laird of Moy Castle and drag her off to get his coin, her captor had omitted to check her for weapons.

Liza still had her dirk hanging from her belt, although the murky light upstairs, and down here too—only a single guttering cresset lit the cellar—meant that none of the three men had noticed.

Even so, it was risky to draw her blade; the man's threat to kill Nettie wasn't an idle one. But in her gut, Liza knew she and her maid were doomed anyway. These three had a coldness to them that warned her they would kill them as soon as she unlocked the strongroom.

The Ghost Raiders had left her with no choice.

Nonetheless, her heart quailed as she made her decision. Her palms were slick with sweat now. There was a chance she'd fumble, that she wouldn't be fast enough.

She had to be brave. Craeg might end up orphaned, the people of Moy leaderless, but at least if she fought back, she'd have a chance.

Do it now.

"Aye," she muttered, her voice faltering slightly. "I'm sure it's this one." She selected another key—this one for the armory—and leaned in, as if to try it in the lock. However, instead of doing so, she grabbed the hilt of her dirk with her right hand and whipped around, drawing it as she went.

The raider was still crouched behind her, his skull-face grotesque in the dim light.

Liza drove the blade into his leg.

The man bit out a curse and backhanded her across the face. She reeled back, bringing the dirk with her.

"Ye shall regret that," he snarled, lurching upright.

Cheek burning, she flew at him once more and stabbed him again. She was aiming for his guts, but got him in the thigh this time.

The raider's meaty fist slammed into her belly, while Tamhas's bruising grip fastened around her wrist, squeezing hard until she was forced to let go of the dirk. "No, ye don't."

She cried out as the fighting dagger clattered to the ground.

"Stupid bitch!" the raider she'd stabbed grunted, grabbing hold of her hair then and pulling her head back so that she stared into his face. The skull was terrifying, as were the glittering dark eyes that glared out at her from the eye sockets. The raider glanced sideways then, to where his companion still held Nettie fast. "Slit her throat."

31: ONE STEP FURTHER

"NO!" LIZA CRIED, struggling against the man's iron grip. Her voice rang against stone. "Spare her, *please*!"

The injured raider hauled her against him, his mailed hand slamming over her mouth to gag her once more. Meanwhile, Tamhas gave a snigger. "Not so high and mighty now, are ye?"

Terror seized Liza by the chest, and she began to struggle wildly, heedless of this man's crushing hold. Meanwhile, Nettie's eyes were glassy, her body rigid as her captor's arm tensed.

He was going to kill the lass, and Liza couldn't do anything to stop him.

The raider holding Nettie jerked then, his big body spasming, before he staggered. An instant later, his hold on the maid, and on the knife, went slack.

Liza stilled her struggling, realizing that something unexpected had happened.

Nettie twisted away, the knife clattering to the stones, and the raider crumpled.

Alec stood behind him, a bloodied dirk clenched in his right hand.

Chest rising and falling sharply, for he'd clearly just raced down through the tower house to find them, Alec's face was cold. "Let Lady Maclean go."

Tamhas sprang forward then, steel flashing as he went for Alec's throat. The two men dueled before Tamhas made a choking sound. A heartbeat later, he slumped to the ground.

The remaining raider growled a curse, the rasp of steel against leather following, as he drew his own dirk and pressed it against Liza's neck. "One step further and she dies." He edged away from the trapdoor then, and the abandoned ring of keys that sat next to it. "Move away from the doorway."

Rankin's gaze narrowed. He hesitated a moment before stepping aside. There was a stillness to him that was disquieting. Pressed up against her captor's body, she felt tension ripple through him. He was limping now, from the two wounds she'd inflicted.

With Rankin here and his accomplices dead, the raider was in trouble—and he knew it. Escape was the wisest choice, rather than attempting to steal any coin, although he needed to keep a knife at her throat if he was to get out of Moy Castle alive.

Liza searched Alec's face, as her captor drew her steadily toward the doorway, looking for a hint at what he was planning. He gave little away. Only the flicker of something in his eyes warned of the anger he now leashed.

The raider hauled her out of the cellar and limped his way up the stairs, pulling her with him as if she were a sack of neeps.

And Alec followed them.

"Keep back," her captor wheezed. "Or my blade will slip."

Liza swallowed, trying to ignore the cold burn of the dirk-blade on her throat. She could smell his desperation now; indeed, he'd kill her if Alec got too close.

They left the tower house, and the raider dragged her down the stairs to the barmkin. The fog had crept in even further, milky tendrils snaking over the castle walls.

The scrape of weapons being drawn, and muttered curses, followed, as the guards posted on the walls spied the skull-faced raider and his captive moving across the cobbled space toward the steps.

And all the while, Alec stalked his quarry. "Mind him," he called to his men. "The bastard's mine."

"I'll kill her," the raider shouted, his voice hoarse with pain now. Liza noted the trail of blood that gleamed in the torchlight upon the cobbles. "Don't test me!"

"Aye … and then I'll end *ye*," Alec growled back.

Liza's blood roared in her ears as the raider mounted the stairs and pulled her after him. Where was he going? Did he intend to throw her from the walls?

Reaching the top of the steps, the raider made his way, purposefully despite his heavy limp, along the eastern wall.

Liza's skin prickled then, realizing that the man knew exactly where he was going. He had an escape planned. His eagerness betrayed him though, for as he dragged her along the wall, toward where the shadows deepened upon the northern ramparts, he slackened the pressure of his blade on her throat.

She seized her chance.

Stepping back into him, Liza stomped her heel, hard, down onto his foot before driving her elbow into him, just below his ribs as Makenna had taught her. She heard his breath whoosh out of him, and his grip on her loosened for an instant.

She twisted away and kicked him viciously in the leg—the one she'd stabbed twice.

The raider hissed a curse, his knee buckling, while Liza rolled away.

Things moved swiftly after that.

Wheezing further curses, the raider clawed himself upright and lunged for the shadows, while Alec leaped over where Liza lay, following him.

She pushed herself up, squinting as she watched the raider lower himself over the wall. She jolted then. Hades, he had a rope.

Alec reached the battlement a heartbeat too late, but he didn't try and follow the raider. Instead, his dirk glinted as he slashed at the rope. It frayed and then snapped, unraveling like a whip while Alec leaped back to avoid being lashed by it.

A startled cry echoed through the mist below.

Alec whirled around, his gaze spearing the guards by the gate. "Find the whoreson!" His warriors moved to obey, unbarring the gate and opening it so four of them could slip out.

Meanwhile, Alec strode to where Liza had risen to her feet and was shakily dusting off her skirts. "Did he harm ye?" he asked huskily, his gaze roaming her face.

Earlier, when he'd been dealing with the raider and Tamhas, his face had been a cold mask, but now concern tightened his features.

Liza shook her head. The two blows the man had dealt her no longer hurt. Instead, rage smoldered in her belly. "I recognized that bastard's voice," she ground out.

"Aye," Alec replied, his voice hardening. His eyes glinted then. "It was Ross Macbeth."

They couldn't find Macbeth's body. Somehow, he'd survived the fall from the eastern walls. The guards returned to the castle a while later, with news that they'd followed a trail of blood down to the shore, where it ended.

The raider had gotten away.

And one of the other guards was missing. Beathan. He was an older warrior, one of those who'd served Leod. According to Alec, he'd been posted near the southeast tower that night.

He'd obviously been the one to tie the rope around the battlement so that the Ghost Raiders could climb up—and when he'd seen Alec rush inside the tower house, he'd likely panicked and used the rope to escape while he could.

Liza's stomach clenched as she received this news, even as Alec growled a curse. Meanwhile, Rae, Kylie, and Makenna— who'd all been called into the laird's solar—looked on. Rae and Makenna had just returned from the village and had been about to go to bed when they heard what had happened.

"Ride to Duart Castle at first light," Liza informed the guards who'd brought the news. "Inform Loch that Ross Macbeth is one of the Ghost Raiders ... and that my husband was in league with him."

This admission brought a murmured oath from Kylie, and Liza nodded, her lips compressing. "Macbeth gloated about it when I took him down to the cellar." She paused then, pulling the woolen wrap she'd donned tighter around her shoulders. After her ordeal, she felt trembly and cold. "Leod's been storing the Ghost Raider's loot in his strongroom ... after taking some for himself. As ye can imagine, his death caused a problem for

Macbeth and his raiders. Luckily for them, they had allies inside the castle … both Beathan and Tamhas."

Indeed, the lanky figure she'd spied disappearing into the undergrowth after meeting with Macbeth the day before was probably Tamhas.

Rae gave his head a disbelieving shake at this. "Yer husband was a chieftain, already a wealthy man … I don't understand why he'd make an arrangement with criminals."

"Neither do I," she admitted. "Although after Loch spared Bran Mackinnon's life at Dounarwyse, he grew embittered, secretive."

"Aye, this was a revenge of sorts," Alec said with a nod.

"It could have been," she murmured, holding his eye across the chamber.

Ever since Macbeth's escape, Alec's gaze had barely left her. She'd told him she was well, had insisted the raiders hadn't injured her; however, he didn't seem convinced.

Liza pushed herself off the window seat, where she'd been perching, and rose to her feet. She then cut her attention back to the guards. "That is all for now."

They both nodded. "Aye, Lady Maclean."

The guards departed, and she surveyed the faces of those remaining inside the solar. "Dawn is still an hour or two away," she murmured. "Return to yer chambers … rest … and we shall talk later."

Makenna gave a jaw-cracking yawn. "See ye in a few hours then." With that, she looped her arm through Kylie's and led her from the chamber. Rae followed at their heel. Rankin then pushed himself off the mantelpiece, where he'd been leaning, and headed toward the doorway as well.

"Alec," Liza said softly before he reached it. "Stay … I'd like to talk to ye."

He halted by the door, his brow furrowing.

"Close the door please."

He did as bid before returning to his former position by the fire. Meanwhile, Liza pulled her woolen wrap even more firmly around her and perched on the edge of the large oaken table that dominated the solar, where she and her family broke their fast together every morning. "Ye saved Nettie's life … I wanted to thank ye."

He inclined his head. "How is the lass?"

"Sleeping, I believe … hopefully, she'll be fine."

"Ye were brave," he said then, his gaze intense. "Macbeth had a knife to yer throat, but ye held yerself together." Liza gave a soft snort at this, yet his gaze didn't waver. "Ye are a formidable laird, Liza."

Warmth washed over her. "Thank ye," she replied after an awkward pause.

Their conversation had become uncomfortable now. She should really bid the man good night so they could both get some rest. Liza wouldn't bother to retire though; instead, she'd remain by the fire here in the solar. Her mind was too full, her nerves still too frayed, to sleep.

Silence swelled between them once more, and she was about to dismiss her captain, when she marked the tension on his face, the way his eyes had shadowed. "What is it?"

He swallowed then, and she realized he was nervous.

"I thought Macbeth was going to kill ye tonight," he admitted, his voice low and strained. "And that ye'd go to yer grave not knowing how I feel about ye."

Liza's heart kicked against her ribs, her mouth going dry. "Alec," she whispered. "I don't—"

"Please let me say this now," he cut her off, "or I never will."

She stared back at him. "What then?"

His chest hitched before he finally replied, "I'm in love with ye."

32: SHACKLED

SILENCE FOLLOWED ALEC'S admission. Blinking, Liza stared at him. Had she heard right?

"I have poor timing, I'll admit," he said roughly before dragging a hand down his face. "This will be the last thing ye wish to hear."

She still didn't answer. Frankly, his words had stunned her.

Alec stepped away from the hearth, stopping when he was a few feet distant from where she still sat upon the table. "I've spent my life avoiding being shackled to anyone," he went on, a nerve flickering in his cheek. "But then I met ye, Liza. Ye made me desire a different future."

She drew in a long, shaky breath, her chest fluttering now. "Is that why ye offered to stay on here?"

Strange how she could keep her wits about her when she had a knife to her throat, but a declaration from Alec Rankin made her feel as if the ground had just given way under her.

She was glad she was sitting, or her knees might have buckled, and that would have been humiliating indeed.

A muscle flexed in Alec's jaw. "I didn't want to admit it to myself at the time … but aye … I remained at Moy so that I could be near to ye," he replied, moving closer. Reaching the table, he sank down onto one knee before her. He then pressed a clenched hand against his breastbone, his gaze piercing hers. "But know this … if I won yer heart, I'd spend the rest of my life leaving ye in no doubt of my love."

Liza's pulse fluttered. "And how would ye do that?"

His blue eyes glinted. "I would serve ye, protect ye, and stand at yer side through all of life's storms."

Her breathing grew shallow. Curse him, he was making her resolve to remain chaste for the rest of her days melt like snow in the warm spring sun. Desperately, she tried to claw back control. "I rue the day we met, Alec Rankin," she rasped, her fingers curling around the table edge.

"No, ye don't," he replied, his lips lifting at the edges.

Her pulse started to throb in her throat. His gaze darkened, and he rose to his feet.

Liza's chin kicked up. His nearness, the scent of leather and salt that was uniquely him, overwhelmed her. And yet, beneath it all, the truth burned as bright as the North Star within her. "No," she whispered, her voice catching. "I don't."

He stepped in closer still, reaching out then and tracing his fingers down her cheek. "We have something," he whispered. "Don't we?"

"Aye," she murmured, even as dizziness swept over her. They did, and she couldn't fight it any longer. "I love ye too, Alec."

And the moment she admitted how she felt, something gave way inside her. Recklessness stirred then, wreathing up from her lower belly into her chest, the heaviness that had sat like an anvil on her breastbone for days now lifting.

Mother Mary forgive her, she was tired of denying herself. She was bone-weary of pretending she didn't want Alec Rankin. Imagining a life where they lived under the same roof but never touched made misery twist under her ribs.

His gaze turned limpid as the pad of his thumb skimmed her lower lip. "I can't tell ye how sweet those words sound," he murmured.

A wave of dizziness assailed her. His touch. His voice. She needed more.

"Kiss me," she whispered, her breathing coming in short, shallow gasps now, need twisting in her gut. "Please."

He made a sound in the back of his throat and bent over her, his mouth claiming hers. His kiss was hungry, desperate—and from the moment her lips parted under his and their tongues began to mate, she was lost.

Gasping against his mouth, Liza entwined her arms about his neck, hauling him closer. An instant later, he was standing between her spread thighs. Reaching up, he then unbound her heavy braid with one hand as he kissed her, teasing it out with his fingers first, before tangling his hand through it and drawing her head back further still.

Liza groaned, thrilling at being completely in his thrall. Aye, she was the laird of Moy Castle and its lands, but when they were alone together, she wanted to be wholly his. His mouth devoured hers wildly, and she started to shiver.

Lord, how she needed him.

However, after a while, he broke off the kiss. Breathing hard, he released her and straightened up. "I shouldn't be so rough with ye, lass," he said huskily. "Not after everything ye have been through tonight." He reached up then and brushed his knuckles across her cheek. "Ye should retire … and try to rest."

"I don't want to go to bed," she replied, her voice choked as hunger dug its claws into her. "What I want is for ye to take me here … on this table."

Alec stiffened. His lips—swollen from their heated kisses—parted, and his pupils flared darkly. "Is that really what ye wish for?" he murmured, a rasp to his voice.

"Aye," she sighed.

He stepped away from her then, and disappointment clutched at her. She watched as Alec walked to the door of the solar, a sigh of relief gusting out of her when he locked the door. He then turned to her, his mouth curving with sensual promise. "We don't want to be interrupted, do we?"

"No," she said throatily, even as her pulse went wild.

He stalked back to her then and proceeded to undress her. His fingers moved with practiced ease—aye, he was a man who'd disrobed a few women in his time—yet she didn't care. From tonight onward, he was hers. And she was his.

Stripping off her last item of clothing, a thin lèine that reached mid-thigh, he tossed the garment aside and stepped in close once more, capturing her hungry mouth with his.

Alec was still fully dressed, and in the past that might have bothered Liza, for it made her feel vulnerable, exposed. Not tonight though, for she trusted him. Even so, her greedy hands wanted to explore his skin, and the quilted gambeson he wore made that impossible. She pulled his lèine free of his braies, her fingers sliding to the hot flesh underneath.

"I'll help ye, lass." He grabbed the hem of both the gambeson and lèine and yanked them over his head. The sight of his muscular torso, kissed by firelight, made her mouth go dry, and Liza leaned into him, bowing her head to let her lips trail down from his neck to his chest, teasing his nipples with her lips and tongue as she went.

Alec growled an oath, his body quivering under her touch.

Liza smiled as her hands slid down, over the flat plane of his belly, toward where his braies sat low on his hips. She wanted to make him react like that again, to hear a groan of pleasure rumble in his chest.

Yet, when she started to untie the laces on his braies, he caught her by the hands and pushed her back so that she lay, spread-eagled, across the table. He then climbed onto it with her and pinned her wrists above her head, a lewd position that made her breasts thrust up into his face. "That's better," he murmured as he lowered his head and licked one of her nipples. "Just where I want ye."

The flesh between Liza's thighs began to pulse and tingle at these words, and when he bent his head and started to suck the aching peak of her left breast, heat suffused her lower belly.

"Oh," she groaned as he moved to her other breast and gave it the same treatment. "That feels so good."

But he didn't stop there. Releasing her wrists, he slid down her body, his tongue tracing the arch of her ribcage and the curve of her belly. His fingers then stroked the dark curls between her thighs. Liza started to tremble in anticipation of what was to come.

Sliding back off the table, he lowered himself to his knees and pulled her close. And then, he spread her legs wide. Liza propped herself up on her elbows and watched him stare between her thighs. His lips were parted slightly, and a flush had risen to his high cheekbones.

"Like what ye see?" she whispered, thrilling at her own boldness. This lusty side—a side only this man had awoken—was a surprise indeed. When she was with Alec, she felt free.

"Oh, aye," he replied, his voice almost a groan as he pushed her wider still, exposing her even more fully. An instant later, he was devouring her, his wicked tongue circling and lapping before it speared into her.

Liza gasped and shuddered, her stomach muscles clenching in response.

She could have lowered herself back onto the table, let her eyes close, and given herself up to sensation, but instead, she continued to watch him pleasure her. Excitement twisted in her loins, her thighs shaking.

By the Saints, this was incredible.

The wet sounds he was making that drifted through the solar now—as his movements grew more frantic, hungrier—would have shamed her once. But now they just made her grind herself against him, harder and harder—until delicious spasms pulsed through her quim.

Panting, she did fall back then against the table, rolling her hips as ripples of ecstasy continued to throb low in her belly.

As she looked on, Alec rose to his feet and dropped his braies, kicking them aside. His shaft thrust up proudly, jerking with eagerness. Flashing Liza a wicked smile, he rolled her over and pulled her back toward him. He then bent her over the table so that her arse met his groin. "I'm going to take ye now, Liza," he said throatily. "And it isn't going to be gentle."

Heat pooled in her loins. "Good," she replied, her voice choked with lust. "Make me yers."

He groaned at these words, and a moment later, she felt him—thick, hard, and hot—pressed up against the slickness of her sex. And then, he was sliding into her, in a long, deep thrust that made her dig her fingernails into the table and bite her bottom lip to stop herself from crying out.

"Stroke yerself," he murmured then. "Let me see ye *own* yer pleasure."

Her breathing hitched at these words. She'd never done anything so lewd before—and Leod certainly wouldn't have encouraged it. However, with Alec, she didn't hesitate. A moment later, she raised a shaky hand from the table and slid it down between her thighs, shocked to discover just how wet she was.

She began to stroke herself then, finding the swollen pearl of flesh Alec had pleasured so eagerly earlier, and circling it with the pad of her finger. She gave a soft, breathy moan.

"That's right," Alec growled. "Don't stop." He leaned forward then and caught her by the hair, tangling his hand in the heavy tresses before drawing her head toward him so that her back arched, and her backside thrust up against him.

And then, holding her firmly by the hip with the other hand, he started to thrust and grind himself into her.

Liza made a choking sound as his rod found a deliciously sensitive place inside her. Continuing to stroke herself, she rolled her hips against him each time he drove into her. "Alec," she gasped as wet heat flooded through her loins. "I think I'm going to—"

She peaked violently, her body shuddering while he continued to ride her. Liza slid her hand out from between her slick thighs and braced herself against the table. She then arched herself hard against him.

Meanwhile, Alec continued to plow her—masterfully. And as he drove into her again and again, deeper still, her core clutched greedily at him.

The Lord forgive her, she could never get enough of this.

Alec gasped her name then, his breath hot against her back, his fingers biting into the soft flesh of her hip. Buried to the hilt, he jolted, a groan ripping from his throat as he spilled inside her.

33: AT YER SIDE

SNUGGLED IN THE hollow of Alec's shoulder, Liza traced the smooth skin of his chest with a fingertip. They lay on a soft sheepskin before the glowing hearth. Despite that they were both naked now, she wasn't cold, for the lump of peat threw out considerable heat. The sweat had dried on their bodies, and a languorous sense of well-being suffused her limbs.

"I was planning to leave, ye know," Alec admitted then, breaking the peaceful silence between them. "I'd told myself it was for the best. This evening, I even asked Rae to carry word to Loch."

Liza propped herself up on an elbow to meet his eye. Alec was looking up at her, his pale hair fanned out around him upon the sheepskin. His expression was sheepish.

"Without speaking to me first?"

He pulled a face then. "In truth, I thought ye'd be relieved."

Her throat tightened. "Don't ye like living here?"

"It's not that," he assured her, shaking his head. "I actually enjoy captaining the Guard … but after I kissed ye last night, I was sure I'd ruined things between us."

"Where would ye have gone?"

"I'm not sure," he replied, his lips lifting at the edges. "I hadn't thought that far ahead."

"Ye wouldn't have tracked down *The Blood Reiver* then and asked them to take ye back?"

He snorted. "No … but I'd have survived. I always do."

Her gaze roved his face. "I wondered if ye'd regret staying on here."

His fingertips traced a lazy path up and down her spine. "I did initially, after *The Reiver* raised anchor," he admitted. "But I had more reason to stay than go. *Ye* were here, after all." His smile turned rueful. "And I was ready for a change, Liza. Even before I met ye, I'd grown weary of plundering the seas … it was only a matter of time before I chose a different path. Meeting ye was a new beginning for me."

Warmth suffused her chest at these words. "I like hearing ye say that," she admitted then.

"Do ye?" His fingers wove through her hair now.

Her mouth curved. "Aye … I've never had anyone look out for me the way ye do."

Something moved in the depths of his eyes. "That's because Leod had shit between his ears. Ye deserve to be cherished, lass … not abused."

Her vision misted, her smile growing wobbly. "So, ye'll stay with me, Alec?"

"Aye." His expression turned tender. "Wherever the future takes us … I will remain at yer side. No one, not even Loch, will keep me from ye."

His vow made her throat ache. Wordlessly, she reached out, her fingertips stroking his chiseled jaw. "Thank ye," she whispered.

Their gazes held for a long moment before Alec favored her with a soft warm smile. He then gave a languid stretch. "The castle will be awakening soon … I suppose we should get dressed."

"I suppose so," Liza replied, reluctantly glancing toward the window, where the first glimmers of dawn were peeking around the edges of the sacking. How she wished she could push back the sunrise so they could spend more time alone. However, there was much to be done today.

Alec rolled lithely to his feet and retrieved their clothing, which lay scattered carelessly across the solar floor. When he handed Liza hers, a groove appeared between his eyebrows. "What happens now?" he asked. "Would ye prefer to keep this … us … secret?"

Holding her clothing to her breast, she considered his question. "I don't want to sneak around," she replied finally. "But I've been widowed less than three months and don't wish to cause an even bigger scandal than I have already."

Alec moved close and reached out, his fingers tracing the curve of her neck. Liza shivered under his touch. Lord, how she wanted to drag him into her bedchamber, turf poor Nettie out, and lock herself away with this man for the next two days, to have her fill of him. But it was a luxury she couldn't afford.

"I can wait," he assured her.

She huffed a sigh. "I know, but I don't wish to. I want to shout from the walls that Alec Rankin has my heart."

He grinned at this admission. "Let those closest to ye know then," he suggested, his blue eyes twinkling. "And meanwhile, we can sneak around in secret … I promise that I shall keep my hands to myself unless we are alone."

Neither of her sisters spoke for a few moments when Liza told them that Alec Rankin was her lover. Nonetheless, the look on both their faces was a picture indeed. It was mid-morning, and the three of them were returning from visiting the ruins of Lochbuie village.

The mist had cleared with the rising sun, the last of it burning away now.

Rae had joined them, his Highland collie trotting beside him, and the chieftain of Dounarwyse had pleased Liza by offering to send supplies to help the villagers. She'd thanked him, but he'd dropped behind the three sisters now, to have a word to Alec. After the Battle of Dounarwyse, he'd been faced with the epic task of rebuilding the village outside his broch, and he had some suggestions for her captain.

And as soon as she was alone with Kylie and Makenna, Liza had summoned her courage and made her announcement.

Kylie was the first to speak. "I thought ye'd decided to keep yer distance from him?"

Makenna cut Kylie a sharp look. "Ye knew about this?"

Kylie ignored her. She was too busy giving Liza a hard stare. "Ye are only recently widowed," she pointed out, unnecessarily. "Ye should be more cautious."

Liza snorted. "I've had enough of caution. Leod put me through six years of misery. There was never any love between us." She paused then, her gaze narrowing as she stared down her sisters, who both walked to her left. "Are ye going to judge me?"

"No," Makenna muttered, even as her cheeks grew pink. "Bed whomever ye wish, sister … it's nothing to do with me."

However, Kylie got that stubborn look she knew well. "Ye said ye would never marry again."

"And I haven't announced a wedding date, have I?" Liza shot back.

Her outburst shocked Kylie into silence. Both sisters regarded her warily now, as if afraid of what she might say next.

Huffing a sigh, Liza halted before glancing furtively over her shoulder to make sure that Alec and Rae were far enough away not to overhear her. Indeed, the two men appeared deep in conversation.

Perhaps Alec was telling Rae that he'd be staying on at Moy, after all. She hoped so.

"I once thought intimacy between a man and a woman only brought humiliation and pain … but Alec showed me otherwise," she said after a pause, noting how a blush rose to both her sisters' cheeks. For all her confidence, Makenna was a maid, and Kylie—like Liza—had found no pleasure in the marital bed. "But there's more than just lust between us," she continued. "There's trust … and love."

Silence followed this proclamation, and Liza's pulse quickened.

She'd never spoken so frankly with either of her sisters and suddenly worried what they'd think of her. Eventually, Makenna cleared her throat. Her cheeks were still glowing with embarrassment. "Ye could have chosen worse than Rankin, I suppose."

Meanwhile, Kylie's gaze searched Liza's face. Her eyes were wide, her expression startled, as if she were seeing her for the first time.

"I shall depart at dawn," Rae Maclean announced as he lifted his cup of plum wine to Liza. "I've stayed here long enough … and Loch will be waiting to hear from me."

Liza swallowed a mouthful of roast fowl and tried to ignore the nervous flutter in her gut. She'd known this moment was coming. Three days had passed since Bealtunn, and Rae had rolled up his sleeves and worked alongside Alec and the Guard to begin repairs on the village. She'd hoped he might stay longer still, to give her more time to impress him with her capability.

"Of course," she said quietly. Around them, the rumble of voices ebbed and flowed through the hall of Moy Castle.

"And what will ye tell him?"

Alec's blunt question made her flinch, and she shot him a warning look. However, her lover's focus was on the chieftain of Dounarwyse. Rae had just met his eye.

Liza's gaze flicked between the men's faces. She wondered if Rae knew about their relationship; she certainly hadn't said anything to the laird. Only her sisters knew that things had changed between her and Alec. And Nettie too—for Liza had taken to sleeping in her solar. Every eve, once everyone else had retired, Alec visited her there. Then, the door locked, they flew at each other.

No, she imagined Rae didn't know—for surely, he'd disapprove. As Loch likely would.

"I will inform Loch that both the lady laird of Moy, and her captain, have settled into their roles with admirable dedication," Rae replied finally, his mouth curving. "And I shall tell him he'd be a fool not to let ye both stay on."

34: OUR OWN PATHS TO TREAD

LIZA'S MOUTH CURVED. "Really?"

Rae's attention shifted to her, his own smile widening. "Aye."

Warmth bloomed across her chest. "Thank ye."

His expression sobered. "Did ye believe otherwise?"

"We had our doubts," Alec admitted. "We're both new to our respective roles … and recent events have tested us."

Rae shrugged. "That's true enough … but ye have shown yerselves capable, and worthy of respect." He paused then, his features tightening. "All those who lead … myself included … have their trials."

"Certainly not ye, Rae?" Alec teased. "Ye give the impression of a man in control."

Rae grimaced. "Aye, well, even an experienced laird makes mistakes. I try not to imagine what my wee brother has gotten up to in my absence. Jack might be finding my chair a little too comfortable."

Alec snorted a laugh at this, and Rae's mouth curved. "My time away from Dounarwyse has done me good though," he added then. "After Donalda died, my life drifted into an unhappy pattern … but things will change upon my return."

"What will ye do?" Liza asked, intrigued. During Rae's stay, she'd been too worried about his judgment to consider his situation.

His gaze shadowed. "I haven't been much of a father to my sons of late. They've run wild. I will take them in hand and see about finding a firm local woman to mind them."

"Sounds like ye need a duenna," she replied.

A groove etched between his eyebrows. "What's that then?"

"A stern older woman hired to chaperone young ladies in Iberia … or in this case, unruly lads."

"Aye, our grandfather told us of them," Makenna added with a grin. "He said ye never wanted to cross a duenna."

Rae sighed, flashing them a wry smile. "If only I had such a woman at my disposal."

"I could fill the role, if ye wish?"

Kylie's announcement made silence fall like a hammer blow at the table.

Liza's gaze snapped to her older sister, expecting to see a teasing light in Kylie's eye. But on the contrary, her spine was straight, her chin held high, as she met Rae's gaze.

Mother Mary, she was in earnest.

"Ye are too young for such a role, Kylie," Liza replied, deliberately brushing off her comment.

"I'm thirty, Liza," Kylie answered firmly. "And I'm not interested in remarrying." Her gaze never wavered from Rae's as she spoke. "I'm good with bairns, Maclean … although I've never had any of my own … and rest assured, I shall tolerate no nonsense."

Rae's fern-green eyes narrowed at this. "Are ye sure, Lady Grant?" he asked, inclining his head. "I'd not wish to encumber ye with my situation."

"Ye wouldn't be," she assured him. "I shall expect a wage for my services … but in return, I will serve ye well."

An awkward pause followed before Rae glanced Liza's way. "Would ye object?"

Liza gave a soft snort. "I'm not Kylie's father."

"And he wouldn't object either," Kylie replied, irritation creeping into her voice. "Indeed, ye will be doing him a favor, for otherwise, I will be underfoot at Meggernie Castle."

Rae's features tightened. "Ye won't stay on in yer late husband's broch?"

Kylie shook her head. "I can't … after Errol's death, I discovered that his debts are many … one of his creditors now owns his broch."

Liza stiffened at this admission. Meanwhile, Makenna's lips had parted. This was news to them both. "Ye never said," Makenna murmured.

Kylie tore her gaze from Rae's then and looked her way. Her oaken eyes were shadowed, faint spots of color upon her pale cheeks. "I was ashamed," she admitted. "Da still doesn't know."

An ache rose in Liza's chest at this admission. Kylie was stoic, private—too much so. She held things close, things that should be shared.

"Aye, well … if ye wish for a position at Dounarwyse, ye shall have it," Rae spoke up then, shattering the tension between the sisters. "I'd be happy to have yer assistance with Lyle and Ailean." He huffed a sigh then. "Lord knows, I need it."

"I wish ye'd told me," Liza said softly as she watched her sister make neat stitches upon the pillowcase she was embroidering. "There was no need to suffer in silence."

Kylie glanced up and grimaced. "As I said … I was embarrassed. The MacGregor pride is strong, is it not?"

Liza snorted a laugh. "Aye."

Like Kylie, she'd been known to weather storms without telling anyone. She'd kept her unhappiness during her marriage to Leod secret, hadn't she?

"Are ye sure ye want to be duenna to Rae's sons?" she asked then. "They sound like a lot of work."

"They're just bairns who've lost their mother," Kylie replied firmly. "And aye, I didn't offer my services just to avoid slinking back to Meggernie Castle and having to explain myself to Da … although it didn't escape me either." She paused then, determination hardening her eyes. "I see ye, and the purpose ye have … and I wish to have something to strive for in life." She shook her head then. "Like Leod with ye, Errol never shared anything with me … I didn't know of his debts until after his death. There were times when I felt like a ghost in our broch, drifting from chamber to chamber, trying to make myself useful yet never quite succeeding."

Liza nodded. "I understand." And she did. Hadn't she felt the same way here once? "We are capable of so much," she murmured.

Rising from her desk, where she'd been counting out coins to pay her bailiff, she moved across the sheepskin-covered floor of the lady's solar to the window. It was another lovely day, and the sky was the color of a robin's egg. Leaning against the stone sill, she gazed outdoors, smiling at the sweet scent of summer grass that wafted over her.

A bairn's laughter reached her then, and she glanced down to see Craeg throwing a stick for Rae's dog. The Highland Collie gave an excited bark and bounded after the stick as it skittered over the stones.

Liza's mouth curved. Her son loved dogs. She'd talk to the hound-master soon and find out when the next bitch would whelp. She wished to give Craeg a puppy as a Yuletide gift this year.

Her gaze traveled over the barmkin and halted upon two figures who sparred with wooden practice swords.

Murmuring an oath under her breath, she watched as Alec attempted to kick her sister's legs out from under her. However, Makenna leaped nimbly aside. Alec's low laugh reverberated off stone. "That's better … ye learn fast."

"What is it?" Kylie appeared at Liza's side, watching as Makenna leaped under Alec's guard and tried to knee him in the bollocks—only his quick reflexes saved him. Kylie then made a strangled sound in the back of her throat.

Liza glanced her way to see her elder sister now wore a look of stern disapproval. "Who is that censure aimed at," she said, frowning. "Alec or Makenna?"

"Both of them," Kylie muttered. "Makenna for insisting on such mannish behavior … when she's supposed to be readying herself to become a wife … and Rankin for encouraging her."

"Makenna believes Bran Mackinnon will forfeit his father's oath to ours … especially once he learns he was lied to," Liza replied, arching an eyebrow.

Kylie scowled. "Da should never have promised the Mackinnons his eldest daughter ... intending to hand over his *youngest* instead. The young clan-chief will see it as a slight."

Liza snorted. "In that case, Makenna will likely be spared." Her gaze held Kylie's then. "Anyway, aren't ye proud of our sister for daring to be different?"

"Makenna isn't just *different*," Kylie said with a sigh. "She flies in the face of convention." She gestured to the barmkin below then, where Alec and Makenna now circled each other, and he was giving her instructions. "And just like yer man, Da indulges her."

Yer man.

The words, carelessly spoken, warmed Liza's chest.

Heedless to her reaction, Kylie continued. "These days, whenever ye remind her of her responsibilities, she gets testy."

Liza eyed her elder sister. "Ye have done so, I take it?"

"Aye. Someone must."

Shaking her head, Liza moved close to her sister and placed an arm around her shoulders. Kylie stiffened a moment, surprised by the spontaneous affection, before leaning into her.

They stood like that for a few moments, watching the goings-on in the barmkin below before Liza broke the silence between them. "Dear sister," she said softly. "Ye care greatly for us all ... and only want what's best for us ... but we all have our own paths to tread." She squeezed her shoulders then, catching Kylie's eye. For once, her sister's expression was unguarded, her brown eyes vulnerable, and Liza's throat tightened in response. "Aye, sometimes we shall falter ... sometimes we will fail ... but ye must let us."

35: ALL I NEED

LIZA AND ALEC stood side-by-side upon the castle walls and watched Rae Maclean and his escort ride away from Moy Castle. As always, his collie ran at his side.

"Shaggy dog!" Craeg cried out, waving a hand. "Goodbye."

"Is that the hound's name then, lad?" Alec asked, his tone teasing as he hitched the bairn up on his left hip. Craeg had wanted to see their guests off too, and so Alec obliged.

"I don't know," Craeg replied. "But I call him 'Shaggy'."

"I think the dog's called 'Storm'," Liza said, her mouth twitching. "But ye are right, love … he is a hairy hound."

Her gaze traveled then to the two women riding with Rae and their combined escort.

Kylie and Makenna would ride with them as far as Craignure before taking a ferry back to the mainland. Kylie would need to organize to have her belongings taken to Dounarwyse and had promised to arrive there to begin her new position at midsummer. Makenna would accompany her before returning to Meggernie Castle in Perthshire.

Liza's eyes grew hot and prickly then, her throat tight.

She wasn't sure when she'd see her sisters again, although once Kylie settled in at Dounarwyse, they could organize a visit with Rae and his sons to Moy—or she and Craeg could go to them.

"I miss them already," she said then, her voice barely above a whisper.

"What … surely not Rae?" Alec replied with a laugh. "That curmudgeon."

Liza glanced left to find her lover grinning. "Ye two got on well in the end, didn't ye?"

"Aye." Alec leaned in then, his breath tickling her ear as he whispered, "Although I thought he was going to try and geld me when I told him that I loved ye."

Liza's eyes snapped wide, and she turned to face him squarely, the guests she'd just seen off forgotten. Meanwhile, Craeg was too busy waving both hands now, singing, "Shaggy dog … shaggy dog!"

"Ye told him *that*?"

"I did." His brow furrowed then. "Shouldn't I have?"

"Well … I didn't say ye couldn't," she admitted, suddenly flustered. "I'm just surprised he didn't challenge me over it." Indeed, she'd have expected Rae to have been thunderous after such an admission, yet his mood hadn't altered whenever she'd seen him over the past days. And indeed, he was taking a glowing report back to Loch.

"I asked him not to."

Liza cocked an eyebrow. "What did ye say to the man?"

To her ire, he merely winked. "Never ye mind."

Liza's gaze narrowed. "And how did he react?"

Alec glanced east, at where the company had almost disappeared amongst the trees between the castle and the village. "Once he'd calmed down, he was almost … wistful."

"Wistful?"

"Aye, I'm not sure his marriage was a happy one."

Considering this, Liza stepped closer to him. And then, she reached out her hand and caught his. It was a bold move, for they weren't in private. But Craeg wasn't paying them any attention at present, and their bodies shielded their hands from view.

All the same, Liza's pulse quickened as Alec interlaced his fingers through hers and squeezed gently.

"Ye have done well here, Liza." He paused then as if considering his next words. "Ye had a mountain to climb when ye took over from Leod … but ye managed it."

A smile tugged at her mouth. "I did." She squeezed his hand back. "But I had some help. Ye could have sailed away … yet ye didn't."

"No," he replied, his voice lowering. "That conversation with Loch was a turning point in my life … I just didn't want to admit it to myself at the time." He cleared his throat. "Meeting ye was the best thing that's ever happened to me."

They stared at each other, and Liza's smile faded. The blend of tenderness and hunger in his eyes made her breathing quicken.

"God, woman, I want to kiss ye right now, right here," he said roughly, "and for it not to matter who sees."

Lord, how she wanted it too, more than she could express.

"And that day will come," she whispered back.

"Aye, but not soon enough," he replied, his gaze roaming over her face. "And I will fight anyone to the death who's foolish enough to ever stand between us."

"Are ye going to fight someone, Alec?" A young voice interrupted them then, and Liza blinked, emerging from the enchantment they'd spun around themselves. Now that Rae's collie had disappeared, her son's attention had shifted back to them.

"Aye, lad," Alec replied, flashing Craeg a smile. "But I require a worthy opponent. Are ye willing to fetch yer wooden dirk and duel with me?"

Craeg squealed in delight before his gaze flicked to Liza, worry shadowing his eagerness. "Can I, Ma?"

Guilt stabbed at her as she recalled his stricken face when she'd yanked him off Alec and scared the wits out of the lad. She wasn't proud of her behavior, although she'd forgiven herself for it. As Alec had pointed out, her marriage to Leod had left scars, and some would take time to heal. "Of course, ye can," she replied. "Come … let's find yer dirk."

They turned from the wall and made their way back down to the barmkin below. There, Alec set Craeg down, letting the lad run indoors to fetch his wooden dagger. He then turned to Liza, his gaze searching. "Are ye sure about this, Liza?" he asked, his voice lowering. "Ye know I'd never harm Craeg, don't ye?"

She smiled, grateful for his concern, yet at the same time embarrassed, for she didn't like to be reminded of that incident. "I don't doubt ye," she admitted. "But the urge to protect him like a she-wolf still rears its head occasionally, that's all."

He flashed her a grin. "And so it should." He stepped closer, lowering his voice as he added. "It's what makes ye such a good mother."

Craeg burst out of the tower house then, waving his toy dirk excitedly. "I'm ready!"

"Right then," Alec motioned to one of the guards posted by the armory. "Fetch me a wooden sword, Hector. I have a challenge I must answer."

EPILOGUE: I WILL SEE IT DONE

Two months later ...

"ALEC ... LOOK!"

GLANCING up from buttering a wedge of bannock, Alec focused on where Liza stood by the window.

She was lovely, as usual, with her dark hair spilling in waves down her back, and her curves tamed by a wine-red surcote—his favorite of all the ones he'd seen her in. In the past weeks, he'd started breaking his fast with Liza and Craeg in the laird's solar, a habit he was enjoying. Before now, he'd eat with his men in the hall below, but Liza's invitation to join her and Craeg in the mornings from now on pleased him more than he'd let on.

Life at Moy was more settled now, especially since Loch had visited a fortnight earlier, to let Liza know she could stay on as laird of Moy. It was the response she'd been hoping for. And of course, if Liza was remaining here, so would he.

"What is it?" He cast aside his bannock and rose to his feet, moving past where Craeg was eagerly spooning porridge into his mouth, to stand by her side at the open window.

"Recognize it?" she asked, her dark eyes glinting.

Alec cut his gaze away from her, looking out at where the morning sun glittered off Loch Buie at high tide. And there, approaching with a billowing emerald sail, was a large cog.

His breathing caught, as he took in her high clinker-built sides and the bloody flag flying from her mast, before a grin split his face. "What are those flea-bitten dogs doing back here?"

Liza flashed him a smile. "It looks as if the crew of *The Blood Reiver* are pining for their old captain."

Still grinning, he turned to her. "Come … let's see what those bastards want."

A short while later, the three of them, surrounded by a handful of guards, awaited on the pebbly shore below the castle. A salty breeze fanned Alec's face as he watched the pirate cog drop anchor in her usual spot, just beyond Eilean Mòr.

Then, as they looked on, the pirates lowered a boat into the water and rowed their way to shore.

Alec's brow furrowed.

"Nervous?" Liza murmured from next to him.

He snorted. "No … but we didn't part on the best of terms, remember?"

In response, she flashed him an enigmatic smile. "I'm sure they've forgiven ye."

"Maybe." Stepping away from her side, Alec strode down to the water's edge to meet Cory, who'd just leaped nimbly from the boat.

The two men clasped forearms, in a typical warrior greeting, before Cory surprised Alec by yanking him into a bear hug. And when they drew back, Cory punched him in the shoulder, his lean face creasing into a grin. "Missed me, eh?"

"Not for one moment," Alec shot back. He inclined his head then. "To what do we owe this visit?"

Cory gave him a secretive smile. "We were passing by, and thought we'd see if Lady Maclean had turfed ye out yet … but here ye are, looking like the cat that got the cream."

Alec flashed him an answering smirk, yet deliberately didn't volunteer any answer to that.

Gunn, Rabbie, Egan, Athol, and Hamish clambered out of the rowboat, and he greeted them all. To his relief, even Gunn and Egan were friendly enough. The pirates didn't appear bitter about it as he'd feared. Instead, they all looked pleased with themselves. Most of them wore new clothing of fine cloth, while expensive jeweled dirks hung at their sides. They'd clearly been spending some of the coin they'd earned after taking Moy Castle for Liza in the spring.

"What have ye been up to?" Alec asked then, before casting a glance over his shoulder at where Liza, her son, and the others looked on. "Or is it best we don't know?"

Cory stroked his beard, his mouth curving once more. "It's been rich pickings this summer," he replied. "Lots of nice fat merchant cogs to be plundered. The Mackinnons of Dùn Ara and the MacDonalds of Sleat will be cursing us now." His smile widened. "*The Reiver's* hold has never been so heavy with loot."

"We heard what happened here at Bealtunn though," Gunn spoke up then, folding his meaty arms across his barrel chest. "That ye had a visit from the Ghost Raiders."

"Aye," Alec replied, pulling a face. "I can confirm they are not phantoms though … for I killed three of them."

"We spied their ship north of Mull," the lad, Rabbie, said then, his blue eyes gleaming. "A sleek cog she was, with black sails and flag."

"Aye, we *chased* her too," Cory muttered, pulling at his beard now, "but she outran us."

"What?" Alec raised his eyebrows. "Nothing outruns *The Reiver*."

Cory snorted. "*The Night Plunderer* did."

"Did ye get a look at the crew?" Liza stepped up to Alec's shoulder then, her gaze sweeping over the pirates. Her gaze was confident and probing; it pleased Alec that this rough lot didn't intimidate her.

Cory shook his head.

"A man named Ross Macbeth likely leads them," she went on. "A big heavyset man with wild dark hair and a beard. Have ye seen him on yer travels?"

The Blood Reiver's captain thought about this description before shaking his head again.

"Aye, well, keep an eye out for the turd-eater," Alec replied, scowling. "He was in league with Leod Maclean … the Ghost Raiders have been storing their plunder in Moy Castle's strongroom."

The pirates all stilled at this news before Gunn gave a low curse. "That'll be why yer husband had so much coin." His mouth curved into a wicked smile then. "Macbeth would have been vexed to discover we'd taken a cut."

Liza nodded. "And that's why they attacked at Bealtunn … they were hoping to get some of it back … but things went ill for them."

"So, is the clan-chief hunting him now?" Cory asked, his brow furrowing.

"Aye."

"Well, we shall keep an eye out for Macbeth, Lady Maclean," Cory assured her, and it warmed Alec to hear the respect in his voice.

"I hope ye will stay for a day or two?" Liza asked, ruffling Craeg's hair as the lad ventured forward and watched the pirates from behind the protection of her skirts. "Ye are all welcome at Moy."

This assertion roused smiles amongst the pirates. Even Egan managed one.

"Aye, thank ye," Cory replied, smiling. "Me and the lads could do with a couple of days on land."

"The castle's inhabitants have just broken their fasts, but there will still be bannocks left over," Liza stepped back and nodded to the castle that rose above them, its broad tower house outlined against the blue sky and the imposing silhouette of Ben Buie beyond. "If ye hurry, ye can help yerself to them ... go on."

Cory and his crew didn't need telling twice. Crusty bannock, fresh off the griddle and slathered with butter and honey, was a treat most pirates dreamed of.

Leaving their rowboat on the shore, they strode up the path and headed for the castle. The guards followed, some looking a little wary.

Alec brought up the rear of the group, with Liza and Craeg. The lad grabbed a piece of driftwood off the shore and capered with it, imagining he was chasing off robbers. Meanwhile, Alec moved close to Liza so that their elbows brushed. What he really wanted was to link his arm through hers, yet he restrained himself.

Most of the castle had likely guessed that the lady laird and her captain were now lovers; all the same, they were careful to keep up the pretense when they had company.

"Admit it … ye *have* pined a little for yer crew these past months." Liza lifted her chin to meet his eye.

"Those feral bastards? Never."

"Ye have no regrets then?"

He saw the shadow in her eyes and halted, reaching out and grasping her arm so that she also stopped and turned to face him. "Not for an instant," he said firmly. "When I told ye I was ready to leave reiving behind, I meant it. Aye, there's a part of my soul that will always live on the high seas … but the rest of me wishes to stay right here, with my feet firmly planted next to ye."

She sighed then. "I'm tired of all this sneaking around," she admitted, moving closer to him. "Of pretending we aren't together."

Alec's pulse quickened, his chest tightening. "What are ye saying?" he asked softly.

Her lips tugged into a smile, the expression chasing away the shadows. "I want to hold yer hand out here in the open … to touch ye … for everyone to know what ye mean to me." She halted then, her breast rising and falling swiftly from the strong emotion that clearly gripped her. "I wish for us to be wed. I haven't been a widow long … but I don't want to wait any longer."

Alec's breathing stilled. "Ye want us to *marry*?"

She nodded. "Shall I send word to Loch … and ask his permission?"

He stared down at her, taking in her lovely strong-featured face and her honeyed skin bathed by the morning sun. "And what if he doesn't give it?"

"He will," she replied, her night-brown eyes glinting with determination.

"Leave it with me," he said firmly, reaching up and stroking her cheek. "Tomorrow, I shall ride to Duart and ask him myself." He paused then, his mouth quirking. "Man to man."

Her own smile widened. "Very well," she murmured. "Have it yer way … and when ye return, I will ask the priest at Lochbuie kirk to wed us."

He nodded, warmth pooling in his belly.

God's blood, he couldn't wait for this woman to be his, to be able to call her his wife. Joy flowered within him, contentment seeping deep into his bones. This was what it felt like to be truly happy. His old life seemed a shallow existence in comparison. He hadn't known it, but Liza had always been his destiny. "We are agreed then," he said huskily.

"We are," she whispered back.

"Good." He stepped into her, both hands cupping her cheeks. "I will see it done." And with that he bowed his head and kissed her deeply, passionately, not caring who witnessed it.

The End

DIVE INTO MY BACKLIST!

Check out my printable reading order list on my website:

https://www.jaynecastel.com/printable-reading-list

ABOUT THE AUTHOR

Multi-award-winning author Jayne Castel writes epic Historical and Fantasy Romance. Her vibrant characters, richly researched historical settings, and action-packed adventure romance transport readers to forgotten times and imaginary worlds.

Jayne is the author of a number of best-selling series. A hopeless romantic in love with all things Scottish, she writes romances set in both Dark Ages and Medieval Scotland, and Romantasy with a Celtic vibe.

When she's not writing, Jayne is reading (and re-reading) her favorite authors, cooking Italian feasts, and going on long walks with her husband. She's from New Zealand but now lives in Edinburgh, Scotland.

Connect with Jayne online:

www.jaynecastel.com

www.facebook.com/JayneCastelRomance

https://www.instagram.com/jaynecastelauthor/

Email: **contact@jaynecastel.com**